Also by Ehud Havazelet

What Is It Then Between Us?

LIKE NEVER BEFORE

LIKE NEVER BEFORE

EHUD HAVAZELET

FARRAR • STRAUS • GIROUX

NEW YORK

Farrar, Straus and Giroux
19 Union Square West, New York 10003

Copyright © 1998 by Ehud Havazelet
All rights reserved
Distributed in Canada by Douglas & McIntyre Ltd.
Printed in the United States of America
Designed by Jonathan D. Lippincott
First edition, 1998

My thanks to Ted Morgan, whose book *An Uncertain Hour: The French,
the Germans, the Jews, the Klaus Barbie Trial, and the city of Lyon,
1940–1945* (New York, Arbor House/Morrow, 1989), provided the basis
for one of these stories.

Grateful acknowledgment is made to the following publications in which these
stories, some in altered form, first appeared: *DoubleTake*, for "The Street You
Live On"; *New England Review*, for "Leah" and "To Live in Tiflis in the
Springtime"; *The Southern Review*, for "Like Never Before"; *STORY*,
for "Lyon"; *Tikkun* for "Light of this World." "Lyon" also appeared on the
National Public Radio Short Story Magazine, "The Sound of Writing."
Excerpts from "There's a Kind of Hush (All Over the World)" reprinted with
permission of Glenwood Music Co. Copyright © 1966, 1967 (renewed
1994, 1995) by Donna Music, Ltd. Words and music by
Les Reed and Geoff Stephens.

Library of Congress Cataloging-in-Publication Data
Havazelet, Ehud.
    Like never before / Ehud Havazelet. — 1st ed.
        p.   cm.
    ISBN 0-374-18762-2 (alk. paper)
    1. Jews, American — Social life and customs — Fiction. 2. Jewish
families — United States — Fiction. 3. Jewish men — United States —
Fiction I. Title.
PS3558.A776L5   1998
813'.54 — dc21   98-12856

For Michael

ACKNOWLEDGMENTS

I would like to acknowledge the following organizations for their support: Literary Arts, Inc.; the Oregon Arts Commission; the Department of English and the Center for the Humanities at Oregon State University. A large measure of thanks to these individuals for their friendship and timely advice: Tom McNeal, Antonya Nelson, Tim O'Brien, Matt Pavelich, Marjorie Sandor, Ted Solotaroff; to Jeff Bens, for a title to one of these stories; to Carol and Fred Seving and Doraine and Denys Potts for opening their homes to me; and to these three, without whom this book would never have been written: Tracy Daugherty, Mark Welther, and Molly Brown.

CONTENTS

Those—dying then,
Knew where they went—
They went to God's Right Hand—
That Hand is amputated now
And God cannot be found—

The abdication of Belief
Makes the Behavior small—
Better an ignus fatuus
Than no illume at all—

—Emily Dickinson

SIX DAYS

Friday nights, after the services and the meal, while the women of the house finished in the kitchen and settled down with books, Birnbaum and his son walked. They headed west, up the boulevard toward the city, or east, deeper into Queens. They marked their passage by landmarks—the Midway Pharmacy, which bulged onto the boulevard; the flat gray edifice of the county courthouse; the bank, which was a replica of Independence Hall in Philadelphia. They recited the neighborhoods they passed into—Rego Park, Corona, Kew Gardens. From odd vantage points they could see bridges—the Verrazano, the green lights of the Throgs Neck; on clear nights, very far off, the GW, or maybe it was the Triborough—they could never be certain.

Across Queens Boulevard they entered the shaded precinct of Forest Park, where the streets were softly lit by gas lamps and black, unmarred lawns lapped serene and elegant houses. Their conversation was muted, filled with a quiet and reluctant awe. Behind bay windows women held record-album covers as men poured wine. There was dancing, right in somebody's living room. Mahogany bookshelves, a special ladder on wheels just for books; on their walls paintings, objects from foreign cultures, even their plates angled for display. His father never said a word but the boy understood that these people had what should be theirs, at least a portion of it, but that never would be. And it was a

measure of the world's perversity, the inherent unfairness of
things, that this would always be so.

They walked down the boulevard into the Italian section, past
restaurants and bowling alleys and bars, people cruising, draped
from car windows to call someone's name. By the Trylon Theater,
kids, not much older than David, boys in jeans and T-shirts, girls
in short plaid skirts and leather jackets, out on their own, smoking cigarettes, kissing, touching each other in full view of whoever passed. Sometimes a bright glance sizing him up, a searing
flash of invitation, then amused smiles all around at him stuck
with his father.

David tried to hurry through these streets but his father liked to
take them slowly. Before the brick-fronted clubs with their neon
signs in looping script, men in knit shirts stood smoking, rubbing
down cars, overseeing the street. David kept his eyes averted,
aware of their Shabbos clothing, strayed from their own neighborhood, while his father distributed Good evenings, How are yous,
as if he knew these men. As if they might say, Good evening to you,
sir, why not stop and have a drink with us?, and he could smile and
say, No, no, my son and I are out walking, perhaps another time.

They walked for hours, talking, not talking. Once they kept
going, ended up in Whitestone, all the way to the water. In a park
under the bridge they were the only people, the gray southern
pylon towering over them like some ancient battlement, a for-
tress's looming wall. Far out on the black water lights bobbed,
fishing boats or buoys, the boy couldn't be sure. After half an
hour, the only ones in the park, Birnbaum said to his son, Did
you see? That Friday they didn't get home till past midnight.

But their favorite spot was not far off, east on the boulevard,
then south on Union Turnpike, a few blocks to the overpass.
From here, they could see twenty-two roads, east, west, north,
south. Four major highways converged at this spot, dumping cars
onto service roads, trading traffic in a maze of interchanges and
swooping ramps that circled high above their heads, doubled

back, and fanned out into more highway. Close by was the IND
subway yard, where trains done for the night would pull themselves across their own bridge with a faint metallic chatter the boy
could make out, tracing the lit windows and the pink circle at the
train's back until it came to rest in the yard and went dark. It was
loud here, a whirring background tumble of noise, and the boy
liked tuning his ears to one road then another, to the trains, the
sound effect of a truck passing above them, spiraling, then disappearing in a stream of taillights toward the east. With their hands
on the cold steel rail, they stood and watched, slowly turning their
heads, feeling the distant flutter of traffic through the tips of their
fingers. His father pointed things out. "Those trucks drive out to
the Long Island farms at night," he would say. "The cabbies are
lining up for La Guardia." "From here you could go anywhere,
anywhere on earth."

The high school where his father taught had once reminded
David of a castle. Older, looking back, he retained the memory,
though he could hardly understand what had given him the idea.
There were two scarred cement columns at the top of a wide staircase, and if you stood across the street and looked, a certain sym-
metry to the tall windows above the entrance, the gilt lettering on
black glass to either side of the portal, in Hebrew and English,
giving the school's name. It was a serious place—it even smelled
serious, something deeper about its mustiness than in David's
school, as if no one here ever opened a window—and no matter
what time he arrived there were always groups of boys huddled
over Talmuds in the harshly lit rooms. There was no playground,
no gym. This was a school for scholars, for future rabbis, and even
the students wore suits and hats. David remembered running
through these halls. A secretary who had long since died or
retired gave him odd, sweet, coffee-flavored candies. Now he was

shy and resentful coming here, fingering the baseball cards in his pocket, hurrying through the first floor, where boys swayed over books, murmuring.

His father's class was on the second floor, down the hallway to the back. On the walls no posters, no maps, not even the little grids by the stairwells telling you where to go in case of emergency or fire. Between two classrooms, portraits of the founder and his father, a famous learned man from the Old Country. The founder was dignified and humorless. The founder's father was in a fur hat and faded striped coat, pictured from the waist up, smiling a smile somehow both kindly and insinuating. He had died protecting his school from the Germans. His eyes followed you wherever you went.

The impression he always got approaching his father's classroom was of books as an ocean, his father adrift among them, possibly going down. There were books on the sills, on the students' wooden desks, on a long table near the window, books piled open-face on each other, threatening to spill onto the floor. There were books on his father's desk, and beside it a worn wooden box, filled with more books. Sometimes David knocked, sometimes he walked straight in, so his father would look up and see him. Other times he stood at the door, playing a game he did not really enjoy, seeing how long it would be before his father, hunched over a smeary manuscript he was translating for some journal, would notice him. David felt uncomfortable standing there, as if he were spying on someone's privacy, and sometimes he was, his father shifting in his chair to pass gas, picking his nose—but, uncomfortable or not, he did it anyway. He watched his father's big head under its black yarmulke, watched his incomprehensible scrawl on the yellow writing paper, thought if he was an Arab terrorist or some crazed sniper like the man who shot Kennedy he could have picked him off twenty times by now. Still other times he just stood there and thought, This is his other world, when he's not home with us.

The response when it came, in any case, was always the same. His father would look up, startled, genuinely surprised to see him there, glad. He would check his watch. "Am I late?" he would say, knowing he was, enjoying the ritual, "Just one more second." And David would bring out his cards to check for Yankees or loiter halfway up the hall, embarrassed in more ways than he could acknowledge, at his father's absent-mindedness—two, three times every week he had to come get him for dinner—at his own unwanted role as messenger, at the shabby familiarity of these rooms and halls, at the way, whether he was ten minutes or two hours late, whether it was snowing outside or blazing hot, his father would look up from his books every time like a man shocked from dreaming, alarmed, happy, smiling to see him.

On the way out, students would nod at his father, occasionally—usually the younger ones—stop and ask a question about their work. There were night classes, and students stayed at least as long as evening prayers, some after that, for dinner. It was a world David was suspicious of, and scorned, but even here he would have liked an occasional wave or smile from one of these serious young men, would have felt then much eased in his faltering sense of worldliness and self-possession. Who wanted what they had? They didn't even seem American.

Older boys sat on the steps to argue, and they didn't rise, as David didn't for his teachers, as his father passed. They said good night in Yiddish or, not pausing in their conversations at all, simply raised their chins at his father, a bare acknowledgment in which David saw condescension, traces of contempt. It galled him that they knew his father in all his weaknesses—his dreamy-mindedness, his affection for puns, his penchant for flying off the handle and his killing remorse afterwards—they knew all these things as well as his own son did. He registered what he believed was the complacent derision in their faces, and recognized much the same in himself, which made him even angrier. He knew his father just that well, and of course he loved him. Did they? Did they love him, these pale boys with their earlocks and green suits, smugly arguing laws nobody but they cared about anyway?

On the street, as his father pulled papers from his suit pocket or tried to relatch his briefcase, which had come undone, as he called, "Wait, David, tell me about your day," the boy would tuck his chin into his neck and walk faster, willing himself deaf and blind.

In Brooklyn, his father's shul was a yellow brick building that, along with another shul next door, took up most of 50th Street between 13th and 14th Avenues. Birnbaum's father had been rabbi here twenty years, was among the city's prominent clergy, on school boards and planning commissions, knew aldermen, councilmen, deputy mayors. The script, though it had never been openly discussed, was that Birnbaum's older brother, Rachmil, would take over one day. But he had not survived the war, the passage from Poland. The honor, the obligation, descended then to Birnbaum. But he was not his father, had other leanings, enjoyed his reading and translating medieval manuscripts, was uncomfortable speechifying, swaying crowds, being the center of everyone's attention. Until the possibility had passed, however, Birnbaum did not himself realize that in idle moments he saw himself up there, dispensing kind wisdom from the podium, leading the congregation with his example of quiet dedication and good works. His father distantly encouraged his scholarship, had even helped him get the job at the boy's high school in Queens — a favor, Birnbaum sometimes thought; other times, exile. Now another man, Alan Ostrow, was being groomed as his father's successor, and Birnbaum, who had managed to publish only a handful of monographs and one article, was not nearly as happy in his choices as he had once hoped to be, as his father's impassive approval made him avow he was. He was disappointed in himself, and disappointed, obscurely, in his father, for accepting him as he had turned out.

At the shul his position was conspicuous if not eminent. He was in charge of organizing the study groups and classes that met during the week, though he taught only occasionally himself. He was on committees, headed, with his Uncle Simon, the charity drive for the orphanage in Jerusalem the shul sponsored. He was well liked, prized for his singing voice, his offhand humor. He sensed the congregation considered him one of them, approachable, one who could take a bit of ribbing, while the rabbi was grand, removed. This was true, and Birnbaum told himself it was all to the good. He tried to see himself as a simple Jew, a humble man who quietly did his duty to God and family and community. If he had doubts, he practiced keeping them to himself.

And, if it was sometimes painful to admit this, given his relationship with his own father, he put great stock in his children. They were bright-eyed, affectionate, favorites among the congregation—it was a special thing to be the rabbi's grandchildren (if not, he sometimes couldn't help musing, the rabbi's son) and they seemed partly everyone's kids. David had his clear singing voice, and Rachel a laugh everyone recognized, turned to smile at. They did well in school and somehow the whole community knew their most recent grades, what their teachers had to say. People would introduce his children as if they were their own: This year he learned twelve *blat* of Talmud by heart, most in his class. She did half the cooking for the seder, twenty-five people they fed.

After the Torah reading David would climb the front steps to sit with his grandfather. As a young boy he had sat on his lap. Older, in his own suit and tie, he sat next to the rabbi, in a high-backed red-velvet chair identical to his and, across the velour-draped ark, the president of the congregation's. You could hear him singing up there. Birnbaum would look over at Ruth, would try to catch his father's attention—here was something they could all be proud of together.

When he had finally moved his family to Queens no one raised an eyebrow. It was nearer the job, after all. They had good schools for the children, the houses were newer, there was room for a man to prosper. It's the right thing to do, people assured him. Brooklyn is finished, they all said. We'll be joining you soon enough.

But to Birnbaum there was defeat, a taint of abandonment in his leaving. He couldn't put a name to it, didn't allow himself to, but he had never thought to leave. All his adult life, when he looked into his future—well, he didn't know anymore what he saw, but he never saw this. Nothing was clearer than the logic of the move, the necessity for it—a man couldn't stay forever in his father's shadow, after all—yet now he was doing it he had trouble keeping his mind turned forward toward the bright new life he and Ruthie had planned. It was reckless, he feared, and there would be costs.

And this foreboding, this bracing for grief was only confirmed for him two years later when he returned to follow his father in the funeral cortege, Borough Park's crowded streets hushed for once, schoolchildren three deep on the curbs, storekeepers, merchants, housewives, everyone in Brooklyn, it seemed, gathered in the streets to pay final respects to the great man. What Birnbaum remembered was the body before him in the box, swaying gently in the hearse, the cold door handle which he wouldn't let go of, all the long walk to the cemetery, the prayers and shattered apologies he offered under his breath.

Sometimes, deep in prayer or late at night, leaning over a manuscript in his study, Birnbaum would get lost in the blunt shapes of the Hebrew letters, or in the incantatory rhythm the words made in his head. He would enter a kind of cottony doze, realize dimly he was wandering into his children's future lives, where there were new children, laughter, spirited, friendly conversation, a sleepily indistinct but recognizable territory where the light was better and you could finally breathe. Other times his reveries were vivid and precise—his house engulfed in flames, past the gruff warnings of firemen he runs in to save a sleeping child; some serious but repairable medical condition in one of his kids, he has to donate something, a vital organ. They tell him how serious it will be. Without hesitating he signs his name to the paper; or less dramatic, closer to his heart—some childhood tragedy, some playground disaster that seems, to the child, the end of the world. Ruth is not home, only he is in the house when the grieving child returns. They sit at the kitchen table over a nourishing snack and talk it over.

He believed, honestly, in the singularity of his children's accomplishments, and he would say to his wife, after David had recited the Gettysburg Address, pointing at a book report Rachel had just completed, "Did you see?"

"Very good," Ruth would say, smiling.

"Seriously. This is something special. Out of the ordinary."

And she would look over at the kids on the floor in front of the TV, seeing them in their pajamas, bathed, their hair brushed, laughing at that secret agent talking into his shoe, then back at her husband, wondering what it was he saw.

"Yes. It's very good."

"You think every child in that school is doing this?"

"No. Certainly not everyone." And she would go back to her book or her knitting, giving him a smile, a look or two that showed she loved him, though he was a bit comic, after all, a bit pathetic. It bothered him to be seen this way, made him feel small, their conversation ended, though he had more he would like to say— there was a sentence here, let him just find it, he would show her what he meant. But she had turned away, and from the carpet the children laughed at the television. He sighed and tried to tune out the noise, put his glasses back on to read the book report one more time.

. . .

It was Yom Kippur, a day astonishingly hot for October, when they were back in Brooklyn for the Holy Day, and the inadequate air-conditioning failed entirely. The super, a black man who had a room in the basement, was allowed to interrupt the services to put fans up and down the aisles of the shul. Most of the congregation had been fasting eighteen hours; the cantor's weak if beautiful voice could barely be heard over the drone and clatter of the fans. The air was overused, hanging. People stood near the back doors for a hint of breeze from the hallway, and when Mrs. Galinsky, one of the oldest worshippers, fainted and had to be carried out, Birnbaum's father stopped the service to announce that younger children should be taken home, to remind those with medical conditions to tend them, remembering God looked for us to first care for each other, then worry about him.

Birnbaum loved Yom Kippur for its pleasant self-abnegation, its clarifying of body and mind. Any day of the week suddenly made significant by the fasting and the ancient mournful tunes, the rising to chant your sins and grievances into the thick, absolving air. The endless hours of meditation, beating your breast as if beating on the door of God's house until he finally listened.

But today was a misery. Though a huge green fan on wheels was aimed directly at him, only its insistent thrumming reached him; he felt not a breath of coolness on his face. His hands were moist, smearing the pages of the prayer book, and droplets of sweat trickled down his back, pooling over his belt, tickling, as if to mock his frayed concentration. He closed his eyes to recite more fervently, opened them to see Louie Weisbrod, one row ahead, slip a sucking candy into his mouth, then turn to find Birnbaum watching. The effort of ignoring Weisbrod's furtive, guilty smile, his blood-red ears, made meditation impossible. At the end of his row Mort Sheinberg mopped his head and neck with a wad of paper towels he had soaked, telling everyone around him, "It's ninety-five in here, maybe a hundred. The human body stops functioning at ninety-five."

He had allowed David to go outside for longer intervals than usual, given the heat, but the boy had been out there nearly two hours now, had not prayed more than a few squirming, distracted moments the entire day. Birnbaum had gone to see what had become of his son, and the boys were bouncing a ball high against the synagogue wall. The ball was small and dark and bounced with incredible force. Anyone walking by could see these Jewish boys, on the holiest day of the year, playing ball in the street. He had taken David aside and told him sternly that this was shameful, that he had two minutes to tell whoever owned the ball it was a disgrace and get himself inside. He had a hold on the boy's thin arm, was twisting his sweaty face to his own. "Do you hear me?" he had said, and David, avid eyes on the game, was nodding fast, his hair pasted to his head, his tie turned into his collar, when the ball, thrown by another boy, took a crazy bounce—he had never seen a ball like this before—over a tree and into traffic, and David broke free to chase it. "I got it!" he called. "Two minutes, " Birnbaum had shouted after him, "I'm not kidding!" as the boys leapt to snatch the ricocheting ball from the air.

That was nearly an hour ago. Over the lambent wail of the exhausted cantor and the rattle and hum of the fans, Birnbaum could still hear the boys in the street.

And he was worried about his father. It was fine to implore everyone else to take care of themselves, another thing to do it yourself. He had a heart condition everyone knew about, blood-pressure problems, still refused, against doctor's orders, to take his medication on Fast Days. He sat before his small table, turning pages in his prayer book, not raising his voice like the others, but closing his eyes and moving his lips. He refused to take out his handkerchief and wipe his face, but Birnbaum could see sweat on it, his white collar growing dark. His pallor frightened

Birnbaum, and as he watched he saw a fat drop of perspiration fall from the tip of his nose onto the page he was reading. His father looked at him and lifted his chin, a signal for Birnbaum to approach.

"How are you feeling?" he said, once he'd climbed the stairs.

"I'm fine."

"You don't look . . ."

"Fine, I just told you. Do you hear that?"

"What?"

"In the street, Maxim. Go out there and put a stop to it. In the street, on Yom Kippur."

"I know," Birnbaum said, whispering so only his father could hear. "I already told them."

His father looked at him, his eyes swimming and his face wet, as if his shirt had grown too tight, and Birnbaum realized how useless and ineffectual his remark made him seem.

"I'm going," he was about to say, when there was a high tap in the room and he turned just in time to see one of the tall green windows, the second from the front of the hall, push inward as if in slow motion, expand in a network of fine white lines, then burst onto the heads of the women praying below. Behind it a hard blue ball fell in, landing first on the floor, then rebounding insanely above people's heads in erratic arcs, like a cartoon version of a cannonball.

People were shouting, running from the glass, his father was up on his feet. The cantor, stupefied, kept singing a moment, then went silent. At the back of the hall, Birnbaum saw David and two other boys run in, look around wildly. The two boys saw the ball, still bouncing, and immediately gave chase. Birnbaum moved up the aisle toward his son. David had his hands up as Birnbaum approached, but by then the boy was on the floor and Birnbaum was in a different place, a red universe where tinted shapes floated between him and the boy on the other side trying to cover himself with his arms and legs. The boy saw his father's eyes, the look in them. He's going to kill me, he thought. Birnbaum leaned over, grunting words he didn't recognize. He tried to reach with his fists, but he couldn't, so he began using his feet on the red-faced creature scuttling away from him on its back near the wall.

On Passover the Jews go to Yankee Stadium—their children have the week off, while the rest of the population trudges on in school. Birnbaum took his son, sometimes his daughter as well, to a doubleheader. He was not much interested in the game, barely understood its rules, and it was with some effort that he responded to the boy's enthusiasm when a favorite—Mickey Mantle, Bobby Richardson—came up to hit, or when something exciting had just occurred and he had missed it, his nose buried in a book, but about which he needed, for the boy's sake, to be surprised, willing on a moment's read of his son's face to be crest-fallen or delighted.

He liked the stadium. After two hours on the subway, after the gray, teeming streets outside, the echoing, dank maze of ramps and hallways, suddenly banners, open sky, the unaccountable burst of green field. He liked seeing the boy with his Yankees hat, his oversized "mitt," the rowdy partisan calls that came from his throat, a different voice, deeper in the chest, male, public. The boy kept score, as he called it, leaned over to tell him Maris was due, he had lined deep to center the last time up, to watch White on first because he was known to take a base now and then. Birn-baum would nod, smile, look out at the costumed men on the field and see nothing. He would make an effort, remark of a tow-ering fly caught near the outfield fence that that was some hit, or praise the exertion of a player who slid into base in a rising cloud of dust. But his son would look baffled at him, might say, It was an out, Abba, and Birnbaum would nod, edified, and return to his book, agreeably aware of the game around him, of people chanting and clapping their hands, the breeze that swirled through the grandstand.

After the game red-vested ushers unlatched gates that opened from the box seats and they followed the patient crowd down, moved on the dirt ring edging the playing field in an orderly line past the three monuments far off by the flag. The boy knelt to fill a plastic bag—brought from home for the purpose—with red Yankee Stadium dirt, which he would add to the box he kept under his bed. Birnbaum thought of his grandfather, in Poland, the tiny leather bag of dust from the Holy Land which he had kept for years, had had buried under his head when he died. He thought collecting dirt from a public facility was unhygienic, also somehow a sacrilegious commentary on the old man's faith. But he hadn't thought of a way to speak of it to his son and, for now, let it go. One day a man in a striped shirt and undersized blue fedora took out a ballpoint and wrote something, signed his name perhaps, right across Babe Ruth's bronze forehead. Birnbaum wasn't surprised. The boy was stunned, talked about it for days.

They sat far back in the reserved section, eating egg salad and tuna on matzoh, and he let the boy gorge himself on Cokes, because that was all he was allowed to buy. Birnbaum took out his pencil and underlined in his book, turned it sideways on his knees to make notations in the margins, references to other books he needed to consult. It was warm, bright and sunny out on the field, but they were in shade, and a breeze lifted past the crowd to cool their faces from time to time, and Birnbaum would look up to see the banners flickering in the blue sky above the stadium walls. Around him were other fathers, he could see boys in yarmulkes, Jewish families pulling out tomatoes, hardboiled eggs, disintegrated matzoh sandwiches in tinfoil. It was pleasant here on a leisurely spring day, pleasant to look up from his book at young men moving fluidly across a green field. On every hit, David stood, glove at the ready, to catch the ball.

Suddenly there was commotion all around them. Birnbaum was alarmed, looked to see everyone standing, moving at once. A woman shrieked, a man spilled his beer and Birnbaum could smell the sour smell. A man with a cigar pushed David so that he fell against Birnbaum, who tried to hold him, but the boy wrenched free to stand on his wooden seat. Hands reached for David, alien, goyish faces, fists, teeth. They were in a mob. Birnbaum's heart pushed into his throat as he reached for his boy to take him and run. Then, above their heads, a white streak, the ball, a few rows behind them a man with a hair-covered stomach bulging from an unbuttoned shirt catching it easily with an outstretched hand. People returning to their seats, a few remaining on their feet to clap. The fat man nodded, took a bow, held the ball aloft like a trophy.

"Are you all right?" Birnbaum wanted to ask his son, but the boy was already turned to him, all smiles, an American boy pounding his mitt. "Jeez, did you see that?" he said. "I almost had it! A home run by Norm Cash!" and Birnbaum reached out to briefly touch his son's hair and they all sat back down to the game. But though it proved to be an exciting finish—the great Mickey Mantle won it in the ninth inning with a home run—Birnbaum could not relax, kept looking from his book to David to the people around them, thinking it would be dark when they left the stadium, then two hours on the subway, and the long walk home.

On occasional Saturday nights, after the services that marked the end of Shabbos, the men of the congregation would take their prayer books out to the street and bless the new moon. In winter in their coats they would gather by the stoop to pray, in summer they would wait on the steps and smoke cigarettes someone had stashed in the shul, until the rabbi and cantor came out to join them. Spring was the best season, the wind, even in Queens, carried smells of ripening, of turned earth. The boys preceded the men, ran out before the services were properly over, craning their necks, the first to see the moon calling to the rest, until someone ran inside and announced it was there, all right, they were ready.

David loved the incongruity of it, released after hours of prayer, the men lighting up cigarettes signaling the return of the normal week, soon home, TV, phone calls, tomorrow baseball. Somewhere a radio played dance music and ahead, on the boulevard, couples walked arm in arm toward the subway, mingled in festive groups as they waited for the bus.

The moon wavered brightly in the high branches of a sycamore, winking silvery light through dark leaves. The cantor came out onto the steps, out of his white gown, a portly man who closed his eyes to sing. David's father motioned him over, so they could share a prayer book, draping a hand lightly across his shoulder. He held the pages open before them and answered the cantor's lead, but David never really mouthed the words, just chanted the melody along with the rest of the men, some bringing cigarettes to their lips, looking around them at the new season, come out to praise God's world and ask his blessing for a few more days of good fortune and peace.

LIGHT OF THIS WORLD

April 1967. In Queens, spring has arrived early, full-blown. Along Jamaica Avenue, in the midday twilight of the El, spindly maples push green tips along their branches and an orange tree, planted by a Korean grocer who doesn't know better, sprouts shiny leaves, no oranges, in a bucket between his store and the barbershop. Doors stay open, cabbies lean from windows to talk, men walk to work with jackets on their arms, and in King Park, for the public's own safety locked two years now, untended crocus and goldenrod bloom, an uncanny camellia three stories high, sending scents up the avenue, where people sniff the air, remembering.

In an alley at the side of the Mid-Queens Hebrew Day School, three boys hide behind an overflowing Sani-Trash Dumpster. They are not friends, and escaping detention together has not changed that. One boy, a pale-skinned child with glasses and thick blond hair, is too short to see over the Dumpster. He stretches. He asks the other two to tell him what they see. They don't.

The tallest surveys the street through a broken desk above the garbage. He keeps his knowledge to himself. The third, apparently losing interest, turns his back and slides to the ground, where he picks savagely at his shoe with a stick.

"What?" the blond boy asks. "Is he coming?" He cranes upward but cannot see. "What's he doing now?"

The tall boy ignores him. This is the last person in the world he need answer. On the sidewalk, Rabbi Klaperman checks behind trees, mailboxes, his face reddening with each step. The tall boy is enjoying himself. Something sweet carries into the alley to mix with the smells of turpentine, rotting milk, and pencil shavings. He spits. "Sorry, Rabbi," he says, softly. "Not even close."

"What's he doing?" the blond boy asks again, not daring to peek around the side. He is trying to keep his mother's disappointed face from filling his brain. He puts a hand on the tall boy's arm.

The tall boy looks at the hand until it is removed. He nods then, acknowledging, and punches the blond boy hard in the ribs. The third boy, his back to the street as if nothing could concern him less, reaches up to add a punch of his own, to a kidney. "Zitski," the tall boy says, smiling. He looks into the Dumpster, aims for a half-crushed Dixie cup, rolls spit into a cartridge on his tongue, lets fly. The spit slaps the paper cup with a solid "thock." Bull's-eye. "Zitski," he says again, enjoying himself.

The third boy snorts, looks up at the spitter. They exchange glances. "Yeah," he says, "Zitski." The spitter snorts, too. "Snotski," the boy continues, "Barfski," and the spitter is doubled over with held-in laughter. "Shitski," the boy concludes, standing, looking right at the small boy, nose-distant, "Ivan Shitski, Mama's love puppy."

The small boy turns away. He upends a wooden fruit box and, climbing slowly, peeks over the Dumpster's metal rim. What he sees is Rabbi Klaperman, whistle and clipboard in hand, a portly man in a black hat, a gray suit worn iridescent at the elbows and knees, yellowed tzizis looped in coils around his belt. Klaperman peers into the back seats of cars, under a few, into the ragged bushes at the school. He doesn't see us, the small boy is about to report, when the box is yanked from under him. The spitter grabs a good dollop of midriff and hangs on. The small boy slips, jackknifing over the side and dipping his hands in something wet: He screams: *"You son of a bitch, I'll kill you, you son of a bitch!"*

Rabbi Klaperman has been musing on what he will do when he catches them. Punitive scenarios loll in his mind. Public humiliation. Calling the parents in the middle of the day—is Avram Klaperman, zoo keeper. Maybe a little twist of the neck, by accident almost, when no one is looking. A hurt for a hurt. He rubs his chest thoughtfully. He can already feel their necks in his fingers, hear their snuffling sounds as they try to walk, almost lifted from the ground. Rabbi Klaperman pushes his hat back and mops sweat with a handkerchief, then takes two white pills from a jacket pocket and puts them in his mouth. Not today, Klaperman thinks. First, a demon of a heartburn—massive, unique, spreading through him like slow fire. Then this, three hoodlums on the run. Not today, he thinks, I got troubles enough.

He sees movement by the janitor's entrance, waits a moment, poised, then darts around to look. He trots on the balls of his feet, silent, nearly skipping. Down three steps by the metal door a gray cat lifts an unfriendly face from a paw and regards him. Rabbi Klaperman looks back, no friendlier, is about to send it flying off his black oxford when one little monster screams. Instantly he is up the steps, whistle at his lips, but already two boys are running toward the avenue and a third, looking fearfully over a shoulder, is not far behind. He gives the whistle two blasts that send the cat pinwheeling through his legs. He does kick this time, hitting air, and he chases, running and whistling a good fifteen yards before his chest reaches up and grabs him. Monsters. Against the hood of a green Oldsmobile he fingers shirt and tie, his chest underneath, twisting socket of all the world's misery. Not today. He shouts their names, slowly, swallowing poison, as he circles them on the detention roll in red: *"Birnbaum, David! Leibowitz, Arnold! Pitski, Ivan!"* But no one is listening. At the corner, three boys disappear in the shadows of the Jamaica Avenue El.

If not truly friends, two boys are united at least in hating the third. Everybody hates Ivan Pitski, and Arnold Leibowitz, acknowledged titleholder of biggest troublemaker in the history of the Mid-Queens Hebrew Day School, sees it as one of his more pleasurable duties to make Ivan miserable. David Birnbaum has never given Pitski much thought until today, but finds with grim satisfaction that hating Pitski is easy.

They hate him for many reasons. For the blue Cadillac with gold-spoked rims his mother drives, for the fancy coats and hats she buys Ivan, the pastel sweaters, though clearly the boy does not enjoy wearing them. For the library his father paid for, the Leon Pitski Reading Room, and the brass plaque that tells you so, every time you go through the door. They hate him for the furs she wears, the skins of animals you never heard of, and for black hair that sweeps off her head like some sleek bird, and for the dresses that cling and slide, dresses slit from Canarsie to the Bronx, and for the fact their mothers don't own, couldn't possibly wear if they did own, dresses so slinky and sheer. They hate him for her lipstick, orange and purple and fire-engine red, and for the kisses she gives Ivan, long, lippy kisses, real-looking, familiar to them from Sunday afternoons in butter-smelling sticky-floored movie houses on Main Street and Parsons Boulevard, and for her throat, movie-queen white, never ending, and for her breasts, most of all, for her breasts, not a thing motherly about them, live under blue satin and black crepe, they rise to where pallid Ivan is passively embraced, breasts a different species entirely from the cushiony plains of their mothers, breasts that are a glory to watch, and which enter your dreams at night.

Hating Ivan is *easy*—David Birnbaum has learned this today— he invites it by his manner, his appearance, he simply asks for it with every move he makes. For Ivan is a wimp, a geek, a pussy, a doughy child with blond corkscrews sprouting on a top-heavy skull. Big water-lidded eyes swim behind glasses so thick it must be a different world he looks out on, and he's a whiner, Ivan, a coward, like all pussies and geeks, a bursting ledger of unspoken hurts, deferred and half-formed schemes of vengeance, for he knows he is hated, and he wears the need for friends like a smell on his skin, sallow baby flesh that asks for— that demands—slaps, hip-checks, pinches, deep body blows that leave him bent against the wall as you walk away, already forgetting. They hate him because he has what they believe they want, and because in his gracelessness, in his sullen, pouty obstinance, he knows it.

She calls him sweetheart, baby doll, loverboy. And after pouring them cups of the sweet dark wine Ivan can barely sip at, she pulls him close and whispers, "My light," looking so long into his eyes he knows she means it. "My only shining light."

His mother is a real beauty, with stark black hair and eyes so blue they seem to Ivan lit from inside, and he can barely look at her. Her delivery of him was long, she has told him, and dangerous. After two days, the doctors feared Ivan would carry her off, kill them both before he'd been properly born. But she wasn't afraid—it had merely made them closer.

She lays out clothes for him. Every day when he comes out of the bathroom they're on his bed, underwear and socks on the pillow, shirt folded neatly over the pants. Weekends, when Leon travels to his out-of-town banks, she lays out suits—blue serge in summer, gray pinstripe for winter. When they come down to the dining room, Carlotta serves them formal meals.

In the high-backed mahogany chairs, Ivan feels like dozing.
The meats settle heavily in him and the candle flames roll on
their wicks, mesmerizing. His mother talks of her youth, of her
suitors from six states, including the son of a United States con-
gressman. But the one she loved, a Gentile boy named Edgar
Atkins, had perished in the Pacific Theater in 1944. She has a picture of him hidden in a jewelry box, and she has shown Ivan the
odd-colored uniform, the grinning doomed boy, his cap angled so
jauntily it must have fallen the moment the shutter snapped. She
tells him how Leon Pitski had arrived after she had received the
news, been kind in her misery, patient, how one thing led to
another. Mistakes had been made, God knew, but out of it all
came a blessing — Ivan, her son, was all that mattered now.

At times Ivan dozes, or feels he must have. As his mother drinks
the sweet wine, as she praises or scolds Carlotta about the food,
Ivan withdraws behind open eyes, dreams out at the world while
he moves far inside himself, finds a quiet place, and sleeps.

After dinner, while Carlotta cleans, there is music, and dancing, Ivan pressed hard into his mother, in among the scents and
powders and smells of food and wine, and she makes him lead,
though he's never been shown how, tells him he is as fine a dancer
as Edgar Atkins, who was known for his dancing. But soon she is
weary, tear-soaked, and Ivan and Carlotta help her upstairs, un-
dress her, and she is crying, calling for him. He hesitates at the foot
of the bed, a shoe in his hand, or a skirt, but Carlotta nudges him,
"Go on, sugar," and he goes to her, strokes her hair, but that isn't
enough, so he climbs into the bed as Carlotta closes the door and
leaves. She holds him to her and sings, whispers in his ear while,
outside, the sun moves slowly behind the trees or rain shifts against
the side of the house or snow silently gathers on the garage tops
across the yard, and Ivan waits there under her hands, dreaming.

·   ·   ·

Leibowitz, Arnold was already in detention when the other boys arrived, in his chair by the window, pretending to sleep. He sprawled backwards, mouth open, emitting sounds. He gave every indication that the slamming doors and rough orders Rabbi Klaperman dispersed were seriously disrupting his slumber. He gurgled and harrumphed, he shifted uncomfortably in his seat, he smacked his lips and yawned like a cat. When Rabbi Klaperman ungently snagged his shoulder, he came alive with sham eagerness and poked deep into his book. The look he turned on David and Ivan as they found seats was sly and amused and full of casual disregard.

Arnold, in the eighth grade, is two years ahead of the other boys, though by the calendar he should have been in high school long ago. He hangs around, as he sees it, to advance his legend. And in the schoolboy mythology of the Mid-Queens Hebrew Day School, no legends rival Arnold Leibowitz.

His vocation is spitting. He is credited with single-handedly driving a substitute science teacher, Mrs. Hannah Corn, into early retirement by inclining his head and spitting high into the air, over and over, catching the downward gob on his outstretched tongue, until the poor woman ran from the classroom forever. On a windy day one November, from the window of Rabbi Mermelstein's Talmud class, Arnold Leibowitz, after several tries, cleared the chain-link schoolyard fence and half the backyard across it, to land a direct hit on a pair of red quilted long johns hanging in the sun to dry. Sammy Gould, the math genius, computed this to be a distance of sixty-two feet, allowing for the sway of the long johns in the breeze. He can hit a doorknob at twenty feet, loose volleys that slalom in midflight to land smartly on your neck, the top of your head, and in the hall between classes, he lets fly random warning shots above the crowd, and everyone goes silent and watches him coming. Arnold has no friends, or need of any; the merest rolling of his cheeks is enough to send most boys, certainly little shits like Birnbaum and Pitski, scurrying for cover.

David slouched into the room, affecting an expression of hardened boredom, and gave Arnold what he hoped looked like a knowing nod. Arnold ignored him. David chose a seat several rows behind Arnold. Ivan followed, was about to sit, when David extended his brown loafers and said, with sudden violence, "Back off, Zitski." This roused some of Arnold's attention. He gave a bare titter and mugged at his book. Ivan backed a couple of chairs away and Rabbi Klaperman said, "Feet off the furniture, if it's not too much trouble, Professor Birnbaum."

David Birnbaum is aggrieved, put upon, a boy who carries anger like a stone in his pocket to caress. As he sees it, his trial is of identity. His late grandfather was a founder of the Mid-Queens Hebrew Day School and his uncle chairs the Board of Trustees. He appears at various functions, sits onstage at graduation, and their pictures adorn the hallway leading to the principal's office. David is reminded of them constantly—his successes reflect their glory, his failures blot the family name. His uncle sells cars for God's sakes, and his grandfather was a rabbi way over in Brooklyn. So what. He hates them with a determined passion—the big shots, the know-it-alls—and is resolved to make a name for himself, if not the one expected for him by the family. He has plans for a vivid future in which he'll pay them all back by becoming a Communist or a Christian or maybe even an Arab. Meanwhile, he engages in activities that baffle the local geneticists: smoking cigarettes on the school roof until the horizon of apartment buildings cants in yellow haze; sneaking out of morning prayer to chalk precise transliterations of curse words on the boards in Hebrew; staying late each day to drop a single holy book out a window onto the heads of the teachers and children lining up on 150th Street for the school buses home. Today, when he was accused of cheating in math—with Ivan Pitski, of all people—David put on such a display of outrage and felt such smarting sympathy for himself that he has forgotten entirely that he *was* cheating, but so what? never with Pitski, never in a million years with Pitski. They hadn't exchanged ten words in ten years and then suddenly Ivan sidles up at the detention-room door with a look, limpid, hopeful—a look, unmistakably, of love—and David is frightened, unbalanced, and he deflects the look with such fierce unfriendliness he can feel it changing his face.

Ivan had been watching David Birnbaum all morning. Mrs. Green, the math teacher, patrolled the aisles and stooped occasionally over students to deliver discouraging noises. The test was multiplication, which Ivan knew, but he had not studied and did not open his exam book. Instead, he watched David Birnbaum. He watched as David pulled yellow pieces of paper from his sleeves, his pockets, his shoes, and with expressions alternately furtive and triumphant copied into his book. Once Mrs. Green stopped behind Ivan, and tapped his arm, but he stared at her through his thick lenses with such imperturbable disregard that she shrugged and walked on.

A miracle had occurred, though no one knew of it except Ivan. In two days he had not slept, had barely eaten, and he felt he even moved differently, as if drawn in his motions by a new gravity.

It was Monday, during recess, when the boys of the sixth grade convened to abuse Ivan about his mother. This was a regular event, ritual to most of them, and Ivan stood against the wall and said nothing, as he always did. Recently, Leon had been out of town an unusually long time. His mother had driven to school one day, upset, and though Ivan knew the boys couldn't smell the wine, they could see the torn housecoat, loosely tied. She had opened the car door and called to him and as she did the housecoat fell, showing the eager boys swatches of thigh and white brassiere, and giving them fuel to torture Ivan for months. They asked if he liked to French his mother, if he had seen her titties. They asked if Ivan and Mommy slept in the same bed while Daddy was in Manhattan with his floozies. They reproached him with all the lurid fantasies repressed imaginations and ignorance could conjure.

This day, Perry Gruber, who fancied himself the expert on all matters sexual or illicit—and by rights, therefore, Ivan's chief tormentor—inquired if they "did it," Ivan and his mom, how often a night and how many different ways. He was a tall boy, with a thick upper lip, which he pulled at with two fingers. Did they do it camel fashion, Perry wondered, or doggie, and had they tried Japanese? Perry Gruber's sad secret was his total innocence of "doing it" any way at all, a fact he cleverly concealed by talking about sex all the time, with the vigor and obscure terminology of the connoisseur. It was probably Japanese, Perry explained to the boys, because of the way his mother walked. You could see it in her walk plain as day, Perry said, that she liked Ivan to do it to her Japanese.

David Birnbaum could not have cared less what they said to Ivan, was no more a friend of Ivan's this day than any other, but he was bored with Perry Gruber and his Brazilian style and alligator style, so he kicked a bottle cap at Gruber and said, "Hold it, Perry. Just what is Japanese style?"

Perry was startled. He had no idea. They were here to torment Pitski, what was Birnbaum's problem? He looked at David blankly a moment, and then, not knowing what else to do, kicked Pitski hard in the thigh. "That's what *he* does, Birnbaum. With his mommy. You want some, too?"

"I get enough from your mommy, Gruber," David said.

There was a scuffle, and the teachers, after watching from the kitchen stoop, where they huddled smoking, came wearily to separate the boys. But the miracle had occurred: attention had been directed elsewhere too long, and when the teachers left, the boys milled off, or broke into groups to play punchball; Ivan was forgotten. He stood against the wall and watched David Birnbaum flip baseball cards with some friends. Soon, as the boys wandered back to class, disgruntled and unsated, Ivan found David, who saw the thanks in his eyes, and to ensure that Pitski didn't get the

wrong idea, body-checked him into the lockers on the way to Jewish history.

Since then, Ivan had watched David. He had composed notes
to David in his mind, invitations to come to his house after school,
suggestions about things they might do together. He had an idea
he would ask his father if he might bring someone, a friend, along
on their summer trip to the mountains. He would ask Carlotta to
make her famous chocolate cake, and after school one day he and
David would go to his house and eat it, listening to records on
Ivan's new Zenith stereo player. He had visions, Ivan, both vague
and somehow brilliant, of a future that involved David. As he
watched David stuff a wad of yellow paper into his desk, Ivan saw
them together, maybe in the mountains this summer, walking
out of the woods onto a bright meadow, speaking in quiet voices.

When Mrs. Green came to a stop behind David, Ivan knew
there would be trouble. She leaned over David, as if to admire his
efforts. She picked up David's exam book.

"Why, David, " she said, "all these answers are correct." She
smiled unhappily. "You've made remarkable progress since yesterday." She was a young woman from the West with ideas about
her life, none of which included teaching multiplication to a
bunch of Jewish boys in the middle of Queens.

"Well, I studied hard, Mrs. Green." David smiled back, looking
directly at her.

"I know, David. I can tell." She reached for the wad of paper.

Before he quite realized what he was doing, Ivan stood and
upended his desk on the floor. The crash was tremendous; all the
students turned and Mrs. Green jumped. She recovered herself
by taking David's exam book, then Ivan's, and scrawling huge F's
on the covers. Together, Birnbaum and Pitski had been sent from
the room.

At the detention-room door, Ivan turned to David, hoping to
have something to say, something humorous and offhand about

Mrs. Green that would both mark this occasion and indicate it was no big deal to tough kids like themselves. But the look he saw on David's face discouraged any statement at all and he simply followed him into the room.

They were to study, without pause or conversation, the next four hours. It could be any subject, but Rabbi Klaperman suggested they study the Bible or simply pray, considering their dubious standing with the Lord. At his desk, Klaperman leaned over a large black Mishnah, alternately rubbing his forehead and sitting back to swallow as his calamitous innards sent alarming signals. He was tormented by indigestion, and the flarings inside soured all of the man—you could see it in his posture, in his expression, in the torpid yellow of his eyes. He was in no mood today. He had a pocketful of white pills, which he chewed while scowling thoughtfully at one or another of the boys. Arnold was a fixture, as regular here as the furniture. A sharp slap to the back of the neck had acquainted him with the foolhardiness of spitting in Klaperman's detention, and Klaperman gave him little thought. Pitski was a lost cause, a strange, unhappy boy, though God knew what reason he might have in that home of his. But Birnbaum was different, not a changeling like Pitski or a Cossack like Leibowitz. That he, with all his advantages, should be in detention enraged Rabbi Klaperman, and watching the sullen glare on the boy's face sent a small breaker of acid rolling in his chest.

"Birnbaum," he said, "are you happy? Does it bring you joy, being a disgrace?" He paused, discreetly, to swallow a belch. "Because that is what you are, a disgrace. To the yeshiva, to your family, to yourself. Your grandfather should see you in this room, with such company." He paused again. "Hoodlums."

Rabbi Klaperman ate a white pill, grimaced, ate another. Gases from foods he did not recall eating filled his throat. "Or your uncle. I should call him, your uncle?" He held an imaginary phone to his ear for heightened effect. "Excuse please, Avram Klaperman with charming news regarding little David." Fish? Klaperman thought. When did I eat fish? "Your uncle, not a busy man. Nothing better to worry about. Perhaps you'd like me to place a call?"

"Yeah, do that," David said quietly.

"Excuse?" Klaperman said. "Did I hear something, or am I mistaken?"

David turned a page.

"I believe I heard something, Professor Birnbaum. We wouldn't want, God forbid, to miss any pearls from your illustrious lips. Would you care to repeat?" He stood.

"It was me, Rabbi," Arnold said, staring at his book.

"Oh?"

"Yes, excuse please, I think I passed a little gas. Perhaps more than a little," Arnold said. "Must be something I ate."

"All right! Enough witticisms," Rabbi Klaperman announced. "As a trio you're delightful. Perhaps we can arrange you should spend the next ten years in this room exchanging witticisms."

David glanced at Arnold, who looked back and widened his eyes in mock terror. To the side, Ivan muttered something and laughed, but neither boy turned to investigate.

"*Silence!*" Rabbi Klaperman roared.

For fifteen minutes Rabbi Klaperman rubbed his raging belly and cursed his life. Images of the shtetl floated before his unfocused eyes, blue skies and grass, children running. Many worlds ago. For fifteen minutes, silence was broken only by the shuffling feet of the boys and the stifled squeals of Klaperman, who chewed white pills and changed color. Arnold watched him. Suddenly the rabbi rose and left the room, unaccountably forgetting to close the door. Arnold was through it before it had swung shut, and David was a step behind, pumping a fist at the rabbi's retreating back. Ivan sat in his chair, looking at the door. He closed his eyes, counted to ten, and bolted after the two boys, catching them just as they hit the street.

Jamaica Avenue, 2 p.m. Freedom. Through the El, a gridwork of light and shadow splashes the storefronts and sidewalks. A green bus rolls by, blaring its horn. A delivery boy on a bicycle rides against traffic, propelling his huge aluminum box before him. Two men push a black sedan down the street while a boy, younger than they are, steers. Overhead, a train roars, and in a moment everything is swallowed in noise, dancing to vibrations sent through steel girders to the street. It passes above them, showering yellow sparks onto the asphalt. Jamaica Avenue in full swing. Free.

Arnold immediately stuffs his yarmulke into his back pocket, and after a moment's pause, David does the same. Ivan fingers his, but leaves it on his head. Two young women in floral dresses walk by with red Coca-Cola cups in their hands. Arnold falls against the shoe-store window. He clutches his heart. "Oh, Mama," he says. The women smile and one of them—the cuter one, with brown hair bobbed short around her face—looks back. Arnold hoots, slaps David on the back, and they tear up the avenue.

In Pete's candy store, they look at comic books and, behind the rack of school supplies, nearly open a centerfold before Pete catches them. He shoos them toward the door, threatening to "get the rabbis on them." Birnbaum and Leibowitz dart for the street, but Ivan coolly continues shopping. He emerges a moment later with two magazines, one about trucks and the other about race cars, and two Hershey bars. Arnold produces a pack of Lucky Strikes he has filched from the counter and lights one with a blue Zippo. He draws in deeply and lets smoke out in plumes from his nose. Ivan sits on the storefront ledge and begins examining the magazines. David takes the race-car magazine and reads about the Corvette Stingray Coupe, which, in trials, has maxed out at 180 mph. Ivan unwraps a chocolate bar and offers the other to David. David begins to eat.

"Oh, isn't that sweet?" Leibowitz says. "Little Ivan and little David. I didn't know you two were engaged."

David feels his cheeks aching again. Leibowitz stands to the side, swallowing smoke. David grabs the candy from Ivan and throws it on the pavement. He holds up what is left of his in front of Ivan's face, then drops this, too, on the ground. Ivan looks from one boy to the other.

"What is it with you?" David asks him, prodding his shoulder. "Did I put an ad in the *Daily News*—Wanted, whiny, fat, rich kid to be best friend? Did I, Zitski?" He stands near Leibowitz. "If I need a friend, I'll write you a letter."

"He thinks you're adorable," Arnold says. "He wants to marry you."

"If I want a boyfriend, I'll borrow one of his mother's."

"I'd like to borrow her," Arnold says, and he mimics a woman walking, hips flared and swinging, cigarette extended. "Zitski, dear," he minces, "come rub Mommy's back."

"Come rub Mommy's front," David adds.

Pitski stands where David left him. He watches Birnbaum and Leibowitz prancing up the street, looks down at the ruined candy. He grinds it into the pavement with a heel, then follows the boys at a short distance.

At Hallmark's, Arnold cops a stack of birthday cards stamped with pink roses. They read, "To Our Darling Niece." David pockets three blue Magic Markers and two reds, and a combination toe-clipper–pocketknife with "NY" embossed on its handle. The two boys spend some time in Sam Goody's, but there is no opportunity to steal anything, so they leave. At the Woolworth's next door, Leibowitz slaps Birnbaum in the chest, motioning for him to look. Inside, Pitski stands before the long, waist-high candy counter. He is filling his briefcase with handfuls of candy, slowly, taking his time. Even Arnold and David are impressed. Ivan finishes, snaps the briefcase closed, and, in no hurry at all, walks out the door. The two boys, guffawing, follow him up the street.

In the Rexall's they get a couple of cigars, a Lady Timex on a plastic stand, and two boxes of Clairol hair coloring which Arnold claims he can put to use with a girl he knows. They swipe two Spider-mans and a Fantastic Four from the newsdealer at the corner of Sutphin Boulevard, and run breakneck through Lilly's Lamp and Statuary, caterwauling, spinning the lampshades on their stands, until Lilly reaches into her desk for the .22 she keeps for personal protection. The boys head for the exit, but at the door Ivan stops, takes a small china figurine from a table, and lifts it over his head. The other two boys are on the street, running. Lilly, with an embroidered handkerchief in one hand, feels in the drawer for the gun with the other. She has never used the gun, a present from a nephew in Syosset, and is afraid to take it out now. For a moment they stare at each other, and instead of throwing the figurine, a delicately painted black-and-white poodle, Ivan sets it back in place, hard, so that a tiny black paw breaks off and rolls onto the carpet. He walks out.

Behind Bohack's, they sit on milk boxes and eat caramels and jujubes, Turkish Taffee and chocolate-covered marshmallow bars. No one likes the soft candies with cream centers, so they toss them over the fence into somebody's yard. They divide the O'Henrys and Chocolate Kisses, and Arnold takes the box of lemon drops, saying a girl he knows is wild about them. They talk about classes they are missing, the suckers left behind.

"Did you see Klaperman chasing us?" David asks, blowing out his cheeks in imitation of Klaperman running. "I thought the old fart would have a heart attack, right in front of the school."

"Old fart is right," Arnold says, and lifts a cheek to demonstrate that spitting is not his sole talent.

Arnold lights a cigar and smokes it, though it sends his stomach barreling toward his chest. David lights the other, has a puff, and passes it to Ivan, who drops it on the ground.

"That's a two-dollar stogie," Arnold tells him.

"What do I care," Ivan says.

Arnold shakes his head, then spits, a low-flying bank shot off the rear wall of the supermarket. "Zitski," Arnold says, then holds the cigar before his face to admire it. "You shouldn't waste a two-dollar stogie."

They take out the greeting cards. Inside is a short poem:

> To our darling niece
> So fair and good
> Upon the threshold
> Of Womanhood
> Happy, *Happy* Sweet Sixteen!

They inscribe one to Doris Goldhammer, in the seventh grade. "I love you madly," David writes. "I love your boomers," Arnold adds underneath. Then one to Rabbi Klaperman: "I want you bad," signed "Lola, the Fox." And one to Rabbi Mermelstein: "Your bald head drives me crazy," signed "A secret admirer."

They write a few more, pass them around, and then Arnold gives one he has written to Ivan. It has a cartoon of a woman sitting on the hood of a car. It says, "Dear Mom, show us some titty," and is signed, "Your loving son, Zitski."

Ivan whips a handful of caramels at Arnold. They slap his face, stinging, and clatter behind him on a stack of tin milk boxes. Ivan reaches into the briefcase again; a handful of jujubes goes flying, then marshmallow bars melted in a heap, until Arnold has lifted Ivan off his seat, has him by the neck against the fence.

"You little jerk," Arnold says, rolling his mouth in a frenzy of preparation. "What should I do with you now?"

Ivan looks at him. "You're shit," he says. "I don't care what you do."

Arnold holds him another moment, then releases him with a sharp smack to both cheeks, sending his glasses to the ground. Arnold lets loose a gob that arcs toward the top of the supermarket, then disappears in sunlight over the roof.

They fill their pockets with candy and toss the rest over the fence. David distributes Magic Markers and they scrawl across the wall of Bohack's. "Mid-Queens Hebrew sucks!" Arnold writes, and "Willis Reed is God." David writes "YANKEES!" and "Doris Goldhammer" in a blue heart. The rear door of the supermarket rattles and the two boys drop their Markers and run up the alley to the street. Ivan ignores the sound. He is over on his side of the wall, working slowly. With care, he writes, "ShitPissMotherfuckerNiggerKikeBastardJew." Over it he draws a large red swastika. He puts his Marker in his pocket and walks quietly out to the street.

At the entrance to the Sutphin Boulevard station, Birnbaum says they should wait for Pitski. "Fuck him, " Leibowitz says, but he stays. A taxi rolls by and for a moment David thinks he sees Rabbi Klaperman against the back seat, with the school nurse leaning over him. But the taxi turns the corner before he can be sure, and then Pitski walks by them, past the columns with the green glass globes, down the stairs to the subway.

Arnold vaults over the turnstile, and Ivan and David run through one of the exit doors. In his glass booth, the token collector follows their movements without expression.

Arnold lives toward 179th Street, in Bayside, and the other boys live toward the city. But it's the middle of a schoolday, an extraordinary Tuesday, and no one is ready to go home.

On the platform, billboards advertise liquor and cigarettes, chewing gum. Four sets of tracks run before them, two inner sets for expresses, the outer two for locals. The tracks gleam silver into the tunnels on either side, where they disappear in darkness.

Arnold shows them how to get penny Chiclets by kicking the handle of the machine. He tries this procedure on the green Coke machine, which moves back an inch or so, but doesn't give out any Coke. They take Ivan's Marker and give Mayor Lindsay a mustache and black eye, and draw glasses and missing teeth on the face of a gentleman advertising English gin. When the express hurtles through the center tracks, the boys stop to watch. Sparks fly from the thundering wheels, and passengers' faces flash by as in old movies, flickering between the pillars. They are impassive, these faces, as are the boys', as though nobody is looking at anything.

As they wait for the local, Arnold and David kick a small stack of newspapers around, but it soon falls apart. David is suffused with hilarity. He can't remember such a wild time. Just thinking about the looks on his father's and uncle's faces fills him with profound fear and exhilaration. A wild time. He takes his yarmulke — a tightly knit cap with his name on the side in blue lettering — from his pocket. He has not taken it off in public before. Even in the house, his grandfather would say, you cannot take more than three steps without a head covering; it is an affront to God. David takes the yarmulke and flips it, Frisbee-style, to Arnold, ten feet up the platform. It carries nicely; David can see his name spiraling in the air. Arnold catches it and tosses it back. Ivan, off to one side, looks away.

When David hooks a throw, Arnold does what he can, but the yarmulke sails off the platform and lands between the rails below. The boys stand on the platform's yellow lip, looking down, and then David jumps, before he can think it over. He grabs the yarmulke, takes a quick look up the subway tunnel — just a few light bulbs in the darkness—then leaps up, getting his torso over the ledge, where Arnold helps him to his feet.

The second time, Arnold goes to retrieve the yarmulke. He picks it up and stands, peering into the tunnel ahead of him. "I think I see it coming," Arnold says.

"Bull," says David. "I don't hear a thing."

"I can see all the way down the tunnel," Arnold says, taking a couple of steps forward. "I see lights on the walls, all the way down, and a red dot. That's the F train," Arnold says.

"Well, get up here, then," David says.

Arnold looks at David and grins. "Why? You want your precious yami, the one Mommy made for her big boy?" He takes another step toward the tunnel. "Come and get it."

David leans over the tracks until he fears he will fall. In the tunnel he sees the back of a signal lamp, red and yellow glass in a long box. That's all he sees. Then, faintly, he hears a rumbling, distant but clear. He wonders if Arnold hears it and looks over. Arnold is still grinning, but at Ivan now.

"How 'bout the little fat boy?" Arnold says. "Why don't you come down here, little Ivan? I think I see your mother with the conductor."

Ivan stands a few feet from the edge of the platform. He has his hands in his pockets.

"You're shit," he tells Arnold. Then he looks at David. "You both are. You came out of my ass."

David looks at Ivan in his plaid shirt and green corduroys. He looks at the glasses and the pale head where veins pulse blue. He takes two steps and snatches the boy's yarmulke. It is a cloth one, a fancy black cap with satin trim. David flings it as far as he can up the tracks. When he looks back, silver light is glinting off the two rails that run into the station.

Arnold scrambles onto the platform by himself, and the boys watch as the F roars from the tunnel to stop in a shattering shriek of brakes. Two men get out and an old woman the boys hadn't noticed gets on, looking at them through a window as the train pulls away. They watch until it turns around a bend.

Ivan moves to the front of the platform.

"That's two steps, Zitski," David says. "One more and God will blast you to hell." Arnold laughs. Ivan steps to the edge, looks down at the skullcap half-floating in a puddle by the far track. He knows what Birnbaum is talking about, but what he sees is himself coming home without his yarmulke; his mother, more superstitious than devout, grabbing him at the door, making him kneel with her to pray, the two of them like that on the floor, half on the street, the door not even closed behind them. He jumps.

He looks quickly up the tunnel but sees no sign of a train. A string of single lights loops away in the dark. He can hear nothing. He picks up the wet yarmulke and wipes it on his shirt, puts it back on his head.

Ivan walks to where the boys stand, and jumps. He is too short. On the second try, he manages to get his elbows over the ledge, but after a couple of seconds he falls back. He looks at the boys above him.

"Need some help?" David says. "You require some assistance?"

"I think he does," Arnold says. "That's what it looks like to me."

"I'd like to help," David says, "but shit doesn't have arms, right, Ivan?"

Arnold hoots once and sends a celebratory round into the tunnel. It flips in the light, seems, somehow, to make a turn, and disappears. Ivan jumps, gets his elbows on the platform again, kicks his feet, hangs a moment. While he is suspended, straining to get his feet over the ledge, Leibowitz hits him right in the eye with a good one. It stretches from his eye to his lip and drops off. Ivan hangs there, trembling with the effort. Not understanding exactly why, David takes hold of one of Ivan's shoulders to help him up.

The moment he touches him, Ivan squirms. He turns his head and they look at each other—David looks right into the magnified blue globes of Pitski's eyes, sees the pale skull the color of eggs under the blond hair. Ivan spits. David feels the warm spatter on his face. With a grunt, he shoves Pitski back onto the tracks. He falls. An express, going the other way, passes behind him. The three boys, two on the platform, one in the tracks, watch the faces in the windows, feel the rumble in their feet until the train reenters the tunnel.

Pitski stands and dusts himself off. He looks at his briefcase, then at the two boys—Birnbaum is wiping his face with a sleeve and Leibowitz is laughing to himself, about to speak. He says something but Pitski doesn't hear it. Before Leibowitz has the chance to repeat himself, Pitski turns his back on them and begins walking, up the tracks, in the direction he assumes will be home.

For C.P.

LYON

To get the money the brothers traveled by bus to Nice, where Jewish money was still allowed in banks. The Jews there lived like people in stories. There was no war going on, no trainloads heading north. The women wore furs to their ankles, bright silk dresses and scarves, the men wore top hats and carried canes. They stopped in the street to light each other's cigars. They walked up and down the promenade in front of the hotels talking in every language—German, Russian, Polish, French. On the beach they lay in striped tents and gave orders to waiters, who ran across the sand and back, balancing drinks and chocolates on small trays. The water was blue like the sky in storybooks. There were white boats bobbing on the waves.

While they waited for the money to be collected, a housekeeper at one of the hotels let the boys sleep in a room off the kitchen. The last night was unseasonably warm, a spring night in February. Two maids they knew knocked on their door with bottles of wine, sausages, a block of hard cheese. They ate on the beach, rolled up their pants and waded in the chilly surf. Music reached the water's edge, violins from one of the hotels, and the air carried clean, salty smells that seemed to come from far off.

The older girl was talkative, with dark eyes and red lips. She put one hand on Rachmil's shoulder, another on his waist. They kissed and took the last bottle of wine behind the dunes. The younger girl was nice, about Maxim's age, chubby and shy and

yawning against the back of her hand. At home, she told him, in
Mirande, she helped her grandmother with the goats. She missed
her grandmother and she missed the goats. She hoped to be going
home soon. Her grandmother was very old.

They watched a light on the water and debated whether it was
a buoy or a fishing boat. They pressed their lips together a few
times and held hands. Soon the girl began yawning harder.
Maxim took his jacket and rolled it into a pillow for her head.

"Why don't you boys stay here?" the girl said from the sand.

He hadn't mentioned why they had come, what their situation
was. But she was a nice girl, maybe she had merely guessed.

"Our mother," was all Maxim said. "Perhaps we will come
back."

It was 1943. The agency that helped smuggle Jews into
Switzerland had sent them, this third trip, to collect money from
the rich and—for the time being—protected Jews in the Italian
Zone. Tomorrow they would be returning with enough money
for six families to escape to Geneva. Maxim wondered what this
farm girl would make of such information. He wondered when
his name, and his mother's and brother's, would reach the top of
the list. He wondered if she would do more than kiss him if he
tried. He looked at her, her full lips and pretty face. She turned
onto her side and pulled his jacket closer.

Maxim stretched out near her and looked at the sea. His head
was lightly spinning from wine. To steady himself he tried to
count a rhythm to the waves, anticipating their landfall, anticipating the whisper as the water pulled back from the sand. He managed for three waves, for two, for three again, but he couldn't do
it. The girl beside him slept, breathing softly. From behind the
dunes he could hear his brother's terrible French, his soft curses
in Polish, the girl laughing. He lay back on the sand and closed
his eyes. He gave up trying to count. He let the waves come when
they were ready.

· · ·

Maxim Birnboym, sixteen, had been in the city barely eight months, still, long enough to learn its weather, and he had not seen a morning like this. He stepped from his apartment and stopped to look at the sky. The wind seemed scattered, coming at him from all directions. Snow blew in gray flurries between the houses, and unfurled like rugs being snapped against the roof-tops. Dry flakes danced sideways, skittered like confetti on the chipped cobbles of rue Docteur Zola. Next door a girl ran coat-less into the street, turned with mouth open and arms out-stretched in the biting cold, until her grandmother caught her, pulled her inside with quick slaps to the back of the neck. The girl smiled at Maxim and stuck out her tongue but the old lady gave him a look as if the girl's depravity, maybe even the weather, were his doing. He pulled his cap over his ears and walked.

At the corner the tobacconist's retired father sat on his chair in a woolen vest, pipe turned down against the wind, red coals falling onto his pants. Maxim raised a hand to him and to the son, visible through the window, rolling cigars on a greasy wooden board, but if the tobacconist saw he ignored the greeting, and the old man was looking past him at the sky, a dim yellow, pulsing snow. Over their heads, a flock of pigeons burst from a rooftop and circled. Maxim looked right at the old man, his grizzled face stained below the lips, his intolerable blue eyes, the blue eyes of a boy, and did not feel afraid until he turned the corner, where without stopping he shifted the parcel under his shirt and com-manded himself to breathe.

It was a long walk to the Agency. His shoes were badly worn but he had the good coat; Rachmil, the felt hat and scarf. Neither had warm shoes. The cold came through his feet as if he were walking on iron. In Cracow, he would never be wearing shoes like this. In Cracow, he would be in Gymnasium now, he and his friends would be sitting in cafés looking at girls in the square. He told himself not to think about it. His mother said they would remember, together, when they got out. Now there was no time.

Dry snow continued falling. There was a cast to the light in the streets, a peculiar dullness. He would be glad to be out of this weather. At the office they would give him a cup of tea and a warm roll. He reached rue Ste.-Catherine and paused. No cars before the office, no soldiers or police. At number 12 he stopped, leaned against the wall, and lit a cigarette. He smoked, watching the street. A mother with an infant wrapped in a blanket hurried past him. It was Monday, the doctor and nurse would be in to see patients, money would be dispersed to Jews who needed it. He wondered if Rachmil was already up there, flirting with Suli, the Rumanian typist.

An old man, in the stovepipe pants and round shoes he must have worn in Lublin, carried an envelope thick with papers through the door. Maxim watched two sparrows bathe in a puddle in the street. Even their tiny weight cracked the lip of ice reaching from the puddle's edge and they pecked at falling snow as if it were corn. *Jest zimno*, he said to the birds in Polish. It's cold. Then the church clock chimed ten and he threw down the cigarette, shifted his weight one last time, and entered the building.

Inside, the unlit stairs, the dank residue of a thousand cooked meals. Newspapers on the floor, a paper sack full of coffee grounds and trash someone had left to be carried out later. On the second floor the door was closed, not unusual, and he heard weeping, probably the mother of the sick child. He grasped the brass handle, stepped in, and saw immediately that, once again, everything had changed.

Two soldiers aimed rifles at him. Another was behind the door, waving his arm inward in mock welcome. A German in a leather coat was speaking to the switchboard operator. "Tell them to come," he said in French. "Tell them it's all right, the doctor is here. We want as many as possible." A little apart, at the back of the room, were the doctor and the nurse. The doctor sat in a wooden chair, his tie undone and his hat in his hand. The nurse held a cloth to his eye.

By one of the desks stood a group of men, one woman. Maxim recognized the laborers who had been replacing broken windows out back, the woman who delivered rolls from the bakery. The woman was drinking from Suli's coffee cup and the laborers were smiling and eating the rolls. On the other side of the room, another group, larger, thirty or forty people pressing against each other and the wall. They wore their coats and hats, though the room was stifling. A few looked at Maxim, then away. No one spoke. The crying came from here, not the mother—the child was asleep on her shoulder—but from the old Pole, bent halfway to the floor, his back heaving with sobs. On a small table were the old man's envelope and a stack of identity cards. One of the laborers made a joke Maxim didn't hear, and the Germans with the rifles laughed. To the rear of the Jews were Suli, red-eyed, and, taller by a head than the rest and staring into the room with no expression, Rachmil.

"Good morning." The man in the leather coat approached Maxim. "Come in, come in." He was young, with lively, interested eyes and Brilliantined hair. He seemed to enjoy speaking French and he raised his chin at Maxim, as if eager for conversation.

"What's this? A raid?" the boy said, trying to steady his voice. He sounded tinny to himself, adolescent and frightened, and to the side he thought he saw Rachmil shift against the wall.

"Papers," the German said, quietly, putting out his hand. He smiled with fine white teeth and it seemed every strand of his oiled hair shone in the light. Maxim, conscious of the parcel, pulled out his identity card, with "Français" under "Nationality," and the name Maxim Bossard by his photograph. His accentless French had won him the card. On the table, he knew, was his brother's—Rachmil had never bothered with languages at school—with *Juif* stamped in red over the name Rachmil Birnboym.

As the man studied the card, bent it and held it to the light, Maxim turned to the group of Jews, casually looking them up and down. His brother stood immobile, their father's gray scarf wound stylishly around his throat. The boy began to panic. They were so similar he flinched to see his brother's face towering above the crowd. Then Rachmil looked right at him. As slightly as he could, without any expression, Rachmil moved his head side to side, did it again, and was still. Maxim understood this. It meant, "There is nothing you can do." It meant, "You don't know me." Rachmil looked away.

"What a country," the German said in his own language. He held the card out to Maxim but, before the boy could reach it, dropped it on the floor. "You can't tell the pigs from the dogs." The German behind the door laughed quietly and the two with the guns smiled. The laborers and the woman with the coffee looked stonily ahead.

Maxim bent to pick up the card and as he did he felt himself tumbling into a great hole, where air sounding like water rushed in on him. He gave his brother one last glance. He had not moved.

"So," the German said, turning, addressing him again. "You have something for me."

"No," Maxim said. "I have nothing."

The German looked at him as if they had been debating the point for hours and his patience was finally exhausted. He shook his head, an exasperated motion, and put a hand to his hair. He stepped forward and, looking away, slapped Maxim hard with the back of his hand. He tore open the jacket to get at the parcel and a button flew off, skated on the wooden floor to the far wall, where it stopped under the window. It was the only sound in the room.

The German held the parcel up to Maxim and raised his hand again. Maxim felt himself flinch.

"This," he said in German. "You brought this for me, yes?" He ripped open the white butcher paper and began counting bills. When he was done he regarded Maxim with disgust. He spoke French again. "You have a love for Jews?"

"Sometimes." Maxim tried to sound indifferent. "One must make a life."

And the German turned away, dropping the parcel on the table with the identity cards. The old Pole stared at Maxim, no longer weeping. "Get out," the German said. "Another day I would gladly show you the cure for such affections. Today I'm in a good mood. Today I have no time." He waved a hand. "Get out."

Maxim had not looked at his brother again. He had not felt anything but panic, hands reaching into his throat from his chest. At the bottom of the stairs he quickly lit a cigarette so he wouldn't cry. He had so much to do. He must call immediately, using the code, to tell them about the raid. He might have to get word himself to the families who expected the money, whose passage would now be canceled. He must go out to the street, get away from this building, find a telephone.

Behind him a door opened and a woman reached for the bag of trash. She looked at him a moment, then put the bag down again. He held the cigarette against his mouth. At home he would find the apartment dark. There would be cups from breakfast on the table, the ashtray they filled with cigarettes, this morning's paper. His mother had hardly left her bed in the weeks since his father had made them leave Cracow. She told them every morning they would be united, they and their father somehow, together, in Switzerland, Canada, the United States. She had believed this. She had asked them to believe. When she heard him, she would call down the dim hallway, waking from sleep, "What is it? Who's there?" And he would close the door and answer her, "It's me, Mother, Maxim. Rachmil is gone."

The door behind him opened again and this time a girl stepped out, his age or a year younger. She wore a heavy winter coat open over a faded blue dress, and there was food on her mouth, a smudge of red jam near her lips. She picked up the paper sack and stood looking at Maxim with flat, angry eyes, as if she had expected to find him waiting there. Maxim pushed the handle and stepped into the street. He could already feel the cold through his shoes as he moved away from the building and began to walk.

THE STREET YOU LIVE ON

Twice a week, Maura had her quiet times. She enjoyed solitude, and on Tuesdays and Thursdays, her nights to prepare dinner, she had a small, pleasant routine David knew nothing about. She would shower and feed Lucy, their cat. She would decide what to make, usually the first easy recipe she found, and start things boiling or thawing or heating up. She would pour a glass of wine, put on some music, and sit in front of the double windows in the living room watching evening come on, smoking a joint. In college, David had gotten high every night—he told her that one entire year he had been stoned—but they hadn't smoked together in ages. She kept two joints in a plastic tampon holder in her purse, and every Monday paid Richie, another teller at the bank, for a week's supply. It wasn't that David would disapprove; more likely, he would be hurt she felt it necessary to hide it from him. But this was *her* time: twice a week, to be calm and peaceful and alone, with dinner cooking and her husband on his way. If David suspected—as she thought he must—she was grateful he let her be. And if he didn't, so much the better.

The dinners had been David's idea. He had been working so hard on Crestview Estates—final presentation was a week away—it seemed they saw each other only at the coffee maker or passing in and out of the bathroom. One day, he noticed something different about her. After he determined she hadn't cut her hair, lost or gained any weight, tried a new makeup or perfume, she told him he simply didn't recognize her. The following day, she had come home to poached salmon with raspberry sauce, and the dinners had begun.

This Thursday, Maura showered, put on a pair of sweats and a T-shirt, and fed Lucy, who had complained through the shower curtain the entire time she was in the bath. While she decided about dinner, she opened a bottle of Chardonnay and played some old Bonnie Raitt. She danced for a while, cutting onions, searing them in a pan, moving her hips and feeling the buzz, as she always did, from the feet up. She held Lucy and sang to her, but when she reached "I want a man to hold me, not some fool to ask me why," Lucy decided she didn't like the smoke, or the entertainment, and twisted out of her arms to the floor. The old LP had clicked itself off and Maura was halfway through the joint, her feet up on the sill, watching the light over the buildings on 108th Street and enjoying the breeze, when the doorbell rang. She rose absentmindedly, on the second ring, and only after she had opened the door on the policemen did she realize the joint was in the ashtray, and not in her hand or dangling from her lips.

"Maura Birnbaum?" There were two policemen, a middle-aged man in street clothes, and a younger one, in uniform. It was the older one who spoke, saying her name again, as if it were foreign. "Maura Birnbaum? 311 West 109th, Apartment 3-A?" He flashed a gold badge at her. "Detective Kasko, Twenty-fourth precinct. You have a moment?"

Her first thought was of David, then her mother. An accident— ambulances, lights flashing, running through hospital corridors not knowing what waited at the other end—her whole life immediately and irrevocably changed. Then she remembered there had been messages from each of them on the machine, both fine, both tired, David late in coming home. So everything must be all right, but her heart still pounded and she had to tell herself to breathe. The detective took off his hat and jiggled a finger in his ear. He was dark-haired and thickly built, about forty-five, with a wide florid face, and he had sweated right through his suit jacket. He probed the ear gingerly and straightened with pain. Maura could smell the pot clearly. She wasn't sure of her rights. Could she ask to see a warrant? More identification?

"I was just making dinner," she said, but it came out sounding like a lie. The patrolman smiled brightly and touched the bill of his cap as if he admired the idea. He continued smiling at her until Maura felt uncomfortable. She crossed her arms on the T-shirt and felt herself move a step back into the apartment. "I'm expecting my husband any moment," she said.

"Of course, miss," the detective said, still wincing. "Five minutes. Tops."

Maura took another step back, uncertain, and immediately the cops were inside. She expected them to go directly for the joint, but the detective stopped in the center of the room, and the patrolman went down on his haunches and whistled for Lucy, who trotted over from Maura's basket of yarn and lay on her back, though she was notorious for her suspicion of strangers.

"Nice place," Detective Kasko said, without looking at it. "You wouldn't have any aspirin in the house, would you, miss?"

When Maura brought the aspirin, they still had not moved. The joint lay in the ashtray, sprouting fronds of white smoke in the air. She walked over and stubbed it out herself. She could see into the bedroom, where she had thrown her skirt and blouse and underwear on the white spread, her blue bra draped over the side. The patrolman was still rubbing Lucy's belly, and she could feel his eyes on her as she passed to close the bedroom door.

"Doctors, huh, Miss Birnbaum?" Detective Kasko said. "One says inner ear, one says middle. One says penicillin, one says anti-inflammatory. I say, Doctors, excuse me, this is fascinating, but what about the guy in my head with the jackhammer?"

Maura waited for him to swallow the pills, which he did, without water. Then he took a pad from his jacket pocket and made a few notations. Every few seconds he shook his head, like a man trying to clear his thoughts. The patrolman was walking about the room, looking at the bookshelves, the pictures of family, picking things up and putting them down. He stopped before the scale model of Crestview Estates and picked up one of the figurines.

"Hey," he said to the detective. "Look at this tiny briefcase."

Detective Kasko joined him at the model. "Here's a little cop," he said, holding up another figure.

"That's my husband's work," Maura said. "Please leave it alone." The policemen stopped and looked at her.

"Right you are," Detective Kasko said. He studied the model, trying to remember where the figure had come from. Finally, he handed it to Maura. The patrolman thought this was funny. He gave Maura his figure, also.

"Look," she said. "Detective. You said five minutes."

"Right you are, Miss Birnbaum," Detective Kasko said again, thumbing his pad. "Would you step over to the window?"

Maura put the figures in the Sun Plaza behind the shopping mall. They were out of place, she knew, but she couldn't remember where they belonged. David could fix it later. The detective was gesturing out the window. She stood near him and followed the angle of his arm across the courtyard and took a quick breath. From the apartment opposite, two men watched her. One held a camera, and the other stood with his arms across his chest, looking directly at her. She stepped back. She started to ask the detective what they were doing, how long had they been there, but he opened his note pad and began to read.

"Sylvia Chafetz, Caucasian, thirty-six years, 284 West 108th. Computer processor. Unmarried. Tuesday, September 27th, killed by intruder or intruders unknown, multiple sharp blows to the head, approximately 7:30 p.m. No sign of forced entry." He looked up at Maura. "Survivors: Mr. and Mrs. W. Chafetz, parents, Long Island City, New York, and brother, Henry, college student in California." He closed the pad. "You weren't by any chance acquainted with the deceased, were you, Miss Birnbaum?"

He fingered his inflamed ear. Maura wanted to ask if she could sit, but was afraid to. Across the way, the policeman with the camera leaned out the window and took pictures of the courtyard. The other had disappeared from sight. Detective Kasko touched her shoulder.

"This is upsetting news," he said. "I'm sorry to upset you. Please. Take a seat."

Maura sat on the couch, and the patrolman brought her a glass of water. "Drink," Detective Kasko said. "You'll be all right." He turned the easy chair from the window. The ashtray with the discarded joint lay on the arm of the chair between them. Maura drank the water and the detective watched, his broad face patient and encouraging. When she was done, he took the glass and handed it to the patrolman, who went to the kitchen for more. "Better?" he said to Maura.

"Yes," she said.

"You're a sensible girl." He leaned toward her. "What we were hoping is you could give us some information. The deceased lived alone. She led a quiet life, kept to herself." He shifted still closer and Maura could see the stubble on his cheeks, the dense sagging flesh around his eyes. His ear was red from the lobe to the crown and looked painful enough to give off heat. "We were wondering if maybe you noticed anything noteworthy the night of the incident. Noises, peculiar goings on, things of that nature." She looked up at him and he turned to the window. "There was considerable damage to personal effects. Being as your apartment is directly in view, we were hoping you might help us out."

Maura looked around the room for Lucy, who had disappeared.

"Think back," the detective said. "Two nights ago. The Yankees played Cleveland. You a fan?"

"We didn't see the game," Maura said.

"Good. Saved yourself some heartache. What else?"

Maura took the second glass of water from the patrolman but didn't drink. "I was here," she said. "My husband came back and we had dinner. We watched a movie, I think. That's all I remember, I'm sorry. I didn't see anything."

"You sure?" the patrolman said. He stood near her, she could see his wide leather belt, a long black flashlight hanging from it, and around to the side the holster for his gun. He was smiling again, his head cocked, brows drawn downward in a look of friendly, somehow intimate, skepticism. "It's right across the way there," he said.

Detective Kasko continued leaning toward her, and Maura was afraid for a moment they did not believe her. Then, abruptly, he stood. He brought a hand to the side of his head. He held the fingers away from the skin, not touching. "Doctors, huh, miss?" He smiled. "We've bothered you long enough," he said, and to the patrolman, quietly, as Maura followed them to the door, words she could not make out.

Detective Kasko handed her a card. "If you remember anything else," he said. When he opened the door, Lucy darted from under the table and tried to escape into the hall. The patrolman caught her and handed her to Maura. Detective Kasko tapped the glass peep hole. "I'd use this, miss," he said, and gestured at the couch. "Especially if I was doing something the whole world shouldn't know about."

Maura waited while David got a beer from the refrigerator. He drank half of it leaning against the sink, then bent to pick up Lucy, who had been whining by his feet for attention. He checked the oven, found it empty, saw the cold pan of onions. Through the door to the kitchen, Maura saw him lift the pan an inch or so, then drop it back on the burner. On his way to the bathroom, he paused before Crestview Estates. He studied the model a moment, and picked up the policeman figurine

Maura had taken from Detective Kasko. Then he noticed the joint.

"Yours?" he said.

Maura nodded.

He put the joint in his mouth, lit it, and spoke between short inhalations. "Secret lives," he said. "The woman. I thought. I knew." He put the figure down by the condominium tower, shifted something by the duck pond, took a long drag, and went in to shower.

When he came out, Maura was still on the couch. He turned on a light and sat next to her, rubbing his hair with a towel. "Bad day?" he asked.

Maura told him about Sylvia Chafetz, about Detective Kasko and his ear, about the patrolman who couldn't stop staring or smiling. She told him about Lucy's strange behavior. She could see David was tired from a long day, and annoyed she had not made dinner, but when Maura told him the murder took place directly across the courtyard, he got up and went to the window. He was dressed only in a towel and he stood there, trying to relight the joint.

"Don't do that," Maura said. "They'll see you."

He ignored her, took a drag off the joint, and held it out to her. She didn't take it. "Which one?" he said.

"Right opposite," Maura said. "Aren't the lights on?"

"Yup," David said. "The old kill-them-and-prop-them-in-front-of-the-television trick. Sandwich is a good touch."

Maura walked over. In Sylvia Chafetz's apartment, the lights were out, the windows open. Something gleamed dully in one of the rooms, a lamp shade reflecting, perhaps, and to look at it made Maura uncomfortable. The apartment David meant was next door, to the left. A woman in a housedress ate a sandwich in front of a TV.

"Hey, I've seen that one," David said, leaning across the sill.

"Sam and Diane get locked in the supply room together. Remember?"

When he saw Maura was not smiling, he stopped. David had a way of making Maura's concerns seem small—matters, simply, of outlook—that she usually found reassuring. Now she stared at him and wanted to hit him in the face. She went back to the couch.

"Sorry," David said. "Too tired for better jokes." He sat near her. He reached out to pull her head onto his shoulder, but she didn't respond. He left his hand on her knee. "Probably a lover's quarrel," he said.

"Why do you say that? The police said she lived alone."

"She wouldn't let him move in, so he killed her."

Maura jerked her knee away, started to stand. "Okay, okay," he said, catching her hand. "What's bothering you, exactly? The crime? You didn't know this lady, did you?"

"We could have seen it, you know." She sat back down, her knees against her chest, not looking at him. "That poor woman. We could have been sitting, just like this, you making stupid jokes, while right out there someone is being beaten to death." He opened his mouth to say something but she went on. "And those cops, coming in here, touching everything, making me feel stupid and vulnerable—hiding my underwear in my own home." She looked toward the bedroom, its door still closed. "I just don't like the way I feel," she said.

"How?"

"I don't know. Different. I just don't like it."

After a moment, he slid over and held her. Water trickled from his brown hair onto his cheek, was collected in droplets on his shoulders and arms. She said, "When I saw the police at the door, I thought something had happened to you."

He shook his head broadly and smiled, whether because he understood what she had felt or because it was silly of her to have felt it, she couldn't tell. She was feverish and restless in his embrace, but his clean smell after the shower was familiar, and she tried to relax.

"We're fine," David said. "Nothing's going to happen to us."

When she met David, Maura had been barefoot. She had just started at the bank, nearly six years ago. It was lunchtime and she was taking a walk, looking in shop windows, exploring a new neighborhood. She had foolishly bought heels for the job, thinking they would make her look taller, therefore older, therefore more serious than the shy twenty-two-year-old she felt herself to be. It began to rain, slow, lazy drops that marked the sidewalk and store windows. She took the shoes off her aching, hot feet. She continued walking, enjoying the texture of the cool pavement through her stockings, not feeling at all foolish until ahead of her she saw a man in a pin-striped suit, lifting a hand to peer into the glass window of a shop. Expensive socks draped from a pocket of his suit, and his shoes, polished black wingtips pointing neatly ahead, were on the sidewalk by his feet.

All her mother's intoned warnings about New York, about men in New York, came back in one moment. The phrase she heard was "Never make eye contact," and Maura, unable to decide if she should put her shoes on first, kept her eyes down and walked faster.

But when she was passing the man he said, "I had no idea they were so big," and she stopped, not meaning to, looking first at her feet, then at his. She said, "What?"

"Look at the size of that sucker," he said, and she saw, displayed in the window of the shop, a fish, a silver and blue-black fish with a ridge of scales on its back and a sharp nose and tail. It lay on its side in a bed of ice, one dull eye facing her. It must have been eight feet long.

"What is it?" she said.

"A sturgeon."

"Wow. So big?"

The man turned from the window and smiled. "Exactly," he said.

David claimed they could read each other's thoughts, and for a while it seemed that way. He would come home with pizza, garlic and red onion, say, to find it was what she had been craving all day. She would call him in the office and he would say, "I love you," before she had said a word, and there must have been something to it, Maura thought, because what if it was the president of the firm on the line, or a total stranger?

They had read the same books in college, liked and were now embarrassed by the same bands. Their lovemaking was patient, quietly passionate—everything he did was what she had just been thinking about, or hadn't thought of yet. He was full of jokes and surprises, seemed to know exactly where he was headed in life, which was comforting to Maura, who felt in herself no such certainty. He knew where he would be in five years, ten, and when he described the houses they would live in, the cars and children they would have, Maura could almost see them, and she felt light with anticipation and love.

Now he told her nothing would ever happen to them and she wanted to believe him. She took one of his hands and brought it to her lips; he shifted his embrace, moving her closer. She felt his body behind her, his chest comforting at her back, and she told herself she was safe. She wanted to be able to talk with him but didn't know how to say it—that it felt as if something had already happened. They loved each other, she was certain of that; yet if she were truthful with herself she had to realize something, something in her, was different. Her mother said she wanted a baby. Richie, at the bank, said she wanted another cat. Maybe David was just working too hard. Lately they'd been living like polite strangers, their times together like negotiations, wary, deferential, each ready to withdraw any proposal almost before it was made. David said it was just work. When the presentation was made, he told her, when the partners were off his back, when ground was broken on Crestview Estates and they were out of the city, maybe even moved into Crestview Estates itself, a four-bedroom condo on the ninth green, the one with the reflecting pool just over the backyard lawn, where sunburned, overweight men in horrible pastel clothes waved from little carts while they sat in the hot tub, sipping drinks, then, David said, they'd be better. Maura had laughed, said they didn't even play golf. We will, David had said. That's when we'll start.

All Maura could come up with, when she asked herself as honestly as she could what the trouble was, was that she wanted things never to change; she wanted people to remain the way they were at first, at their best; she wanted the days back when she would suggest a movie to David or a walk by the river and he would smile and put his arms around her and she would know he had been thinking just that, that she had said exactly the right thing.

And now, as had often seemed the case lately, she had no words for what she felt. A woman she didn't know was dead, killed where they could have seen it from where they were now sitting, and she didn't know how to tell David that somehow, in some small way, that changed everything.

He held her the way she liked, both arms around her, his hands over her breasts. She leaned back into him, resting. "Sweetheart," he said. "It's scary. It's upsetting. I'm upset, too." He kissed her ear, pushing the hair away. "But we have to look at the statistics. Maybe two thousand people live on this block, right? And one of them gets unlucky. That's terrible. But New York isn't even one of the most violent cities. Did you know that?"

"Yes."

"It's worse in Detroit, it's much worse in Miami or Washington, not to mention Casper, Wyoming, where some liquored-up rancher would take you for a deer and blow your head off." He played with her hair, twisting it on his finger. "Right? What can I tell you? This is the city. You're going to run across things."

"I know," Maura said.

"I know you know," he whispered. "You're sexy when you know." He reached around and kissed her cheek softly. He turned her to

him and moved his lips onto hers and when she allowed him to
he kissed her and then he took her hand and put it under the
towel. She was on her feet and had her hands behind her in fists.
He put his hands up beside his head as she had seen athletes do in
basketball games they watched on TV. "No harm," was what the
gesture meant. "No foul."

"Okay. We'll talk later, all right?" He was up now, gathering his
wet towel and heading to the bedroom to dress. She could tell he
was angry. "All right?" he said. He pulled some underwear out of a
drawer and slipped it on under the towel, opened a drawer and
pulled out a shirt. "You didn't ask me a thing about my day, did
you?" he said, and with a twinge of regret Maura realized she
hadn't. "Williams says tomorrow the shit hits the fan. The investors
don't want to wait until next month, never mind that's the deadline
we've been working toward for a year and a half. They want it
tomorrow. Williams says all our asses are on the line." He threw the
two wet towels on the bed, near her pile of clothes, and came out of
the bedroom in a white T-shirt and worn jeans, dragging a comb
through his hair. "Look, we'll talk later. I'm not mad but you didn't
make dinner and I've got about seventy hours of work between me
and bed. I'll make a Chinese run. Want to come?"

She shook her head.

"You okay?" he said at the door.

Maura nodded. He blew a short kiss at her and was gone.
Maura remained on the couch. She thought about relighting the
joint, putting on some music, but didn't do either, and when
Lucy climbed into her lap she barely stroked her head and the cat
moved apart on the couch and went to sleep.

Hours later she couldn't tell if she was dreaming or not. She lay
in bed, half awake, remembering their wedding, David's family
there, hers, except it had to be a dream because Richie and
David's sister were passing a joint to David's old aunt, who
accepted it like an expert, and Detective Kasko was there, and
the patrolman, holding Lucy the cat. Music played dimly, half-

muffled salsa, and somewhere toward the back, people danced. Maura couldn't make out the guests seated in the front rows, women in hats, long-haired, their faces obscured by shadow. David was barefoot and he was having trouble crushing the glass at their feet. It kept rolling away, and Maura decided to ask him right then what she'd been meaning to ask since they'd met—on the sidewalk that first time, had he really been standing with his shoes off when she had passed, or had he seen her coming and taken them off?

Maura woke to find David in bed with her, pulling at her pajamas. For a moment she didn't know where she was, then she opened her eyes and saw him. He smelled of beer and mumbled something but she couldn't tell if it was to her or not. She adjusted herself so David could get her pajama bottoms off, helped him with two buttons of her shirt, and when he climbed on top of her she tried to waken just enough to feel his warmth. Over his shoulder she could see the drafting table in the living room, empty Chinese cartons, beer cans and paper on the floor and the couch. He moved on her, lifted his hips and breathed in her face. His elbow pinned one of her arms. "Ready?" he said.

She waited until he was asleep. On her way to the bathroom, Maura stopped to close the windows. White curtains blew into the room. She reached to pull down the window and saw, across the way, the woman still there, still in front of the television, now doing her nails. She had a bottle of red nail polish on the plate where the sandwich had been, and every few seconds she held her hand out before her, fingers splayed, as if she were showing Maura. Maura held the window in her hands, feeling the nubbly, soot-dusted paint she could never get clean, and wondered if the woman knew what had happened next door, not twenty yards from where she sat. She wondered if the police had questioned her as well, if she felt, as Maura had, guilty, somehow, the minute they appeared at her door.

As Maura watched, the lady blew on her nails one last time and capped the bottle of polish. She stood. She was a stocky woman, in her thirties, attractive in a rough sort of way, with hennaed hair in thick ringlets about her face. Arms outstretched, she let out a massive yawn that Maura could hear, faintly, all the way across the courtyard. The woman poked a plant on the windowsill and covered a bird cage with a bright-colored cloth. Maura thought she could hear her singing to the covered bird. Then she yawned again, shifted something under her housedress. Maura felt she was intruding; she was queasy from the pot and from not eating and she felt panic gather in her fingers and at the back of her neck. But she could not make herself look away. She waited until the woman turned out the light and left the room. In the faint illumination of stars and reflected streetlamps, the two apartments, the woman's and Sylvia Chafetz's, were identical.

She had seen her. Sylvia Chafetz, in the next day's paper, a photograph, smudged-looking, blurry, taken from the side as she was already turning away. The caption read "Victim was thirty-five," and Maura tried to concentrate on the article, which recounted the facts she already knew with some neighbor reactions—"quiet girl," "always had a smile and a hello"—but she was drawn back to the picture, a young woman, younger-looking than thirty-five (hadn't Kasko said thirty-six?), with high cheekbones and long dark hair, just beginning to smile as she tried to elude the photographer's gaze. She had seen her.

Maura recognized her from the bank, from the Red Apple on Broadway, from the all-night Korean grocer where they bought their fruit. She had seen her many times. They had never spoken, but she was a neighbor, one of the faces Maura recognized on her block, a face you nodded to, or, even if you didn't, were glad to see, as a sign you were nearing home.

One night the previous year, when they were to leave the following day for a week in Vermont, the four washers in the basement of their building had been occupied. Maura had gone upstairs for the shopping cart and wheeled her load around to Broadway and the Laundromat on 106th. Even here she had to wait for a washer to open and she had settled in with an old *Vanity Fair* for a long stay.

There were several other people in the Laundromat, which, with its nearly unbearable bright lighting and the heat and hum of the machines, seemed to Maura like the set of some futuristic thriller. Faces passing on the street looked through the steamy windows and a homeless man with a blue tarp over his belongings banged a shopping cart through the door, took the seat farthest from the front, dropped his head onto his chest, and was immediately asleep.

A nervous-looking man in Lycra biking shorts and a racing cap signaled Maura he was done with his three washers. She got up to approach, but then he glanced around and saw there were no empty dryers, though several had stopped, the heaped clothing through the doors oddly still in all the motion of the place. He looked at Maura, raised his eyebrows and hands theatrically in the air, and, with a turn so elaborate Maura wondered if he was joking, began pulling armloads of clothing from two dryers, piling them in metal laundry carts he then rolled away with a flourish. Maura smiled distantly, aware she would not be too happy if she came in and found her clean clothes handled by some stranger, aware also that she would be annoyed if, when her clothes were done, someone had left the dryers full. She nodded at the man in passing, said thank you when he handed her a dropped sock, sorted and started her clothes washing, and sat back to her magazine.

A few moments later the cowbell over the door clattered and Sylvia Chafetz walked in. She was wearing jeans and a sweatshirt with "St. Thomas" on it in faded gold lettering. It was her clothing the man had removed from the dryers, and he looked over at Maura. Sylvia Chafetz gave them both a quick smile, in turn, and gathered the two carts with her clothing. The man, still annoyed, stared at her, as if daring her to question him. The cool air that had followed Sylvia Chafetz into the Laundromat reminded Maura how hot she was, that her head had begun aching a half hour ago, that she had forgotten to leave David a note. She was tired and hungry, and she had meant to spend the time waiting for her clothes with a glass of wine and some music, at home. Over her *Vanity Fair*, she stared, too.

Sylvia Chafetz began folding her clothes. She did this slowly, neatly stacking her linens with the folds to the rear in tight piles, folding the T-shirts so they were centered down the front. Unlike Maura, who would throw her clothes and David's into the laundry bag to be sorted at the apartment, Sylvia Chafetz had brought hangers, Static Guard, a lint brush. On the hook jutting from the wall she hung her blouses carefully, smoothed wrinkles, turned cuffs, buttoned buttons. She zipped the pants before hanging them from the hook and made short piles of her socks and underwear, taking her time. She was watching the small ritual of a person who lived alone, Maura realized, and she was embarrassed, as if she were intruding on this woman's privacy.

Then from the bar across the top of one of the carts Sylvia Chafetz began hanging her lingerie, smoothing each item with her hands. The man, sitting on a washer across from Maura, again caught her eye, cocking his head and further opening his eyes in a pantomime of heightened interest. Sylvia Chafetz had four or five simple nightgowns, thigh-length, unadorned, pretty, much like the ones Maura had in her own drawer at home. But she would never hang hers in public this way, she thought, embarrassed for Sylvia Chafetz, who seemed unconcerned, though the man in the bicycle cap was openly smirking. She finished folding her clothes, loading the piles into a shopping cart identical to Maura's, draped the blouses and nightgowns from the handlebar. When she passed the man on the way out he swung his feet dramatically in the air so she could get by, though there was plenty of room. In case he felt like more conversation after Sylvia Chafetz had left, Maura closed the magazine and leaned her head against the wall and shut her eyes.

She remembered this encounter—was it even that?—all day as she cashed checks and counted out bills from behind the brass-barred window at the bank. Sylvia Chafetz—though of course she hadn't known her name then—had seemed just as everyone described her—quiet, unassuming. She had been like everyone else there—except the annoying man in the bicycle cap—tired after a work week, wishing she were somewhere more exciting than the neighborhood Laundromat at seven on a Friday night. Watching her, Maura had felt something sad in the unhurried, practiced motions of this woman, not much older than she, after all, had felt she should go over and start talking, break the insult-ing tacit alliance the man had formed with her, maybe help Sylvia Chafetz—as she would have any woman—fold her clothes faster and get out of there. She would have liked to remember they had talked, at least exchanged glances. But of course they hadn't.

Sylvia Chafetz had worn round horn-rimmed glasses that slid down her nose and a sweatshirt from an old vacation. She was stockier that night than in the photograph in the paper, and she had her hair pulled back in a patterned scarf. Maura could see her perfectly.

That night at the Laundromat, the poor night's sleep she had had, the way Sylvia Chafetz's face kept looming at her from news-papers as people waited in line all weighed on Maura through the day like an intimation, like a fever coming on. She tried to call David at lunch to tell him about it, but, as she expected, his secre-tary said he was unavailable. She called again later and this time the secretary put her hand over the receiver and Maura thought she could hear muffled shouting. No, no message, she told the secretary.

In the break room after work she found the card Detective Kasko had given her and dialed the number. A woman asked her to hold. Behind her Richie was telling a story about a woman in his line today whose dress was so low cut he had lost all concentration and given her five hundreds instead of five twenties. He realized his mistake as he counted them out and was blushing, fumbling in the drawer for the twenties. "She leans over again, I swear, just so I could get another look, and I hand her the bills. And when I say 'Thank you,' she smiles and says, I swear to God, 'On the contrary. Thank *you!*'"

The woman came back on the line and asked if she could help Maura. She sounded as if she had been laughing. Maura asked for Detective Kasko.

"He's out on assignment," the woman said, and from behind her in the police station Maura heard more laughter. She asked if she could leave a message.

"What? Yeah, sure, of course," the woman said, and then, "Hold the line." Maura heard her yell something, then return.

"This is Maura Birnbaum," she said, spelling it for the woman. "Could you ask him to give me a call? He said I should call this number if I remembered anything."

She expected the woman to ask when she had spoken to Kasko, about what case, but the woman simply said, "Sure, honey, I'll tell him," and then she shrieked "You bastard!" at someone and the phone clattered in Maura's ear as she hung up.

Outside, Richie and the other tellers were going to Cannon's for a beer, but Maura declined. She walked away from the noisy group toward the darkening river.

It was dusk, though in the city you could recognize it only by a deeper, bluer light between the buildings before night set in. The air was cool, carrying up from the park just a tinge of smoke, the first night of fall. In front of the shoe repair, a boy in a jeans jacket kissed a girl in a Catholic school uniform. She had her hands in his back pockets, and he held her under her gray plaid vest.

Maura could hear their breathing as she passed. People sat on stoops, reading newspapers in the failing light, listening to radios. She passed the discount cosmetics store where the old Greek lady in the black kerchief sat on a folding chair all day, but she had taken her chair and gone inside already. Maura considered stopping at the Cuban restaurant for one of the colorful fruit drinks she enjoyed in the summer, but the noise from the juke-box somehow turned her away. She crossed the avenue toward home.

Nearly at her door, Maura heard footsteps. She gave a fast look, saw it was a man, saw dark glasses and something in his hand, then she thought she heard the footsteps quicken. She was aware of her hysteria rising; part of her stood off and watched in surprise. She was unable to think clearly, though she told herself she must. She told herself not to as she began to run, and as she reached the door of her building and fumbled for her keys, she was not certain if what she heard was the man behind her or her heartbeat or something else entirely.

Mr. Cohen, who lived alone on 5, stood behind the thick glass door, smiling. "Good evening, Mrs. Birnbaum," he said, pressing down the handle and letting her in. She pushed the heavy door behind her until it clicked shut, and after a few seconds a man passed. He walked slowly and in his hand had a paper bag. He turned to look at Maura and Mr. Cohen through the door, but under the dark sunglasses his face bore no expression.

Mr. Cohen, a retired fur cutter who always stopped to chat with Maura and often sat on the bench in the lobby with the evening *Post*, was blinking at her from under his plaid fedora. Maura tried to smile and allowed herself to breathe. He held his string shopping bags.

"At the Red Apple," Mr. Cohen said, "they got a special in rutabagas, also summer squash. You want I should get you some?" He held up his shopping bags, showing her he had two. "It's no bother."

"No," Maura said, "thank you," taking his dry hand for a moment. He smiled at her and he tipped his hat and went out onto the street.

At her floor, leaning against the wall, appearing to be dozing, was Detective Kasko. The entire left side of his head was covered in a thick white bandage, and as he stepped forward to greet Maura, he held his head stiffly at an odd angle. His eyes were bright with pain.

"Hello, miss. I got your message," he said. "You believe it?" He gestured at the bandage. "Wait and see, the next doctor tells me, 'Kasko, to control this infection we have to cut off your head. You understand, Kasko?' And I'll say, 'Sure, Doc, be my guest.'"

Maura unlocked the door and the detective led the way in. David was not home yet. On the couch, Lucy turned an indifferent shoulder and went back to napping. Maura noticed the joint, shortened by a hit or two, exactly where it had been the previous day. Detective Kasko sat heavily at the table.

"You wouldn't have a glass of water, miss?" he said.

Maura brought the water, and he took two pills from a small cardboard box and swallowed them. "Doctors, huh?" he said, and swallowed two more.

"Where's your friend?" Maura said.

"On a Friday night? You got to be kidding."

Maura took a seat and waited for Detective Kasko to speak. Instead, he looked at the tabletop and made minute adjustments in the position of his head. Maura could see him probing the inside of his mouth with his tongue. Occasionally, he grimaced.

"Detective?"

"Yeah." He did not look at her. "I'm with you." He reached into his jacket and pulled out two photographs, which he slid across the table to Maura. One was the photo from the newspaper, a grainy black-and-white. In her arms—this had been cropped from the newspaper shot—Sylvia Chafetz held a bottle of beer. Behind her, also cropped from the newspaper, were two other people, laughing. It looked like a party. The second photograph was also black-and-white, more sharply focused, an official photograph of the kind you see in passports. Her hair was cut shorter and she was not smiling. She stared directly into the camera, her eyes slightly widened, as though startled by the flash.

"Sylvia Chafetz," Detective Kasko said to the floor. "I hoped these would jog your memory."

"I saw her," Maura said. The detective turned to her, too quickly, for he had to turn halfway back and shift his body instead. "I don't mean that night," Maura said. "I mean I saw her around the neighborhood, before."

Detective Kasko nodded. "Still no recollection of the incident?"

"No, I just recognized her from the neighborhood. I don't guess that's much help."

"And your husband?"

Maura handed him the photographs, and he stood. "Well, thanks again, miss," he said. "We'll be in touch if there's anything else." He shook his head gently. "You got a motor running in here somewhere, miss?"

"No," Maura said. She followed him to the foyer. "Detective?" He paused with his hand on the door. "Are you going to find who did this?"

Detective Kasko looked at her, then at the windows. "I could lie to you, miss," he said. "I could lie but my head's gonna roll onto your carpet any minute, so I don't feel like it." He looked back at her. "We'll never get this guy. Nobody saw anything, nobody heard anything, nobody remembers a single thing from that night. She let somebody in and look what happened. We'll never catch this guy." He opened the door. "A lousy break. Thanks for the water, miss."

. . .

A secretary at David's office, sounding upset, told Maura he was in a meeting, overtime. No way of telling when he'd be done. But I need to speak with him, Maura was about to say, then caught herself. "He says eat without him," the secretary said. "He says he doesn't know when he'll be home." After a moment she added, "I'm sorry."

Maura made a dinner of leftovers for herself and put out a bowl for Lucy. She opened a can of beer, then, after tasting it, poured the rest down the sink.

She sat at the table with one of David's magazines, and picked through the cold chicken on her plate. Across the way, she noticed, the woman next door to Sylvia Chafetz was in her house-dress again, vacuuming. She had the TV on and seemed to be vacuuming the same strip of carpet, moving the machine back and forth while she kept her eyes fixed on the set. Finally, she turned the vacuum off, and Maura could hear the small roar subside across the courtyard. The woman sat in her easy chair and began to watch the TV in earnest.

Maura tried to become interested in an article about the rejuvenation of a Southern town. Someone had unearthed the original plans, and there was great hope that, once these were realized, the town would become the center of learning and commerce it had been a century earlier. When Maura looked up, she saw the woman had a visitor.

She could not see much, only that the visitor was a man, and that he had not taken off his coat. The woman was having a drink, and when the man reached out for the bottle, the woman wouldn't let go. He pulled her up out of the chair, the bottle still gripped between them, and for a moment it seemed they were performing some strange dance. When the breeze shifted in the courtyard, Maura heard their voices, shouting. Then, calmly, pausing first as if to think it over, the man hit the woman in the face with the back of his hand. She released her hold on the bottle and fell.

Maura was out the door, running, before she had any idea what to do. She raced down three flights and onto the street. She stopped, looked around for a police car, then ran again. She was aware of what she saw only in glimpses: Lucy arching her back as Maura ran past; a man giving her room on the stairs; two girls watching her, open-mouthed, from a stoop across the street.

The door to 284 West 108th was open. Maura slapped the intercom panel but did not wait for anyone to respond. On 3, she found the right apartment and pounded the door with her fists, then her feet, chipping flecks of blue paint onto the hall floor.

When she heard someone fumbling with the locks, she backed away. The woman opened the door but did not undo the security chain. She looked out at Maura.

"Harry," she said. "It's a lady."

"What's she banging on the door for?"

"I don't know," the woman said.

"Well, what's she selling?"

Maura stood by the opposite wall, breath rising like a fist in her chest. The woman was still in the housedress, though several of the buttons were undone. She watched Maura through the opening over the door chain and she did not seem hurt or frightened.

"Rosie," the man said. "I thought we were in the middle of something here. Close the goddamn door."

The woman looked at Maura for another moment, then softly shut the door. Maura listened for noises, but heard none. At the far end of the floor, a man stuck his head into the corridor. He looked at Maura, then pulled his head back inside. Maura heard him tell someone, "I don't know. Some nut."

Maura started to leave. Nearly at the stairwell, she turned back. Before Apartment C was a small pile of yellow police tape. The door swung open to her touch. She stepped inside and closed it behind her.

It was a two-room apartment, much like her own, and smelled strongly of paint. Everything was white, the walls, the windows, their bare sills. Carpets had been pulled and studded runners were naked by the walls. Through the open windows squares of moonlight lay on the hardwood floor. A phone, the only furnishing left, sat by the right window, unplugged, wrapped in its cord.

Maura went into the bedroom. It, too, was picked clean. There was not a postcard, a forgotten piece of clothing, an overlooked box—nothing that might hint someone had lived here a week ago. She walked to the kitchen, stepping lightly to avoid causing echoes. In the refrigerator, she found an orange, starting to brown, and a small bottle of Vitamin C tablets. She put the vitamins in her pocket. In the back of a drawer by the stove, she found a ballpoint pen, and a torn envelope with a recipe for date-nut bread copied on the back. She read: 2/3 C dates, pitted. 1/3 C chopped walnuts. Raisins??? She put the pen and the envelope in her pocket. On the top shelf of a hall closet she found a blue kerchief, and in the bathroom cupboard she found the nub of an eyeliner pencil. She looked these items over carefully and took them back into the living room, where she sat on the floor to wait.

After an hour, perhaps longer, she heard it. She rose and went to the window. Across the way, David closed the apartment door. He walked from room to room, stepping in and out of view, looking for her. He walked in heavy, leaning strides, and she could tell he had been drinking. He got a beer and went into the bathroom. When he came out, he did something with his feet, and then he bent to pick up Lucy. He held her by the back of the neck and threw her, hard, swinging his entire body, in the direction of the bedroom. He sat at his drafting table for a moment, drinking. Then he walked to Crestview Estates. He held the beer high over the model and poured, moving slowly, from the shopping mall to the Sun Plaza to the condominiums. Then he threw the can down on the model and looked around him.

He could tell something was wrong. He looked behind him, to

his left and to his right. He looked into the bedroom; he took a couple of steps toward the kitchen, but stopped. He looked out the window, onto the street, into the empty courtyard below. He took the curtain in his hand. About to pull it shut, he looked across the way and saw her there.

LEAH

1

As far back as I can remember, Leah was preparing herself for marriage. Not for love, exactly, not for romance—unlike the rest of us, with our dewy notions of cars and cigarettes and boys' broad shoulders—but for marriage, for sacrifice and a lifelong abiding. She was my cousin, a week older to the hour, a thin girl with rich, pleated hair, searching eyes, and olive skin taut over bony points, flat inconcealable planes. She was polite and diffident, so you could never tell what she was thinking. She was starved for attention and consequently did everything to avoid it. She lacked what I later understood to be intensity, and in my family that was the greatest lack you could have, but she saw everything. That is my memory of those years, of life as it happened, vivid and unexplained, and Leah off to one side, not missing a beat, silently watching us all.

Before bed—we were young girls, eight or nine—Leah recited a prayer her mother had taught her, asking God to protect the unknown boy who would grow to be her husband. She prayed for his safety, his moral development. She prayed God would give him brains but not a swelled head, good looks but not vanity, money but a sense of charity, decorum. She prayed he was off in his own room these nights, praying for her.

When we played Barbie dolls, she didn't take hers to the beach, or a dance concert, or a picnic, where they could lie under some shady trees. Her dolls were endlessly married, set up in modest houses with patios and backyard grills. They were in shul together, at holiday meals, their plastic heads bowed in gratitude over the bread. My Barbies, even then, were restless, insurgent. They borrowed the family car without asking. They smoked cigarettes behind the Dream House. Partly to annoy Leah, they kissed constantly. Hers brought babies home from the hospital in little bonnets, did good works for the Jewish Sisterhood. They wed and grew old serenely, they emigrated to Eretz Ha'Kodesh—the Holy Land—they even died (usually Ken, after a long, uncomplaining decline), Bridal and Malibu Barbies, Midge, and Barbie's sidekick, Skipper—minus the arm our neighbor's dog had chewed off—all gathered solemnly around a shoebox grave to weep.

At the time, of course, I didn't find Leah mysterious, even interesting, just odd in that painful, embarrassing way cousins, whom you didn't get to choose any more than you did brothers, could be. Even at that age, she had a capacity for misery, she seemed marked for it, and too young for knowledge of luck or instinct or plain irrefutable fate, I sensed she would be in for a hard time. The one thing we knew about Leah was she wanted to be married; and the one thing we knew about the world was it would never happen, not to her. About this, about some other things, we were wrong.

My grandfather was a rabbi, his shul, with its high-set sea-green windows, and the brass eternal flame flickering before the velour-draped Ark, three blocks from home. My mother and I sat to the side, a few rows back, in the women's section, while David weekly climbed the steps to be with our grandfather at the front. Here I was allowed only on special occasions, when, if no serious prayer were being conducted, girls might join the boys in the main sanctuary.

Rabbi, scholar, community statesman, my grandfather was acknowledged family leader, but his status was tested constantly by Simon, my mother's uncle. If not himself a spiritual adept, Simon was Brooklyn's fourth-largest Chevrolet dealer, with a lot on New Utrecht Avenue and another in Bensonhurst. At the shul, Simon was alternately president of the congregation, chairman of the building fund, secretary of the men's club. He was devout, in his way, thinking he could outdo anyone in adherence and good religious sense. He loved biblical commentary and nothing would make my father go silent and grim around the mouth quicker than one of Simon's obscure finds, offered usually at mealtime, in mock humility—"I'm not a rabbi myself," Simon might say to a Shabbos guest, "but anybody can read."

Leah's mother was Simon's younger sister. She had married late and had one child, about whom she worried with a fanatic devotion. She was a flighty, kind woman, my Aunt Esther, given to overexcitement and meticulous superstition. She had prayers— and she taught them to Leah—for rain and drought, thunder and lightning, for the moon in its four quarters, for dressing in the morning and undressing at night, prayers for a new pair of shoes, for an old one, for perspiring, for headache, for your time of the month, for someone else's, for killing the chicken, plucking its feathers, and putting it in the pot. Aunt Esther sewed a red thread into Leah's underwear because this would bring a good husband, and when a one-eyed neighborhood cat named Duke picked among our trash cans, she would spit three times and make us turn to the north. For six months she was possessed by the spirit— and the heartburn—of an acquaintance of hers from Detroit, a recently deceased stenographer, a vindictive person, she told us, impossible to get along with. She walked around holding a blue bottle of Bromo-Seltzer, belching mournfully into a handker-chief. From my grandfather she begged an exorcism, until he threatened to banish her from the congregation.

Friday afternoons, school let out early. In the alley between the houses we played baseball with my brother—whom Leah voicelessly loved—and Barry Diamond, me in jeans and a sweatshirt (I was allowed to change after school) and Leah (who wasn't) in the long-skirted cotton dresses her mother sewed, with the woolen knee socks and black shoes. They wouldn't always let us play, not when they were about the manly business of making believe they were Yankees or Mets, and when they did allow us, it was mostly to laugh, to make comments between them as if we were deaf or too stupid to understand. That was boys. But I liked baseball. I liked the running and being outside. I liked the sting of the bat in my hands when I hit the ball, and I liked watching the boys hit it, occasionally, over the hedge into Mrs. Cohen's backyard. I liked knowing that soon it would be sundown, all of us indoors, a veil of silence and muted light drawn over the day as Shabbos approached, but now we were running, filling the air with our shouts, free.

One day we were girls against boys. It was autumn, you could feel the weather changing. Above the garages, wind shifted the oaks and sycamores and we stopped to watch as the leaves turned, filling the big trees with red and yellow light. Soon it would be time for my brother to dress for shul, for us to go in and set the table. The boys spent a lot of energy mimicking us, splaying arms and legs spastically, meaning to imitate our girlish ineptitude, while we said nothing about the mighty swings they took, hitting air, or the balls that bounded under their gloves, between their legs. Baseball was their game, and if we wanted in, we had to put up with them. But that didn't mean we had to lose.

The boys made smug concessions—they'd pitch easy to us, they'd play short in the field. They'd pitch left-handed, Barry offered, and blindfolded, David said. "C'mon," I said to Leah. "Let's show these fools."

We did. We scored a run in the first when Leah, closing one eye and swinging from her heels, hit Barry's garage on a fly, a ground-rule double, and then came home when the puffing red-faced boy chased a grounder of mine all the way to the swing set. My brother didn't like to lose. He didn't like to play fair unless he was winning and could make a show of it. David was a boy constantly on the edge, of laughter, of panic, of some unaccountable act of friendship or some meanness that would leave you stunned. I never forgot I was around him, and Leah watched him as if the sun rose over his shoulders every morning.

He could be nice. Before the game started he had shown Leah how to hold the bat, bringing his arms around her to demonstrate the correct angle, flaming her cheeks a pretty red. She stood there, holding the bat, his hands on hers. "You see?" David said, and she nodded, but I knew she wasn't seeing the bat, or the green garage door she faced. She was off in some landscape of her own, with his voice as company. "Good," David said, not unkindly, when he let her go. "At least you look better than my sister."

Now, down by a run, he was angry. He flipped the ball in the air to himself after Leah scored, and when she laughed suddenly at his grim expression, he managed Brooklyn's most grudging smile.

Why was any moment in any day suddenly the last straw to boys, the ultimate line in the sand, pride staring down disgrace? I thought he was ridiculous. I thought of saying something funny, something to ease the tension. We all felt it. Barry was trying, jumping foot to foot behind David, saying, "He-ey, batta-batta-batta, no-o batta-batta," pounding his silly mitt. But with David you always thought of saying something; you never did. Some invisible signal he gave off warned you to keep away.

I think Leah was enjoying herself. We hugged at home plate, and when she fell in the field next inning, dirtying the side of her blue dress, I thought she might go inside to admit the damage to her mother, but she just shrugged and pounded Barry's mitt as she had seen him do. We held them to a double and came up to bat in the second and—daylight quickly draining from the trees—final inning.

David seemed all right. They were still down a run, but they had the bottom of the inning, plenty of time. As I came up they made jokes.

"Show her your scroogie," Barry said.

"You think? It might make her cry."

"Show it to her once, man. Give her something to remember."

Adrenaline. Annoyance at my brother and his motor-mouthed friend. Some melancholy in the fading light that signaled the coming end of the year. I don't know. The ball met the bat with a feeling I had never had before. I swung right through it. I connected with it, as the boys would say, as if everything—the ball's flight, the tracking of my eyes, the slow acceleration of the bat in my hands—were the progression of an inevitable mathematical theorem. I creamed it.

A low liner, the ball pierced Mrs. Cohen's hedge more than cleared it. But there it lay in her azalea patch, at the end of a little furrow it had dug, a home run for all to see.

Leah and I hugged and ran around the bases together. I told her it was easy, to go up there and do the same thing. Then I looked at David. He waited for the ball, glove raised, and when Barry flipped it to him, he held it in his hand, looking to the side, his fringe of brown hair concealing his eyes.

Leah could sense his anger. She walked up to the plate and asked him if she was holding her bat correctly. "That's fine," David said, not looking.

"C'mon, Leah," I said. I could hear the nervousness in my voice. "You can do it."

The pitch came hard, high over Leah's head. It bounced once on the cement and then off our house at the other side of the alley. I ran to get it.

"What was that?" I called, angry now myself.

"A pitch," David said. "A slider, if you really want to know."

"Good one," Barry said behind him. "Now show her your scroogie."

I picked up the ball and thought of just going inside. This was how it was with my brother—at any moment the showdown, the crisis unavoidably arrived. Instead, I threw it back, over his head intentionally, and sat on the steps of our back porch to watch.

There was no way Leah could have gotten out of the way. David turned, lifted his leg in the manner I'd seen them practice with Barry's older brother. He brought the ball close to his chest, gathered himself, and threw as hard as he could. The ball hit her squarely in the face, with a sound like a piece of fruit dropped on a wooden floor. It made me sick even as I heard it. She fell straight down, the ball rolling feebly behind her, down the alley toward the street.

We reached her at the same moment. David helped her sit and Barry took the bat from her. I stood with my hand over my mouth.

"Are you all right?" David said.

"No blood," Barry said, leaning in to see. "That's gotta be good."

"Shut up, Barry," David said. "Leah, are you okay? Where did it hit you?"

A purple bruise was already spreading under her eye. I wanted to take the bat to him.

"Can you stand?"

"I'm all right," Leah said, and she let him put his arms under hers to help her.

"I'm sorry," David told her.

"I'm all right," she said again.

He helped her up. When he let her go to brush off her sweater, I saw the expression on her face. She was looking at David. In her eyes not the pain or shock I expected to see, but something else, something I didn't understand. It was as if she'd been waiting years for her turn to be hit in the face with a baseball. She looked at him with forgiveness, with wonder, even joy. I pushed him aside and put my arm around her.

"Good job, superstar," I said.

He shoved me from the back. "You think I meant to hit her?"

"You hit her, David," I said, turning around with Leah a moment. "You hit her and you knew you would, or could. You knew."

I took Leah inside and our mothers, draping the thick white cloth over the table for the meal, came running. Aunt Esther took one look at Leah and began opening and closing her eyes rapidly.

"Mom," I said, "she's going to faint."

"No she isn't," my mother said. "Esther, go into the kitchen and get a cold compress. With ice."

We were all late that night, the men to shul, the food to the table. As Leah and I stood in front of the candles while our mothers said the blessing, I could hear my father calling David in the yard. I heard him go up and down the alley, calling, his voice rising each time, then finally David answered and the shouting began. Then there was quiet, which could only mean my father had hit him. I knew the neighbors were listening, quietly pulling back their curtains to watch. I felt sorry for David, I always did, but now this night and what had happened would be about him. I looked over at Leah. They had held ice over her eye for half an hour. It was swollen blue and below it were the distinct imprints of three stitches from the baseball. She was praying, swaying slightly from side to side. Her eyes were closed and her lips moving slowly, something like a smile playing over them.

2

We moved to Queens later that year. By fourteen we were smoking joints in the space between the garages and by fifteen I was

involved with a boy from around the corner, Albert Fogel, who
wrote love poems and planned to be an optometrist and wanted
me to go all the way. He was a tall boy, with a diffuse smile and
thick curly hair like a cushion for my head, my hands. I would lie
with my head on his chest, listening to the breathing sounds, the
unerring thump of his heart, while he smoked Winstons, read
Marvel comic books. He copied out an e e cummings poem for
me, complete with the famous inverted characters, and seemed
so certain I would catch him in his poetic larceny that I didn't
have the heart, and told him it was his best poem yet.

He wagged his head at me, side to side, I swear he did, that
loopy smile, perhaps starting to think if I believed he wrote it,
maybe, somehow, he had. He kissed me and told me he loved
me. Did I *know* he loved me, he asked. I know, Albert, I said, of
course I know, and kissed him back. I wouldn't go all the way with
Albert Fogel because he would leave me then, that's what I knew,
and the night I finally loved him, that's just what happened.

It was a Saturday, the night of his senior dance. The family had
gathered, as they often did since my grandfather's death, at our
house for the weekend. Albert had left early to meet me, made off
with one of the table arrangements—a black-eyed Susan and two
daisies minus petals, like missing teeth—and a six-ounce bottle of
kiddush wine. As Albert had gone into the storage room to lift the
wine the band was playing "There's a Kind of Hush," a popular
song from a few years back, and he was humming it now. Inside,
they were doing the after-Shabbos rituals, my mother and Esther
finishing the dishes, putting them in the cupboards, Uncle
Simon's boys, maybe Leah, on pillows in front of the TV. We did
that every Saturday night, the same shows, movies in rotation,
redress to the prohibition on TV the day before. David talked
constantly about the shows we couldn't see—*Twelve O'Clock
High, Wild, Wild West*—as if an entire culture was out there
and we, hostages to religious zealotry, were being kept from it.
From the windows on the shifting breeze I could hear the women

talking in the kitchen, the rasp of the TV as the credits for *Chiller Theater* rolled—a hand lifting from a steamy swamp, six fingers waving—and behind it, classical music from the living room, where the men sat with newspapers and listened to Rubenstein or Heifetz. Albert began singing, "All over the world, you can hear the sounds of lovers in love." We sat on a front seat Barry and David had pulled from a derelict Buick the summer before, the flower arrangement beside us in the dirt, our feet on the tin milk box where we kept our stash. We held hands and looked at the sky between the trees. To the east, a faint glow was gathering, moonrise over Flushing Meadow.

We settled in comfortably and watched the view. Albert sang the song for me, but he couldn't remember the words. "So listen very carefully, da-da-da and dee-dee-dee what I mean . . ." We kissed and when Albert put his hand down my shirt I let him, we'd done this many times, and he left it there contented, under my bra, as you might leave a hand in a pocket. Albert drank the wine and I rolled a joint. When he passed it back to me there was a purple ring around the lip end, residue of the sticky wine. That was Albert.

"Penny for your thoughts," he said.

He killed me. "I don't have any change, Albert."

"Really. What are you thinking about?"

"Nothing. I'm not thinking about a thing."

"You must be," Albert said. "It's Saturday night, we're together. I'm graduating high school next week. I mean, we're in love, aren't we? You must be thinking about something."

"I was just thinking," I told him, "how nice it is to be here with you, smoking this joint and hearing my mother in the kitchen, while Mothra attacks Tokyo, just being here with you and not thinking a thing. That's what I was thinking."

But Albert was pensive. We shifted on the car seat, I leaned into him, smelling the warm woolliness of his shirt. He put the wine down on the ground and looked at me before he spoke. This wasn't easy, what with his hand, my wire-supported bra, the shallow car seat, but Albert managed. He took my hand with his free one.

"Rachel," he said. "What do you hope for?"

"Hope?"

"Yeah, you know, what are your dreams? Where do you see yourself in ten years?"

"Ten years? From tonight? I don't see myself anywhere in ten years."

"Okay. What do you hope for now, then?"

"Well, right now I'm hoping your hand doesn't fall asleep."

No, Albert said, he was serious, and he was, looking at me with slow, blinking eyes. "All right," I told him. "Okay."

So as the moon rose through the trees, as my mother's voice in Yiddish mixed with the screams of Japanese teenagers running from a forty-foot moth, I told him lies I hoped he wanted to hear. I hoped for these things: a nice home, a tree-lined street, a backyard with shade trees, maybe room for a garden. A career, I told him, some service kind of thing, nurse or teacher, you know, people work. He seemed happy, so I went on. A good marriage, with a man I could admire. Friends, women I could talk to. Mid-morning, after the chores (did I really say chores?), they would come over to my patio, or I would go over to their well-lit kitchens, the breakfast dishes still glistening in the drying racks, and over coffee we would discuss tuition, how fast kids went through clothes, recipes. Albert had his smile back on. He gave my breast a soft companionable squeeze. Travel, I continued, Italy and France, Hong Kong. Copenhagen, I threw in for the sound of it, Budapest, for no reason at all. Sri Lanka. And children, of course, several, boys and girls, matching sets. Larry and Lulu, I'd call them, Minnie and Mo, but this was going too far for Albert and I kept it to myself.

He reached for the bottle and nodded, his eyes above me somewhere, where he saw me in a trim apron in some sunny kitchen alcove, cutting meat for stew, pausing to look out the window and count my blessings.

"Yeah," Albert said.

He was a sweet boy, the only boy I had known who would listen to me, no matter what I said. I liked the way his man's body seemed to have caught him by surprise, the way he clunked around in his brown work boots, as if his feet were things he had to carry, the way his flannel shirts hung out of his pants, part man's indifference, part boy's unaware sloppiness. He liked to hold me, I could tell from the way he shifted, settled his arms around me, moved so there was room for me on his chest. In polite ardor, he would recite his poetry: "High upon a windblown crag, I climbed to think of you, And there, amid the roiling clouds, my melancholy grew . . ."

I told Albert I hoped we could see each other after he went off to college. When he looked at me, I turned away, concentrated on relighting the joint. I passed it to him after taking a long toke.

"Sure," he said. "You bet."

Then he spoke of his dreams, I'd heard them before, to be an optometrist like his Uncle Danny, go to conferences in Miami Beach, live in a home with a circular drive. I knew the rest—he would move out to the Island, learn to play golf, date blond girls who'd never heard of Queens. At restaurants, they would pour his drink the minute he came through the door, and they would call him by first name. He would marry somebody whose dream it was to marry an optometrist on Long Island and who would buy them coordinated outfits. They would actually have kids named Minnie and Mo. They would be happy.

He was sweet and earnest and the night was fresh and full of breezes. He loved me, he said. Did I *know* he loved me? From inside I heard the teapot whistling for tea, and Mothra, having devoured the populace of several towns, had retired ominously to the hills. The moon, white as a dinner plate, shimmered upward in the sycamore behind the house. Albert swung the bottle like a small pendulum between his knees. It was one of those spring nights they tell you invoke newness, rebirth, possibility, but which to me are always edged with sadness, full of time's passing and the many things that will never be. I know, I told Albert. I love you, too. I took the sugary wine from him and finished it off. I took his hand out of my shirt and then unbuttoned it. I kissed him on the mouth and undid my bra. The look of surprised delight as I pulled him onto me I will always remember.

When he got up from the car seat to stretch in the blue moonlight, he told me he had just that day been accepted to a college upstate. They had a major in optometry and eleven fraternities that allowed in Jews. It would be so great, he said, buttoning his clothes. Soon, I would be old enough to drive, I could save up for a car—heck, my rich uncle would probably *give* me one—and I could drive up every other weekend to see him. It would be so great. He lit a cigarette, lay back near me, his billowy Afro nudging my neck like a small pet. When he fell asleep with the cigarette in his mouth, I took it and smoked it down, looking at the moon laced with thin gray clouds.

I heard laughing behind us, then voices, Barry and David, back from wherever they had wandered, talking to someone else. "There's no rats in here," Barry said. "There hasn't been a rat in here for weeks." As if he were already in his home and heard the gravel crunching up front, my first love Albert jumped up from the Buick seat to welcome guests.

"Hey," he said, before they had made the turn to see us. "We're over here."

David came first, holding a pint bottle. "Oh," he said. He looked back at Barry. "They're over here."

Barry pushed past him and said, "So that's where you are. Terrific. Now in case anybody is ever looking for you we'll know." He moved past Albert and dragged the milk box from under my feet. "You guys roll any doobies?"

Behind David, half in the shadow of the garage wall, was Leah.

From the way she stood, one arm extended before her, I realized
Barry had been holding her hand.

"C'mon in," Barry said to her, "cop a squat. Hey." He slapped
my foot. "Shove over."

The tearing pain I felt when Albert first pushed into me had
mostly subsided, but when I had pulled my pants back on I saw
there was blood. I could feel it now, warm between my legs. I
didn't move.

David stood at the other end of the clearing, tipping the bottle
to his lips. When the amber liquid hit the light, I saw the bottle
was nearly empty. Albert kept his eyes on David as Barry took
Leah by the hand and brought her over to the Buick seat. "Here,"
he said, guiding her, and to me, "You wasted or something? Make
some room." She sat next to me and we exchanged quick glances.

"We were just hanging out," Albert said, moving a foot in front
of him as if there was a rock there to kick. "You know, talking."

"Yeah?" David said. "About what?"

"You know, stuff. School stuff, summer plans, stuff like that."

"Yeah? You have summer plans, Albert?" David said.

"I usually wait tables at the Concord, you know, where my parents spend a few weeks. Sometimes I teach swimming."

"Swimming. Like, to kids."

"Kids, yeah. And adults. Anybody who wants to learn to swim, I
guess."

I knew Albert would flip desperately for minutes around David,
until, like a fish on a line, he'd give up and silently wait to die. I
reached out and pulled him by the pants pocket onto the seat
beside me. There was barely room. He was scared by David,
which I found endearing, and a sign of good sense. David was
deep into his glowering, sarcastic phase. He had grown his hair as
long as he could without inciting outright war with my father and
I saw him every day combing it delicately, then messing it up,
over and over, until he achieved just the right look of accidental

fashion. He was seventeen, smoked whatever dope Barry left for him, had some connection for Southern Comfort, maybe Barry's older brother back in Brooklyn. The liquor was nasty, sweet and sour and biting, like medicine, and I couldn't swallow a mouthful. But for weeks now David had been coming to the garages with pint bottles, the label with the Southern mansion and the riverboat on the front, drinking the stuff until he got sick in Mrs. Segal's irises or fell stuporously silent, hunching his neck deep into his collar, not saying a word.

"Want a hit?" He gave Albert an unfriendly smile and passed the bottle.

"Sure," Albert said. "Thanks, bro." I felt the shudder pass through him as he drank.

Barry was rummaging in the milk box, collecting papers, the Baggie of marijuana, the *Playboy* he used to separate the seeds from the buds. I saw Miss April, in a bow tie and fishnet stockings, spilling her breasts halfway across the page.

"Albert," Barry said, opening the magazine to the centerfold, "have you read the article in here on our flawed Vietnam policy? I tell you, it makes you think."

"No," Albert said, staring as the glandular marvel of Miss April unfolded in sections to the light. "I haven't read it."

"Albert," I said, taking his hand. "Don't speak."

Like a teacher at the front of the room showing a picture in a text, Barry displayed Miss April to each of us in turn, his grinning face stuck to the side like a salacious gargoyle. She was a blonde, not much older than me, I guessed, in a lacy shift that covered nothing, lordosing to beat the band, a pose only boys could find intriguing. I felt the oozing wetness in my pants, squeezed my legs together for the almost reassuring stab of pain it sent through me, and wondered what this cotton-candy phantasm had to do with the brief, breath-filled encounter (And there amidst the roiling clouds . . .), half pain, half pleasure, I had just had with Albert.

Once Albert had a sufficient study, Barry turned her to me, but I smirked at him. David, by the wall, ignored her, as if just one more naked woman today could hardly be of interest. But Leah, beside me, was rigid with attention. I was sorry I had not tended to her more. Normally, I would have, would have screamed at Barry and David to leave her alone, led her back to the house. But tonight I had other things on my mind.

Barry moved the pinup closer to her, holding it top and bottom. "This," he told Leah, "is what today's gentleman refers to as beauty."

I looked at her. Her face bore no expression beyond the stiff-jawed determination to reveal none. Her hands were in the pockets of the coat she wore, or was made to wear, even on this warm night. Leah, fifteen now, still rail-thin, still watching through soft, wary eyes, still dressed as she was when we were children—the heavy dress, black braids, the laced shoes and white stockings. I wondered what she was doing here. She never came out back. Another night, an earlier year, I would have protected her from this. She stared at Barry and Miss April without flinching.

"Put it away," I told Barry.

"Why? Aren't you an admirer of the female form?"

"Shove it, Barry," I said, and he leered at me, then Leah, even Albert, then shrugged and busied himself with the pot and the papers.

Leah looked at me, but with gratitude or fear or confusion, I couldn't tell. She sat on the seat beside me, her hands thrust into her coat pockets. It was a spring coat, had been fashionable when it was new, brown wool with big buttons in two rows down the front. I tried to catch her eye and smile but she had looked away. David passed the Southern Comfort back to Albert, who took a showy, manful slug. This time he nearly retched. Barry had rolled two fat joints and handed one to me.

Leah and I had grown apart, if you could say so—from what earlier intimacy had we deviated? We still shared the same room, weekends, when her family stayed over. We were still lumped together, the female support staff, assigned chores in tandem — set the table, girls, make the salad, iron the spread and napkins. And we still talked. Leah, not allowed to be around boys herself, was insatiable for knowledge of them. She never quite said as much but I could tell. When I started dating Albert, I told her. She wanted to see a picture. Who needs a picture, I said, he's around all the time. Wouldn't a picture be nice? she said. We could look at it in our room, together. So I got her one and she kept it by her bed, at night when her mother didn't know, propped up against the lamp. I didn't care. She asked me if he went to shul and I said I don't know, I guess so. She asked if he was polite to me and I said sure, Albert was as polite as they came, and she asked me if we talked about the future and I said, yes, Albert talked about the future day and night.

When I told her Albert wrote me poems she demanded to see one. I found one and read it, declaiming, waving my hands around, and we laughed so loud David banged on the wall next door. Then I made the mistake of telling her I had let Albert put his hand down my shirt. She seemed genuinely shocked, and I was sorry to have upset her, but later, praying by the side of the bed, she kept glancing at me, and I realized she was praying for my redemption, which shocked me and kept me angry for two days.

She still prayed, sometimes so long and fervently I'd stay awake just to watch. She prayed for the boys facing off with the Arabs in the Sinai desert. She prayed for her father's gout to disappear. She prayed for Mort Sheinberg, a man from my grandfather's shul running for city council, and when Uncle Simon went into Maimonedes for a hernia repair she kept a vigil into the night, all night, for all I knew, finally falling asleep myself in stupefied awe. She no longer prayed, at least out loud, for the welfare of her future husband, and aside from our talks about Albert's studies, his plans for the two of us, I never heard her speak directly about boys. When they dragged David off to a psychiatrist, for general recalcitrance, for mouthing off and skipping shul, she was nearly hysterical.

The grownups sat on the front porch and talked about him as if he had become a stranger, were gone already, committed to a life of crime or insanity, disappeared into the one-way hole of the goyim's world. In our room Leah pulled me down on my knees next to her, held me there. If we prayed together, she said, maybe we could help him. Fine, I said, and closed my eyes and listened to her fervid whispering. Then she asked if she could burn herbs in my room, and I ignored her and got into bed.

One night the spring before, she lay in bed under the covers, did not get out to kneel on the floor. After the final prayer, speech was forbidden. "Hear, O Israel, the Lord is God, the Lord is One." After that, silence. Those were the last words God wanted to hear from you that night. Aunt Esther told us this. She also told us that in the moment before birth God took each new child in his hands. He looked at it and kissed its forehead, which meant it would be born, alive and healthy, into our world. But his kiss also left a number, invisible, under your skin. This represented the words you were allotted to speak in your lifetime. Your whole life. When they were done, you were done, finished, no more, don't bother asking. Aunt Esther had an aunt, back in the Old Country, who had lived to be ninety-eight and couldn't utter a single word the last four years of her life. Could we imagine anything more terrible? This old woman—a happy enough individual in her youth—walking around scowling all day, holding a cup of cold tea. She knew what had happened. Well, Aunt Esther asked us, sitting on my bed and whispering, was that the future we wanted?

This night, instead of climbing out of bed after we'd finished reading, Leah lay under the blankets. I knew she wanted to talk. From somewhere in the street, music played on a radio. I couldn't hear the words or melody, but the rhythm came through, barely pulsing in my ears. I ran my eyes up the trellis of roses on the wallpaper, a pattern repeating until I lost sight of it in the dark near the ceiling. Then she spoke.

"I had my time," she said.

I didn't answer. I wasn't sure what she meant.

"My time," she repeated. "Last week, at school."

"You mean your period?" I said. "You got your period?"

"In history. I thought I had had an accident. I thought I had wet myself. I ran to the bathroom. I had to wait there two hours for the final bell."

"Oh, Leah, I'm sorry." I sat up in bed and looked over at her in the gray half-light. She lay still. I could see her hands motionless on her chest. I pulled the pillow from behind me and held it in my lap.

"I had my first one in gym last year. We were jumping over that stupid horse, you know? It was my turn, I got up from where we were sitting by the wall and I felt this trickle. But I was concentrating on the stupid horse, you know? On not making a fool of myself. So Sheila Schivelowitz announces to me and everyone else in the room there's blood running down my leg. 'Gross,' she says. 'Oh, my God,' she says, 'that is just so gross.' It was in my sneaker and everything." I fluffed the pillow and leaned over it toward Leah. "I flicked some right in her face." Leah looked at me and I laughed. "I didn't. But I wanted to. It didn't hurt. You know, cramps, a little, but nothing else." I tossed the pillow at her. "Anyway, cousin, welcome to the wonderful world of womanhood."

The pillow lay where it had landed, across her legs. She didn't answer and I thought—as I did often—I had said something to offend her. I looked out the window, across the driveway, where I could see the lit kitchen in the Segals' house. The brown Motorola radio on their table was playing music, it might have been a waltz. Every night I would watch them in there, Mrs. Segal ironing clothes, making coffee, which they drank from green cups while they listened to music from the radio. No one was in the kitchen now, just the radio playing soft music and a breeze shifting the corner of a curtain.

"Do you use something?" Leah said.

"For my period? Sure."

"Did you see a doctor?"

"For tampons? Why? I got some from my mother, then bought my own at Rexall's."

"Your mother knows?"

"Of course she knows. Doesn't yours? Didn't you tell your mother, Leah?"

"I found something in her drawer. I took it."

She got up from bed, went to her small blue suitcase, came over, and handed something to me. I was about to turn on the light when I remembered it was Friday night. The light from the windows was enough to see by. It was a puffy contraption, a long thin diaper snapped to a belt by metal clips. The belt was worn and beige, the white diaper downy with cotton, thick in the middle and tapering at both ends, where it attached to the belt. The napkin was long enough to wear as a headband.

"What *is* this?" I said.

"You wear it. In your time every month."

"You do? How? I mean why? Don't you know about Tampax?"

But this was the wrong thing to say, or not what she'd hoped to hear. She got back in her own bed and I, full of exasperation and self-reproach, went to my drawer and got out a tampon. We weren't supposed to tear anything, not even paper, on Shabbos, but I ripped the paper wrapping off and let it drop to the floor. I sat on Leah's bed and showed her how it worked, the string, the cardboard applicator. She looked at me as if she had no idea what I was talking about and I was so mad I would have pulled my nightshirt over my head and *showed* her, but she said, "Thank you. I see," and rolled over on her side to sleep.

"Oh, Leah," I said. "It's nothing, you know? I mean, it's not nothing. It happens to everybody, that's all." She didn't turn or make any response. From my bottom dresser drawer I got a handful of Slender Regulars and tucked them into her suitcase. I said "Good night," but couldn't hear her murmured reply. Later, as I was just beginning to dream of Mrs. Segal putting down the iron to dance around the kitchen with her husband, I heard the sheets rustle and the bed shift as Leah climbed out of bed to pray. I didn't open my eyes.

Barry was smoking one joint, holding the other. "This is killer weed," he said to Albert. "*Yo soy blotado*, bro, *et vous?*"

"Killer," Albert agreed.

"I'm wasted. Like, okay, like, I wouldn't know my own head if I sat on it, you know? I mean, where'd you *get* this stuff, man?" He put a hand on Albert's knee. "Righteous bud, man."

Barry was on the ground, in the rubble and gray dirt. He lounged on one side, his head cupped in a hand as if he lay on a rug in somebody's living room. He offered the joint again to Leah, who had declined a dozen times, then passed it to me.

"I thought it was yours," Albert said.

"Mine?" Barry said through held breath. He had the other joint now and was contorting his face dramatically to trap the smoke in his lungs. "I live in Brooklyn. Where would I get weed like this, for Christ's sake!" He looked at Leah. "I mean, by gosh," he said.

"It's his," I told Albert. "He's just making fun."

"Seriously, bro," Barry continued. "This is A-1 marijahooch. You gotta cop some more, I'm begging you."

He half walked, half stumbled over to the car seat. He tried to squeeze in between Leah and me, but there was no room. He sat on the ground and dropped his head in her lap.

David had finished off the bottle, with some help from Albert, who now sat with his hands between his knees. From the way he looked fixedly at the ground before him I knew he was angry.

"Hey, Albert," David said.

When Albert did not respond David said it louder, then a third time, stressing the second syllable. "Hey, Al*bu-u-urt!*"

"That's Alvin," Albert said, still looking at the ground.

"What's Alvin? Your name is Alvin?"

"No," Albert said slowly, "when you said Hey Albert just then, that's not what they say. They say Hey Alvin."

"Who says?"

"Those chipmunks. That's what they say," and he looked at David, nodding his head as if his patience were being sorely tried. "In the cartoon. They say Hey Alvin, not Hey Albert."

"Wait a minute." David turned to me. "Did you know his name was Alvin? I thought it was Albert. Didn't you tell me it was Albert?"

"It *is* Albert," Albert said, and I could feel him start to rise.

"Oh, sure, now it's Albert, a minute ago it was Alvin. You see my problem? How am I supposed to keep up?"

"David, you asshole," I said.

"That's Hey Asshole, isn't it, Alvin?"

"No," Barry said, half asleep, or pretending to be, in Leah's lap. "I think it's just plain asshole."

"Yeah?" David shoved himself off the wall and came over to the seat. "Well, what I mean is, Alvin, why it's so important and all, is just that my sister should know who's fucking her. That's just courtesy, don't you think? I mean, does she say 'Oh, fuck me, Albert!' or 'Oh, Alvin, that feels so good!' You don't want to get these things wrong."

Albert stood. "David," I said.

"I just want to know. Is she hot? When you fuck my little sister, Alvin, does she bring you pleasure?"

I was woozy from the pot, but not enough so I couldn't stand between them. I felt the blood move in my pants. "David, shut up. I'm warning you to shut the hell up."

"Why? It isn't true?"

"It's none of your fucking business is what it is, even if it was true, so just shut the fuck up."

"Oh, I see. Pardon me."

"Asshole," Albert said and moved toward him. David nodded broadly, encouraging Albert forward. I sat back on the seat.

Then Leah gave a quick moan, a swallowed shout. Barry had his head nestled in her lap. A joint smoldered half smoked in his lips. His hand, moving, had disappeared under the folds of Leah's skirt.

"There," Barry said, contented. He smiled dreamily at her and lay his head back down.

Albert threw a punch at David but missed, grazing his hand on the stone garage wall. David stepped over the milk box and shoved Albert hard against the opposite wall, where his breath left him in a rush. When it returned to him he started to shout.

"You fuck! I'll get you, you fuck!"

Immediately my mother's voice reached us from the kitchen. "David, what are you doing out there? David?"

David stood in front of Albert with his hands at his sides. He held the empty liquor bottle before him, then let it fall to the ground. He smiled at Albert, taunting him until Albert stood and swung again. He missed, but the third time connected, hitting David hard in the mouth. Blood was on David's face, from his mouth or Albert's hand, I couldn't tell.

"Hey, look, Alvin," David said, touching his face. "You got me."

He walked over to Barry and yanked him up by the shoulders. "Party's over," he said. "Say goodbye to your friends." Albert, giving David and me one look together, tramped off through the garages one way while Barry and David headed off the other. "You bring the doobies?" Barry said.

"Yeah, I got 'em."

"Hey, man, watch it," we heard Barry say. "You're bleeding on me."

Leah was sitting beside me, still rigid, her hands inside her pockets. I leaned over and pulled the skirt of her coat around her. She made no sound, no movement. I wanted to cry. I wanted to hold her and be held and cry with her. When my hand touched her, on the way to her pocket, she flinched, and I looked at her, saw her lips moving. I lay on the car seat, my head brushing her coat, my feet hanging over the edge.

"Well, cousin," I said. "It's me and you again."

She didn't answer me, and by the small rocking motions she began making I measured the duration of her prayer. After a while she sat still. I didn't know if I should say something to her. I hoped she would say something to me. She didn't. She got up and went indoors.

The moon, framed directly above me between the garage roofs, was a bright disk, an opening and closing eye. I watched it, clouds rippling before it high in the wind. What had Leah prayed for? Vengeance? Absolution? Understanding? I never understood what you were meant to pray for. In shul we thanked God for healing the sick, bringing in the crops, crushing our enemies. We bore witness: Hear, O Israel, the Lord is God, the Lord is One. Was that what she had prayed? Nighttime's prayer, the last thing God wanted to hear from you.

I lay on the car seat, hoped for a while Albert would come back. I listened for him. He would be smiling, embarrassed, putting the whole thing behind him with a joke. That crazy brother of yours. He would hold me, he would hum songs in my ear. I would listen to his poems, I would let him make love to me again if he wanted to. Upstate was a dumb idea, he'd tell me, he wouldn't be going after all. He would stay.

But Albert didn't come back. It was getting colder. Soon my mother would be calling, or worse, out looking for me herself. From the yelps and hurrahs of Uncle Simon's boys I could tell Mothra had succumbed in flames, the countryside was safe, the villagers could return to their homes. I lay there watching the moon in the clouds until I heard my mother say my name, a quiet question from the kitchen window, as if she knew I was close by and could hear.

3

Leah's first marriage was a neat disaster.

Rabbi Solomon Memmel was a short man, with small glittering eyes that fastened on what he saw. When the food went around the table he watched it, as if unbelieving that any would remain by the time it reached him. When he lifted his hat to wipe sweat from his forehead, his yarmulke peeked through, stained pink to purple, and his mouth, through his thick ungainly beard, was a wet red hole glistening with teeth. Rabbi Memmel had a small, ultra-Orthodox congregation in Williamsburg, where they called him Reb Shlomo. He encouraged everyone to call him this, even my father, ten years older than he. "Call me Reb Shlomo," he said to me, with a damp hand leading me to the couch in my mother's living room. Passing me the cake, the lemon slices for the tea, he sat so close I had to keep moving my legs.

Reb Shlomo lectured us about the responsibilities of the Jewish wife, about the rites and sancties of marriage, including the marriage bed. He leaned into me, smiling confidentially, and gestured at the bowl of fruit. As he talked he peeled an orange by sinking a thumb past the knuckle in the soft meat, then tearing outward. He announced with satisfaction that Leah was a good girl, modest, dutiful, a hard worker. She understood—and he looked around the room here, as if to suggest not everyone did nowadays—what it meant to be a Jewish wife. Wiping his hands on a napkin, he told me I would be welcome in their home any Shabbos of the year, weekdays, too, and when I showed him to the door, he took my hand again in both of his, fixed me with his moist gaze, and whispered, "Now we will be family."

The marriage was annulled within two years. I never learned the whole story, though the fact that Leah remained obstinately without little Memmels surely played a part. I heard from my

mother, who sadly shook her head, of Leah showing up in tears
at Aunt Esther's house in the middle of the night, without a coat
or change of clothes or money to pay the cab; of prayer sessions,
with incense; of entreaties to rabbis for an exorcism of the child-
killing spirit Aunt Esther believed had encamped in Leah's
womb.

I was off in college then, a small school in Ohio. I didn't get
back East often, and when I did, too much urgency was focused
on me—my hair, my clothes, my friends, my life—to talk about
my cousin. She wasn't going to have an argument with me, my
mother said once, before I'd shrugged my pack to the floor, but if
I came into the house again without a brassiere on, she would
send me back to Ohio for good. And those boys—Paco and H.,
long-haired boys in sunglasses who had dropped me at the house,
given me a kiss, each of them, waved to my mother happily, and
driven off without a word—they weren't Jewish, were they?
Weren't there any Jewish boys in Ohio? And what was I telling
her, his name was H.? His whole name? What kind of name was
H.? I could have asked for money for a bus, I didn't have to ride
halfway across America with boys with names like secret agents.

Later, in the kitchen, after watching me unpack my things in
bated sadness—where were the nice dresses I left home with?—
she would tell me of Leah and Aunt Esther, but not with much
spirit, her worried eyes coming to rest on me, the kitchen falling
silent around us.

Leah's second marriage was more placid. An old man named
Miller—old*er*, my mother insisted; yes, I said, older than anybody
else still living—a retired fur cutter on a good pension in Rock-
away Park. Even my mother had to admit it was odd that such
a young woman—Leah was twenty-three at the time—would
agree to the match, but everyone saw how the old man loved her.
He redecorated their entire flat in the latest colors—burnt-orange
shag for the living room, pale lime for the cabinets and trim in the
kitchen—installed a new range and refrigerator, an auto-drying,

pot-scrubbing dishwasher. While Leah sat in the living room he would insist on serving guests himself, shuffling in slippered feet to the kitchen to prepare the tea and cut the cake, whistling quiet old-man ditties to himself. When he talked about his long soli-tude—he had lost his first wife nearly forty years earlier—and about how happy Leah made him, his eyes would swell red at the edges. "My *neshomale*," he called her, "my little soul." For two winters he took Leah to Miami Beach, deluxe accommodations, strictly first-class—I wondered if they ever ran into Albert Fogel there—and they sent picture postcards of the Millers, Mr. and Mrs., in chaise longues on immense white beaches, in sunglasses, matching robes, funny hats.

To no one's surprise, except Aunt Esther, who took to her bed for a week, Mr. Miller died. After returning from Florida their second winter, he sneezed once or twice, ran a slight fever, was told to stay off his feet. Leah pushed fluids, boiled soup, blasted steamy showers in the bathroom for his runny nose. In a week he was dead. On a Sunday morning she found him, slumped in his chair by the window, wrapped in the blue robe with the hotel monogram on the pocket, the Yiddish paper fallen in his lap. He looked so peaceful there in the sunlight she didn't think to disturb him at first—what really was the rush, now?—until the strangest thing happened, no one had ever heard anything like it.

As she watched from across the room, a black bird with yellow eyes and strange red feet, like a sparrow but bigger, flew in the open window and landed on Mr. Miller's head. It stood there, pecking at his few gray hairs, until Leah, horrified, ran to the kitchen for a broom.

And this is what sent Aunt Esther to her bed. Couldn't we see? It was a dybbuk, as plain as the nose on a dog, a dybbuk, the old man's foul spirit—yes, he *seemed* a quiet old gentleman when he was alive. Who knew?—roosting on the corpse, leering at the young wife, pecking like a balabos there on the warm dead head. A disaster. Had Leah touched it, Aunt Esther kept asking. Had it looked her in the eye; worse, spoken any words? No, Leah reported, it stood on Mr. Miller's head until she shooed it with a broom. She gave it a bad scare, she thought, and it knocked Mr. Miller's glasses off in its escape, but after a short breather on the curtain valance it had flown back out the way it came in.

After a brief examination Esther's rabbi proclaimed the new widow free of all visitation, demonic or otherwise, except the grievous luck we had all predicted for her, and Aunt Esther, with great trepidation, dragged herself to the cemetery. She would go nowhere near the grave, however, and stood ten feet off with the men who would fill in the hole, one holding a shovel and reading a magazine, the other in a slouch cap, chewing an unlit cigar.

So my first year out of art school, apprentice and lover to a Manhattan stained-glass artist who monthly retired, told me sadly we were finished over a bottle of Chianti, called his broker to put the studio up for sale, then got back on his meds, hired more help, fired his broker, took me off in the middle of the afternoon to a downtown hotel to make love with the TV on, then order room-service pizza and urge me into the shower so he could call his wife in White Plains, I was not entirely surprised to receive an invitation to my cousin's third marriage. The sober stationery had a bare black garland around the border, some puny leaves, and was covered with a lengthy Bible quotation about the joy of wedlock. "The hour of the songbird is upon us," it proclaimed in block letters. "The call of the dove is heard in our land." I immediately got on the phone with my mother.

"It's terrible," she said. "This one will be worse than the other." "Which other?" I was about to ask but she went on. "He's a scholar, God help her, a serious man." And all the way across the river I could see her shaking her head. "That poor girl."

Bernard Finkel was indeed a serious man. At twenty-six he had already received his rabbinical degree, authored nine scholarly articles of his own, four in Hebrew, and, with his professors at Yeshiva and the New School, co-edited a lively volume of essays

on the decline of moral standards in the Jewish family. He was of
the new breed of learned men, adept at contemporary discourse,
a modern at home in several languages and literatures, one who
out of clear-eyed zeal, not some weak-kneed atavism, cleaved
unto God's Law in all its terrible majesty. He was thin and ascetic-
looking, and had the preoccupied gaze of a man with too much
on his mind. He was discussed, consulted, admired. He was
invited to shuls to deliver Shabbos sermons. He was on panels,
talk shows, was photographed with a gloomy assemblage of religious leaders convened to discuss ethnic relations with an assistant to a deputy mayor. He suffered shattering headaches, epic
insomnias. No wonder. Who could sleep after so much thinking?
Only tea and warm toast could anyone, even Leah, coax into
him, though she was often asked—Aunt Esther, who was terri-
fied of the man, told my mother this—to stand behind his desk
chair and rub his closed eyes with her fingers, lightly, making
no sound. He was a great catch, this was obvious: where in the
whole city would you find another like him? And that he would
marry an older woman—Leah and I were barely twenty-eight—
showed him to be a man of sound character as well as searing
intellect.

But something troubled Aunt Esther. At the engagement lunch
Esther never emerged from my mother's bedroom, and a constant shuttle of family ranged from the kitchen to the back of the
house until only Uncle Simon, my father, and I remained at the
table with the guests of honor. We were eating honey cake and
fruit. Uncle Simon had had two slices, was eyeing a third.
Bernard Finkel sat in his suit and hat in front of his untouched
cake—he had sliced an apple and carefully placed a section in his
mouth—looking like a man at an interview for a job he knows is
beneath him. Uncle Simon was very interested in Bernard
Finkel's rabbinic views on finance, and was becoming his closest
ally. He was just asking Bernard what kind of car he drove when
my mother called me from the room.

On her bed lay Aunt Esther, a dampened handkerchief on her forehead, another forgotten in the top of her blouse. "She's fainted twice," my mother told me.

"Three times," Aunt Esther said feebly from the bed.

"I only saw two."

"You were in the kitchen," Aunt Esther said. "I couldn't wait."

My mother leaned out the doorway to look down the hall, shaking her head.

"I can't do it, sweetheart," Aunt Esther said to me, taking my hand. "Darling, I beg you, I haven't got the strength." She pulled me onto the bed near her. "One more minute, bubele, a little mercy, please." She closed her eyes and breathed. "Don't worry, I'm coming. Just help me up. Is he gone yet?" And she tried to sit up, if lifting one wrist can be counted as such, then succumbed, eyes fluttering.

"Number three," my mother said from the door.

From behind closed eyes, Aunt Esther whispered, "Four."

After Mr. Finkel had gone away, Uncle Simon came and sat on my mother's bed, where Aunt Esther lay recovering with a small tray of chocolates and candied fruit, and pronounced Bernard Finkel a rare animal, a biblical scholar of the first rank with—and this was truly unusual—a good business sense. He thought he might put him in an Impala. What was all the commotion, Uncle Simon wanted to know, glaring at us balefully. Rabbi Finkel had some fascinating ideas on what the Law had to say about running a modern automobile franchise, but we had missed it and it was too subtle to re-create.

The bride was purchased a gown, snow-white, by her husband, who also determined the menu, the guest list, the flowers, and the music. For a honeymoon they would travel to Boston, where Bernard had an appointment and had purchased a house, which he described to Leah with vivid detail, so she could see it in her mind's eye. He had, Leah told my mother, thought of everything.

At the wedding, the women sat in the bride's dressing room while in another room the men gathered with a bottle of Scotch to review the marriage contract, discuss the ancient rites of property transfer — of bride from father to husband — dowry, payment. Leah's father, my Uncle Lew, had been dead for years. My father stood in as surrogate proprietor, but he was nervous around Bernard Finkel and his intellectual friends, and I had glanced in the room, seen the black-coated backs of Bernard's friends leaning over a table, and my father, an empty whiskey glass in his hand, hovering nearby.

In the bridal chamber, a room walled completely in mirrors, maroon velvet, like a walk-in jewelry box, I watched as Leah had her hair combed by Miriam Finkel, Bernard's younger sister, whose own hair, henna bright, was festooned impressively from all sides of her head. On the vanity before them were atomizers, hair sprays, tubes of gel, cans of mousse, a pink travel case stuffed with makeup. Bernard wanted a floral bouffant, Miriam explained around bobby pins in her teeth, and it was not going well. She tugged Leah's hair like she was hauling in an anchor, constructed something first to the left, then the right, then the left again, pausing only to stare in the mirror one outraged second, then tear the whole thing down to begin again. At her feet, small piles of daisy and lily-of-the-valley were ground slowly into the carpet.

On a couch to the side, my mother held Aunt Esther's hand and Aunt Esther held a bottle of smelling salts. She looked grimly arrayed in a white suit — courtesy of the groom. She had agreed to some sedation and stared stonily ahead of her, as if she had been invited to view her own destruction, not see her daughter wed a third time.

My mother, too, seemed agitated. There had been some commotion, raised voices in the attached powder room when I had first arrived, and when my mother and Aunt Esther emerged together, Esther was red-eyed, tottering in her new silk shoes, and my mother was erect with anger. When Esther saw me, she put some spirit in her wobble.

"Esther, don't you dare!" my mother said, and Aunt Esther found the seat where she was sitting now. I had gone over to offer a kiss and congratulations. She grabbed both my hands and started to pull me down, crying. My mother, her mouth a straight line, nabbed a girl who had come in to lay out more towels and ordered a pitcher of whiskey sours to be brought in.

"Ma'am," the girl said, "the bar's not open."

"I'll give you five minutes," my mother said.

She had replaced me by Aunt Esther, taken her hand, and when the whiskey sours arrived, she ignored them. I didn't. Though the sweet fizzy mixture was nauseating, I sensed this might turn into a day that required some fortification. I drank one, offered one to Miriam, who had no time for it, so I drank hers, too. Leonard, my boss/lover, who needed the narration of talk shows to drown out his guilty bleatings in bed, had taken up with a new glass cutter in the studio, Stephanie—"She's got a fine steady hand," he told me. I'll bet she does, Lensky—younger than me, who watched him with that secret, limpid, adoring look I was absolutely disgusted to recognize from my own face in the mirror barely a week earlier. Not even a bottle of Chianti this time. After pouring several glasses and offering them around, I drank one at a time from the five cocktail glasses on the tray, and watched Leah's torment.

She was beautiful. It shocked me to see this. She was as pale as ever, but the harrowing thinness had left her. She seemed, after all this time, to have grown into her body, and it was softly con-toured, lovely. She had breasts, nearly obliterated by Miriam in powder, but there they were—I had from time to time admitted to passing fits of nostalgia for the pre-braless days, junior high, when you could change shape weekly, courtesy of Maidenform and Kleenex, and there would be boys who would have stepped over you bleeding in the street the day before regarding you all of a sudden, stopped in their tracks, prayerful hunger on their silly faces—and here was my cousin, grown to womanhood, some-body's dream date, somebody's wife. Her eyes, looking occasion-ally at me in the mirror, were—I was unprepared for this—happy.

I wished then we were back in my room, years ago, saw us perched on the edge of our beds in the dark, holding pillows and whispering, the doorframe outlined in light, the sounds of grownups on the other side. "What's happened to you, Leah?" I wanted to ask. I realized I wanted to talk with her, to tell her about Leonard. I hadn't spoken about Leonard with anyone, but I wanted to tell Leah now, how I was sure I'd lose my job, a job I needed, how he had told me just today it was so painful to see me now, how he kept looking over my head, couldn't look me in the eye, and other things, the little "hunh"s he gave out when we were making love, the way he screwed up his eyes and made me hold completely still so he could come undistracted, the way he patted his semi-flat stomach and liked to sit around in striped bikini briefs. All this I wanted to tell Leah, waiting to marry her thin-lipped rabbi, but here, today, I could say nothing. The pitcher was empty and Miriam Finkel was cursing under her breath when, after a particularly savage tug to Leah's head, she had snapped her second comb. I went over and put out my hand. Miriam looked at me a wild moment, as if she would plunge into my hair next, then exhaled, surrendered the half comb and brush and left the room with two bobby pins still vised between her teeth.

"I can do a French braid," I told Leah, "sometimes."

She smiled quietly in the mirror.

"They're going to live in Massachusetts," Aunt Esther said from the rear of the room, as if someone had asked a question. "Cam-bridge. In Massachusetts. You know it?"

"Yes," my mother said absently.

"That's where they'll be. In Cambridge, Massachusetts. He has an appointment."

"I know," my mother said.

"He bought a house," Aunt Esther said. "A yellow house. Three floors. I saw pictures. In the garage you could put at least two cars."

"How's that?" I asked Leah, pulling the hair back to show her what I intended. With hair like hers, I'd have worn it down, wedding or not. She nodded, and for a few moments I made believe I knew what to do with the pins, the spray.

"She looks beautiful," my mother said. "Esther, wake up, tell her she looks good."

Esther nodded sadly.

"Bernard found us a house," Leah said to me. "I haven't seen it yet. It's near the campus, so he can walk to the library."

I shook my head enthusiastically, a barrette between my teeth.

"If only Elazar was alive," Esther said, meaning my grandfather.

Leah and I paused, looked at them in the mirror. My mother straightened her hat, sat stiffly. "Yes," she said. "Well, he isn't."

Esther took two deep breaths, opened and closed her eyes, and slumped against my mother, who pushed her ungently away. *"Genug shain!"* she said. "Esther, enough!"

"He wants children right away," Leah was saying. "He says it's already late, most of my child-bearing years are behind me."

From the couch, a soft groan.

"He's a distinguished man, Leah. You must be very proud."

She smiled again.

I was braiding her hair now, moving down her back. Before I had thought about it I heard myself say, "David called. To say congratulations."

"He did?" She turned around in the chair to look at me. "I'm glad. Where is he now?"

"Out West," I said casually, as though I knew more but was deciding to be vague. Actually, that was all I knew. He had quit architecture a year earlier, about the same time his marriage had collapsed. When he had come back to tell my father he had left the firm the argument had carried them out of the house, the shouting bringing out the neighbors, until a man from across the street had approached with his hands in the air and David had run toward the subway. That was the last we'd seen of him.

He called from time to time to say hi, relate some funny anecdote about the town he was in, the job he temporarily held, twice to ask—though he never really asked, somehow managed to let me know an offer would be accepted—to wire him money. He was heading out to Oregon now, or Washington, anyway, the Coast. What would he do? He would know when he got there, and he would call. "He's still traveling," I told Leah.

"You know," she said. "It's silly, on a day like this . . . I used to hope . . . I mean, when we were young . . ."

Her hair was done. Before me in the mirror, swimming above her head in the five whiskey sours I had poured into me and in the tears that unaccountably pushed their way into my eyes, was an image of the three of us as we had never been—I knew that— children together, unworried, sharing spacious and sunlit days. I shook my head. The whiskey would make me sick. "I know, Leah," I said. "I know."

I wove a spray of white belled flowers into her hair and turned her from side to side so she could see. A knock and then outside the door a soft voice said, "Time."

I walked to the front of the chair to look at her and bent down to kiss her lips. "You do," I said. "You look beautiful."

She looked at herself in the mirror.

"He sent flowers," I said, gathering up the pieces of comb. "From Seattle. They should be here by now." He hadn't, of course; had reacted to the news about the marriage with no more than a snort, but I'd sent an arrangement in his name. With a funny note, "Don't forget your favorite cousin."

"Ready?" I said.

The sanctuary was full, and when we entered, Aunt Esther and my mother first, then me, then Leah and my father, they all turned to look. The violinist from the band took up a Yiddish air. The old ladies from my family were in tears, gazing at us, bright with hope and sadness. On Bernard's side, strangers, though behind his aged mother and the bonfire of Miriam's hair were several empty seats. Ahead stood the rabbi in his white ceremonial robe, under the flowing canopy, prayer book in his hand.

Everything was ready. But the groom, who should have been waiting under the canopy, was missing. I looked at my father, but beyond a certain stiffness around the mouth could see nothing in his face. We stood to one side to make room for Bernard and his attendants, and waited. The violinist had come to the tune's end, but after a moment of silence that seemed to swell into the room, he began again. Leah took my hand.

In the front row, as if moved by the lugubrious melody, Aunt Esther began to sob, and my mother worked the bottle of smelling salts into her hand. I gave my father a questioning look but he had his teacher's face on, calm, unreadable. He gazed steadily up the aisle at the rear doors. The rabbi held the prayer book open, busied himself turning the pages. On a small table beside him, the wine, brimming in the glass for the wedded couple to drink, vibrated almost imperceptibly.

Two chairs were knocked to the ground as the doors to the rear burst open, and Uncle Simon strode in, holding a piece of paper above his head. He took two steps and stopped, breathing loudly, glaring at us all with pop-eyed wrath.

"Woman!" he shouted, and waited for the room to fill with his voice. "What have you done!"

He stood there, both arms upraised now, seeing himself, I'm sure, as an Old Testament prophet summoning God's destruction. But he had used the same pose for an ad in the local paper—Fifty Cars Under Twelve-Ninety-Nine!!!—holding in each fist the dollars his lucky customers would save. I saw now he had the Hebrew marriage contract in his hand.

"A lie," he proclaimed, "an insult," and he began walking slowly toward the front of the hall, as people rose from their seats. "An outrage before God."

People were standing by their seats now. The rabbi, a professional smiler, looked up mildly, though he couldn't keep wrinkles from gathering near his eyes. Bernard's deaf mother looked about happily and Miriam leaned into her ear. "I told you," she shouted. My mother had her arm around Aunt Esther now, who sobbed openly. My father walked quickly to Uncle Simon, pulled him aside, and talked with him in strained whispers. The rabbi joined them. I saw him look back at Leah. We were the only two left under the canopy. Leah held my hand, did not move, and looked down at the floor where the wineglass lay wrapped in a linen napkin, waiting to be shattered by her husband at the ceremony's end.

Uncle Simon made a dramatic turn and walked from the room, nearly tripping on an upended chair by the door. My father came up to my mother and Aunt Esther.

"Is it true?" he asked.

"Yes," my mother said.

"The contract says she's a virgin? A woman who has had two husbands?"

"Yes," my mother said quietly. "How did he find out?"

"You knew?"

"Just a few minutes ago. How did he find out?"

My father stared at her, uncomprehending.

"About Memmel," she said. "About Miller."

"Simon. They asked Simon to look at the contract."

"They who?" my mother asked.

"They who? They, who do you think, they? The friends, the professors. Someone got suspicious, someone started asking questions."

Esther let out a small whimper, and for the first time since Bernard Finkel had entered the picture I heard my father raise his voice at her. "A woman's married two times already and her husband's not going to know? Who thinks like this?" And he looked up the aisle now, where not a person was still sitting.

My mother shrugged, raising both her palms as if to say nothing could be done now, or to tell my father enough had been said. Aunt Esther was in full collapse beside her, shaking with near-silent moans.

Then, as if this was his cue, the doors to the rear exploded again and Uncle Simon made his second entrance, arms full of coats. "Come," he declaimed, in the general direction of his wife but loud enough to include us all. "We're leaving this place." Behind him were Bernard Finkel and several serious-looking men in black suits. They moved up the aisle like Jewish Secret Service men, they didn't look left or right. Bernard gathered up his mother, an old woman in a huge brocade gown who came docilely, still smiling, used to being moved from place to place, like a potted plant. To Leah, all Bernard said was, "I'm disappointed."

Then they were gone, all of them, Bernard and his mother, Uncle Simon and his wife, his boys, grinning delightedly over their shoulders, Miriam, who, after glaring at Leah a moment— as if nothing would surprise her from a woman whose hair wouldn't take a back comb—stomped noisily from the room. The news spread quickly, a buzz filled the air. The violinist, looking unhappy, picked up his instrument to start again. Then a woman I did not know ran up and whispered in his ear. He dropped the violin from his shoulder and looked at us. People, as if they had to choose sides, either left the room—this was the majority—or huddled near my family, what was left of it, looking shamed.

I didn't know where to look. The rabbi, beside us, was gathering up his papers and book, hurrying, as if he meant to catch up to the departed crowd. My father was gray with rage, looking at him and away, and my mother stared out patiently before her as if she were on a steamship, land days and days from view. I thought I might laugh or I might sit down and cry. I watched the swinging doors at the rear of the room, heard loud voices beyond them, Uncle Simon's the loudest, apologizing, assigning blame. Leah had not raised her eyes from the floor, but the expression on her face was composed, unsurprised. "I asked her not to," she said, looking only once at her mother. She still had not let go of my hand.

Then, as if on a cue of her own, once the crowd scene was ended, a groan, a guttural plaint, and, for the first time since I had known her, my Aunt Esther really did faint. She collapsed to the floor and lay there, mouth open, head back, her thick wig lifting slightly from her mottled white scalp.

One of her arms nudged the linen napkin slightly, releasing the water glass—not a wineglass, after all—inside. No one moved. The glass rolled across the room in a wavering line until it reached the far wall and the baseboard heater, where it came to rest with a tiny click.

4

My guy was a cabdriver, a chess player in Washington Square Park, a Rumanian on an expired visa who read philosophy paperbacks in three languages, phoned his mother in Bucharest every Sunday, wearing a clean shirt and tie for the occasion, and sold nickel and dime bags in the park so we could shop at Balducci's once in a while, eat at Panetta's Steak House on Fourth Street, and dance—we did this twice—to the Harmony Makers Jazz Band at Roseland uptown. His name was Alex. I loved him.

We had plans. Summers hiking in the West, a flat on the Left Bank where he would pursue his philosophy degree while I waitressed evenings, did my stained glass all day. We would traverse

the world by sea, following Magellan's route. We would open a
bagel shop in Rio. We would spend some time among the Hopi
or the Navajo or whatever tribe would have us—Alex wrote away
for information. We would live wherever we decided to, Alex said,
wherever the life was, and when we had money we would send
for his mother and sister to join us in New Orleans, Dubrovnik,
Montevideo—if not in time for the wedding, then for the chris-
tening of the grandchildren.

The police said he was lucky to survive such a beating, that
anyone who would fight three men so hard for fourteen ounces of
marijuana was either lying or had a serious wish to die. They were
guys we knew from the park, just young guys who hung out,
sometimes bought dope from Alex, sometimes shared beer with
the rest of us. They danced to the conga circles, they checked out
the girls. They had names, but I didn't know them. It was a Tuesday, early spring, the grass starting to push through the pounded
dirt, everybody's juices running. They were all in the park. Alex
would go there after getting off shift, to mellow out, play some
chess, talk with the local philosophers. He was besting the old
Belgian with the beret and the Chihuahua for the third consecu-
tive game when these guys came over and lingered, that look on
their faces. "Sure," he probably said to them. "I got you." After the
game, he invited them up to get high, to sample the wares. There
was an empty Budweiser 40-ouncer in the stairwell, Alex had
probably shared this with them on the way upstairs. What happened next he wouldn't tell me or the police. He had been stupid
enough to leave the pot with the money he was saving under the
bed—all of it, just rolled up in rubber bands and shoved in a box
under the bed like some farmer from the Old Country—and
maybe it was seeing the bills that set these guys off. Maybe it was
something he said—if he was angry Alex was capable of saying
anything. Maybe they had it planned all along. All I know is they
called me at the studio, told me to get down to St. Vincent's right
away. "What is it?" I asked, not able to breathe. I was standing

near the round window overlooking the street. I watched people talking, entering stores, waiting for the light, trying to get myself to breathe. "What's happened?" "There's been an assault," the nurse told me, and gave me his name. Behind her I could hear a siren and loud voices.

He was on a bed in the emergency room, hooked up to a whole wall of machines, smiling at me like it was an elaborate joke. "They have good drugs, your American doctors," he said, grinning around a broken tooth. He had a fractured wrist, a contused kidney, four broken ribs, a blood bruise behind one eye the doctors said could leave him brain-damaged if the swelling was not controlled. His arm was broken in six places, he would need to wear a pneumatic cast for two months and then have surgery. He smiled and waved me over with his chin. He looked comfortable, stoned, amused. His face was so blue and battered I couldn't even touch him. I just stood in the doorway and cried.

The studio I worked in, maybe to help me get out of town for a while, sent me on assignment to Baltimore, where they had contracted to clean the windows of an old Presbyterian church. It was absorbing work, the crew was friendly and liked the job, they even got me to go for margaritas one night in a dive across the street. After three weeks I took up my mother's constant suggestion and gave Leah a call. She had lived in Baltimore almost four years now, was married to a man I'd never met, had two little boys I'd never seen. "I knew you were here," she said. "I was hoping you'd call." She invited me for the weekend, for Shabbos—the new husband wasn't a rabbi, thank God, but a lawyer—but I said no, I didn't do that anymore, and Leah changed the invitation to the following day. So on a Sunday afternoon I borrowed a car, put on a dress for the first time in months, and followed Leah's careful, elaborate directions out to the suburbs.

They lived in a two-story house on a gently curving street lined with young trees. There were hydrangeas out front, a bank of irises to either side of the door, and around the side of the house a rope hammock slung between two maples. There was the smell of barbecue in the air, and a radio played the Orioles game next door, where two men were carefully re-oiling a driveway with big push brooms. The older man stopped to wipe his forehead and waved his cap at me.

The door was opened by a boy in a plaid shirt and a large yarmulke, his hair crew-cut on top, wrapped in small peis around his ears, where it had been allowed to grow on the sides. He looked at me seriously a moment, then left the door open and ran into the house, calling for his mother. Leah said, "I'm coming," and the little boy stopped in a doorway up the hall to stick his head out and peer at me sideways.

In the moment it took her to walk to the door, I fought the urge to run, get in the car before anyone else saw me, drive, not back to my hotel, not back to New York, just somewhere away from here, fast. There was a nameless rebuke in her happy face coming toward me, in this quiet street with the ball game drifting from the radio next door. Then Leah threw her arms around me, and with the older boy leading the way and the younger laboriously pushing a plastic truck into the hall before us, she brought me inside.

I sat in the living room with the older boy, Joseph, while Leah called her husband in from the yard. Through the sliding rear door I saw him put down pruning shears, and he waved to me from the kitchen, a large man sweating freely behind a thick brown beard. He smiled and tugged at his shirt collar to indicate he was going upstairs to change. Leah and the younger boy, Sam, were in the kitchen, preparing food. Joseph sat on the sofa opposite me, his sneaker soles straight out before him. He held a brown bear with a battered white nose in his lap.

"I know who you are," he said.

"I know who you are, too."

"This is Bo, my most famous stuffed animal."

"Hello, Bo," I said.

Joseph shook his head. "He doesn't talk to people."

Alex had been gone two months. He was gone five days after the beating, still dizzy, still pissing blood, only out of the hospital thirty-six hours. Someone had asked some questions and Alex was convinced the police had turned his name over to Immigration, and it was clear, at least to Alex, he'd be jailed for the drug charge — though they'd found less than an ounce in what was left of our room — then deported anyway. He was leaving for Bucharest, if he could find the money. There was no choice.

We had just come from the hospital. We were standing in our kitchen drinking iced tea. It hurt Alex to sit down, jarred the dressing around his chest, and he tended to knock his pneumatic cast against the table, which the doctors told him wouldn't hurt but did. I had taken the week off from work, made us a lunch of soup and cold salads from Balducci's. I had bought a checked cloth for the table and some flowers from the cart on Sixth Avenue. I had made a sign in block letters and funny designs, "Welcome Home!" but the place, the "crime scene" — for two days yellow police tape had barred me from the door — didn't feel exactly like home anymore, and I had left the sign in a drawer. I had done what I could with the bedroom, though the blood in the carpet would never come out, and the glazier had not come to replace the window as he'd promised. In the cab Alex had told me he was leaving. Now he poured his tea into the sink and with one clumsy hand found the Scotch in the cupboard. I could have helped but I didn't. He opened the bottle by holding the cap in his teeth, poured a glass full, and smiled at me. "I have no choice," he said, and took a long swallow. "This way I beat them to punching me." He laughed, wincing through the pain. "Is joke, no?"

There was no one I could talk to. My father didn't know about Alex; I was sure my mother had kept the information from him. She had disavowed all knowledge, too, telling me one Sunday last summer in Central Park. Alex was going to join us at Bethesda Fountain for a picnic, his first chance to meet my parents. I was at

the subway stop with the basket, and when my mother came up
the steps alone, without my father, I grew concerned, but she
looked festive in a blue summer dress and I hugged her gratefully
and took her arm. But she wasn't staying. There on the avenue,
with tourists unloading from a bus behind us and the summer
breeze buffeting our dresses, my new straw hat, she told me as
long as I was with this man she would rather not know about it.
She looked me in the face, then turned away and said if I didn't
care what I did to my own life I could at least care about the pain
I caused others who loved me. She kissed me solemnly on the
cheek and was gone, down the stairs, lost in the crowd of people
blinking their way into the sunlight.

When Alex met me by the fountain, I had thrown away the hat,
the picnic, basket and all. I couldn't talk to him at first. We
walked around the park until it grew dark and lights came on in
the high buildings on the avenues. We walked down to the duck
pond, then up to the reservoir and back, not talking, until at
Sheeps Meadow Alex stopped me and took me by the shoulders
and held me hard until I could begin to cry.

So I had no one to call. David knew about Alex, was ambigu-
ously sympathetic—"My God, you made a *picnic?*"—but he
would just magnify it into an age-old pattern, a constellation of
familial pain in which David's star burned most bright.

Alex called Bucharest several times, spoke loudly to his mother,
had a shouting match with someone he later told me was an
uncle. He had been drinking since early morning, had smoked
some hash the police hadn't found in the freezer, was washing
down pain pills with Scotch every half hour. When he finally
screamed something into the phone and hung up, he turned to
me with a tight smile.

"They have no help," he said. "You must get money for my
plane."

I did. I emptied my bank accounts, including one he didn't
know about, where I had been depositing forty dollars a month

for our future travels. I reserved the ticket over the phone, packed his heavy leather suitcase, his box of books, while he supervised from the couch.

At Kennedy Airport the following day he boarded the plane, his head in a big colorful Rastafarian cap I'd bought to cover the swelling, his shattered arm in its cast sheltered up near his chest like a sleeping child. In the coffee shop he had talked about sending for me in a few months, about meeting in France in a year, but I wasn't really listening and soon he stopped. As he went through security he tried to wave, but a stewardess came up behind him, jostling him down the ramp. I saw him try to turn, but he couldn't, and then I began waving. He couldn't see me but I waved anyway. All I could see was the festive woolen hat, concentric rings of yellow and red and green bobbing down the walkway. I waved until it was out of sight.

The younger boy enjoyed planting his feet in his father's lap and tugging with both fists on his father's thick beard. Avram, Leah's husband, didn't seem to mind. We ate sandwiches with coffee in the kitchen, except for Joseph, who explained that Bo wasn't hungry and he would eat when Bo did.

"Will Bo be hungry soon?" Avram asked.

"I *told* you, he doesn't talk to people!"

"All right," Leah said and put a sandwich in front of the boy, who soon took a few bites and asked for milk.

We talked about the neighborhood, the religious school the boys would have to be bused to across town. Avram seemed to know all about me, which I found touching, and the delight he took in his two boys, the quiet way he watched Leah, made some age-old verity in me dissolve away, made me glad for my cousin and at the same time made me know I couldn't stay here very long. After the meal, Avram took the boys upstairs for a bath, and Leah, as we had done all our lives, cut lemon, boiled water, and brought tea in glasses to the table.

"You have a beautiful family," I told her.

"Yes," she said, and I was grateful she didn't say any more.

"How's your job?" she said. "Still making windows?"

"Well, cleaning them most of the time. I like it. I'm good at it and I like the work."

We sat in Leah's white kitchen, with its sink and stove under gleaming copper-bottomed pots in the center of the room, with the soft garland of flowers circling the wall near the ceiling, with the long shadows of late afternoon reaching across her flower beds and the children's toys left in the yard, with the tea steaming between us, and suddenly I wanted to tell her everything about Alex, about my life with him, about the idiotic dreams we half believed in. I wanted to tell her how his thick red hair had so many cowlicks he wore a hat most of the time rather than wrestle it with a comb, how his beard tended to grow inward, piercing the skin and causing painful blisters, and how I would tease the hairs out gently with a pin. I wanted to tell her we liked taking baths together, using a huge pink sponge, the kind they use at car washes, on each other's backs, that we liked to go see Chinese movies in Chinatown, no subtitles, how the Chinese women would knit and talk back at the screen, how the kids would play in the aisles, sometimes come right up and climb in your lap, how vendors walked up and down during the movie and sold sweet candied noodles out of little trays. He was a large man, I wanted to tell her, but somewhere he had learned how to dance, and he had taught me, and he would talk with anyone—if someone stopped us on the street for money he'd ask what they needed, where they would spend the money, until I dragged him off, handing out dollar bills as tolls to reach home. I wanted to tell her he snored like a diesel engine, was the only man I ever knew who liked to hold me after we made love, how he thought he was a talented cook when he was a terrible one, how he liked to sing Jimi Hendrix tunes when he had no idea of the lyrics. I wanted to tell Leah I loved Alex and he was gone and memory was a tricky thing to live on; it shifted on you like cards in a deck, until you didn't know any longer what it was you were remembering.

Our last night we propped up the bed with a milk crate we found near the elevator—one of the legs had been knocked off in the fight. Alex was in great pain, and had been through a bottle of Scotch. Now he was drinking red wine and talking to me in Rumanian part of the time. He had gotten very angry when I couldn't find his Husserl essays and when I asked him if he wanted any of our travel books he said I should keep them. I said I didn't think I wanted to and he said fine and opened the front door and threw them into the hall. He had followed them out and taken a long walk while I finished packing. When he came back he was silent and I took him to bed, undressed him, changed the bandages over his eye and on his chest, bathed him with a damp cloth and warm water. He was asleep when I finished. I found some music on the radio, took off my clothes, and got in next to him, listening to the music and his thick breathing.

Sometime in the night he woke me. He was unable to move without wincing, so we kissed for a long time. I tasted Scotch on his breath, wine, and his skin smelled of smoke. I moved, kissed him on the hair, the cheeks, the shoulders and neck. I whispered nonsense in his ears. After a while he stopped kissing me back. I had drunk most of the wine, Alex had taken more pills. He said something to me, too quiet for me to catch, as I slid down his belly to take him in my mouth.

I was making love to him when he said it again. "Jew."

"What?" I picked up my head.

"Jew. Jewess. Daughter of Abraham."

"Alex, what the hell are you saying?"

"Daughter of martyrs. Miserable bone-faced Auschwitz to teach us all how to suffer."

I was sitting in bed now. I tried to get out, but Alex caught me by the arm and dragged me back. He pushed my head back toward his penis.

"There. You see?"

"Let go of me, you fucker," I said.

"What do you see?" he said angrily, this time pulling on my hair.

"You," I said. "I see you."

"This is uncircumcised cock. Look." And he reached down with his other hand, I heard him groan and he lifted the half-erect organ closer to my face. "Uncircumcised cock of infidel dog. Cock of dog. Is what your mother saw."

"No, Alex," I tried to say, but with a call of pain he sat halfway up in bed and forced my mouth down over him.

Leah asked about David. He was married again, I told her, had a little boy just about Sam's age.

"Cousins," Leah said.

I drank some of the tea and Leah went to get more hot water. She had started to gain weight after the second child. She thought it was funny, after a life of praying she could put on some weight, her prayers had been answered all at once. Her hair was short, and I was relieved obscurely that she had not covered it with a wig. She wore a white blouse with a blue skirt and battered Adidas on her feet. She moved lightly around the room, called up the stairs when Joseph yelled a question from the bath, and watched me patiently during my silences.

"It's nice to see you this way," I told her.

"Yes?"

"Like this. Happy, I mean."

"I am," she said. "And I hope you will be."

"Oh, you know, I have my moments." I stood to help her with the kettle.

At the table she spooned sugar into her tea. Then she said, "It was always easier for me," looking down at her teaspoon, turning it in her hand.

"What?"

"Easier. I always had an easier time, or I always thought I did."

I had no idea what she meant. I remembered the trussed and constrained child, the timid girl who could not choose her own clothes, where she went, whom she talked to. I remembered her inability to hold even a simple conversation, and her eyes, always wanting. I had been the free one, I had been outdoors, unsupervised, able to speak my mind, my convictions.

"I don't think that's true," I said. "I always . . . I'm sorry, but I always pitied you, Leah, you had so many rules, so many fears."

"Yes, that's true. I was afraid of everything. But somewhere in all those rules and superstitions and fears, I understood what I wanted, I learned what would . . ." Here she paused, looking for the word. "What would be enough."

"I'm glad," I said. Something was in my throat, a pressure building behind my tongue. I tried a sip of the tea and looked at her, then away.

"I'm sorry," she said.

"And me?" I said. "What did I learn, Leah?"

She pushed the saucer of lemon slices aside and reached across for my hand. I pulled back, lifted the warm glass near my face.

"You never learned," she said quietly. "I've watched you my whole life and you've never known what would be enough for you."

"That's not fair," I said. I heard Joseph running upstairs and Avram's voice calling in Yiddish. I thought of Alex walking away from me toward the plane, of my father, who had not spoken with me since I had come home the night after Alex left, in tears, and he had learned of him for the first time. He had prayed for me that night, prayed to God and to his ancestors for guidance, for forgiveness. I thought of my parents, steeped in sorrow like good Jews, of Leah, emerging from it and looking back at me from her remote and inscrutable calm. Where in all this had I asked for too much? I thought of what Alex had called me. "That's not a fair thing to say to me," I said, standing at the table.

"I'm sorry," Leah said, rising, too, "I didn't mean . . . All I meant was . . ." And again she paused, and I raised my voice.

"What? All you meant was what?"

"All right," she said, and sat down, looking at me. "It's not about wanting, I don't think. Everyone wants. It's about looking around and finding the world, I don't know, sufficient. You saw everything, nothing slipped by. Maybe you saw too much. You saw right through people's words, what they meant to do, to the ways they failed. You always had to forgive them. I saw less. I had less to forgive."

Sometime later Avram came down and said the boys were ready to say good night. We followed him upstairs, where the boys, one in train pajamas, the other in a red suit with a smiling dinosaur across the shirt, were saying their prayers. They said good night first, Joseph throwing his arms around me, and putting his lips on my face. They got into bed and said the "Shema," the prayer Leah and I used to say before bed. Then they added the prayer David had been taught, the prayer for boys. "May the angel who keeps me from all evil bless these young boys and speak of them in my name and the names of my forefathers. And may they grow to prosper in the heart of their land." I stood in the lit doorway near Avram, while Leah sat on Sam's bed, and wondered if in other dark rooms somewhere there were little girls praying for these boys, praying for their future husbands. And I wondered who prayed for those girls.

Downstairs, they invited me to spend the night, to stay and listen to some music or sit on the patio out back. I shook my head, said I had a crew who would sit and drink coffee until I showed up and got them started. They walked me to the door, came out to see me to my car. The night was fresh and still, the oil from the drive next door shone dully in the moonlight, and from somewhere behind the house I could hear wind moving in the trees. Leah and I kissed. She made me promise I would call soon and kissed me again. Avram shook my hand warmly and put his arm around Leah there on the walk. I got into my car, turned on the ignition and lights. They waved as I pulled away from the curb and I waved back. But at the corner I stopped, looked in the rearview mirror, where I could see them still standing on their walk. They looked around the street a moment, Avram picked something off the lawn, and they moved back toward the house. I watched until I was certain they were safe indoors, then slowly slipped out the clutch and turned the corner.

PILLAR OF FIRE

Something made him turn around. He had said his goodbyes and was halfway down the walk to his car when something made him stop. It couldn't have been the gravel, the way it popped and slid under his feet, and it couldn't have been the light in the trees ahead, the way the air shimmered the leaves. It couldn't have been these but he felt it was, as if for a sudden sickening moment he could feel the earth moving through space. He stumbled, then stopped. He turned around.

They were there still, on the elegantly sagging porch, among the plant hangers and chimes, his wife and this man, Oliver, one padded arm across her shoulders. They were watching him. In Maura's face David saw a flicker of concern—she must have known he would see it and he thought this was why he stumbled, what he had turned to see. But then Oliver lifted a beefy hand and called out "Safe travels," and David watched his wife look at the man, saw the raised eyes and dip of the shoulder, the happy, intimate surrender to the embrace. He found his keys this time and reached the car, gunned the engine, feeling a hollow pleasure at the sound the tires made, the spatter of pebbles he left behind.

He drove fast. He pulled onto the road fast and didn't slow down. He tapped the accelerator and the big car responded. He breathed the wind, felt the gears mesh deep in the engine, and told himself he was all right.

It was the sweater that got him. Not the fact that she had left him. Not the fact that she had left him for a potter—named Oliver, for God's sake—a potter who *looked* like an Oliver, all furry eyebrows and nodding concern, smug fingers praying in front of his face. You're angry, Oliver had said. You're in a lot of pain. They were in his artistic living room, books piled everywhere, bowls, knickknacks, curios, cultural artifacts, African, Chinese, casually heaped in the corners. I can see it in your face, the potter had said, tilting his head to show he meant it, and David wanted to clock him. But that wasn't it. Not his tacky Berkshire château, with the wind chimes and hummingbird feeders and happy gargoyles. Not even that the potter seemed to enjoy David's company, inviting him for dinner. Couscous and salad, Oliver said, homemade bread. Stay and eat. We'd like you to. Sure, David had thought. We. And after dinner do *we* go upstairs with my wife?

Well, that wasn't what got him, though you'd think so.

It was the sweater, white and a thick lumpy blue in some pathetic amateur crosshatch. It sat on him like a wool sack. All their years together Maura had knitted—socks, scarves, mittens, whatever—without finishing anything. As far as David knew, she had never completed a single piece. There was a wicker basket in their living room full of abandoned efforts, it made him sick to look at, a little woolen graveyard in the corner by the TV. Then all he had to do was take one look at the sweater Oliver wore, the way it bunched in the shoulders and tented at the waist, to know it was Maura's, she'd finally goddamn finished one. And for some reason this is what stuck with him, came up in his throat to choke him.

He didn't know everything, he knew that. He thought he had made that clear. He wasn't perfect and he'd made mistakes. He knew that, too. But here—here was craziness. David, she had said, this is Oliver. Like he was a neighbor in the building, some guy in the street—except he had his hand on her back at the time, except he stood there in the world's ugliest sweater, *his* goddamn ugly sweater, if anyone was interested, or that should have been his.

Seven years they had lived together. Maura was his wife — did that mean anything? They paid the mortgage on the co-op. They had a bedroom suite and a dining-room suite, a stock portfolio, they owned this car. They ate Chinese twice a week, liked *every* Schwarzenegger movie, preferred MacNeil to Lehrer and thought the show had gone down — what were they doing, if not building a life? Didn't they have plans? — moving out of the city eventually, children, trips to South America, Europe, all over the place. When David looked into his future he saw Maura there, nothing else.

He had sat there, them on the couch, he in a chair covered with some itchy Indian rug, drinking tea that smelled like roots out of one of Oliver's mugs. I want to stay, Maura said, smiling at them both. I'm happy now.

Well, it was crazy. They sat there, three people drinking tea as if they were normal, as if the day was, but it wasn't, they weren't. It was insane. There was an order to things, David wanted to explain, but how do you explain anything to crazy people? You didn't just wake up one day with a wife and go to bed that night without one. You didn't make plans, live your life a certain way for thirty years just to have it disappear one afternoon at four o'clock because some bearded guy in the woods gave you tea and told you he felt your pain. Did anyone else see that? There was an order to things. If you broke that up, what would be next? And what did she mean, "now"?

He careened down the middle of the blacktop, looking straight ahead, both hands holding the wheel. His throat hurt, his head ached as if he was coming down with something, a rare and sudden disease. He hoped he was. He hoped they found his body in the morning. Would serve her right. He took the curves at sixty-five, seventy, fishtailing, rear tires catching roadside brush. He pressed the accelerator, not caring, faster on the straightaways, glimpsing houses behind barriers of hedge and lawn, a man cutting his grass stopping to look as David roared by, gripping the wheel and leaning into the acceleration, feeling for the floor of the car through the pedal, until a wooden fence sprang up to fill his windshield and he slammed the brakes, sliding. The car fanned slowly behind him, came to rest at an angle to the fence. He could reach out and touch it if he tried. Ahead, a pasture sloped away to a white barn on a hill. Not five feet from him a Holstein, munching grass, lifted a massive indifferent face, its black eye, a huge wet marble, glistening dully in the light. David cursed the cow, the fence, the barn, floored the car in reverse, squinting through dust and rubble until he managed to turn it around.

He didn't understand what happened next. Five hundred yards from the highway he must have done something—swerved, slowed, who knew?—because suddenly in his rearview mirror there was a black muscle car, a Mustang maybe, honking and flashing its lights. "That's right, you sonofabitch," David muttered, saying it louder as he slowed and signaled he was entering the highway with the car still on him, high beams and horn going, white face hovering in his mirror, so close David wasn't sure if he felt a tap, screaming now, "That's *right*, you sonofabitch!," pulling over on the tight curve of the entrance ramp, some kind of flowering bush streaming up his hood. He stomped the brake, one wheel off the road, branches scraping his windshield, dust sifting through the open windows. He stuck his head out to call "Die, you fucker!" as the driver, a kid with long hair and a baseball cap, lightly gave him the finger and disappeared behind grillwork and red taillights.

He had had his affair first, Rhonda, an intern at the firm. He wished she were waiting for him now, in her two-room apartment

near the park. He was still up-and-coming then, the partners' darling. The Crestview deal hadn't collapsed yet, he was twenty-nine
and overseeing a $50 million investment, and he knew he was
watched, talked about. He felt as if he was in a movie, the camera
always on him.

Rhonda was fresh from the Virginia program, one of this year's
eager crop, her cubicle right outside his office. Her first day he
helped her hang a Hockney print and they couldn't get it straight,
no matter what they did. They joked about how many thousands
of dollars had gone into their architecture degrees, with the result
that together they couldn't hang a picture. He made her laugh,
and when she caught him looking at her she seemed to like it.
That was all it took. He knew he could have her. She was beautiful and talented and smart and she carried herself with the
seductive air of someone who knew she would get whatever she
wanted. For a while, six weeks, maybe, this had included him.

David had thought it was love, because it changed everything.
New vitality stunned him. He rose early to get to the gym,
watched what he ate, made sweeping design modifications to the
project without needing to consult anyone. He was witty with the
partners, firm with the contractors, airy and patient with the interns
and staff. He took up cooking, started reading again. His physical
reflexes seemed to have improved, if that was possible. All day
he was aware of Rhonda's whereabouts—as he showered in the
mornings he could imagine her rising from bed and moving
through her darkened rooms. At the office he could sense where
she was, in the conference room, at the coffee machine, as if they
were hooked up by radar. Their movements seemed charmed,
synchronous, touched by some mysterious and happy significance.
They talked about this, whether people's lives moved along a pre-
ordained path, if their meeting had been in the cards from the
start. Rhonda told him he had looked strangely familiar, even that
first day, and David told Rhonda—this was past midnight, in his
office, take-out boxes and clothing scattered on the floor around

them — that he felt drawn to her almost magnetically. She had a glow, he told her — he'd never seen anything like it — in her eyes, her hair, around her shoulders, and it was as if he walked in it all day. He could breathe it. It was something he had never felt before and he was certain it was love.

He was so certain, when he told Maura he believed she must have known, felt it on him, smelled it on his skin. It was a terrible thing to expect her to understand, but this wasn't about them — not ultimately, not in its deepest sense. He had come home after she was asleep, had woken her, the words rushing out as if by their own momentum — he couldn't lie anymore, it wasn't fair to anyone to lie, not about this, it was too big. What was happening to him was unusual, if it happened to you once in your life you were lucky. Could she try and see that?

But she had not known. When he told her her jaw actually dropped open, her eyes stretched wide as if he had hit her in the face. She sat on the couch in her robe and nightgown, hair pushed sideways from sleep, and when she started to cry he was desperate to do something, hold her, get her an aspirin, take it all back. He stood there — realized then he still had his coat on — and said, "Can I do anything?"

Her laugh startled him. She looked up at him, her eyes wet, as if they'd been laughing a good long time. She shook her head as if this was a joke she'd remember and when she moved past him to the bathroom put a hand on his shirt. "Thanks," she said. "You've done enough for one night."

When she came out of the bathroom her hair was brushed and she held a glass of water. Her eyes were dry. He stood by the couch with his coat on — it was hard to move, hard to look at her — while she asked him a few questions. She held her jaw in a hand and looked at the floor as if she could barely stay awake.

"So this is the big one," she said.

"Yes."

"The one we all hear about. The lifesaver."

"I think so."

"Right," she said, rising, pulling her robe close, and moving toward the bedroom. "You'll have to excuse me now. The rest of us mortals untouched by bliss need our sleep."

She gave him a week to decide. When he told her nothing had changed—it had, he had lied; Rhonda had taken the news of his confession coldly, was even then moving subtly away—Maura had nodded once, as if a bargain between them had been sealed. "Okay," she said. "Are you staying for dinner? Frozen lasagna sound good?"

Over the next few weeks, brochures appeared around the apartment—skiing, woodworking, Outward Bound, pottery classes—and sometimes Maura wasn't home when he arrived. Twice there were notes taped to the refrigerator, saying she'd be gone for the weekend, back Sunday night, late.

He got out of the car to check for damage, saw nothing obvious, not much he could tell from where it sat, tilted off the road, covered in branches. One of these whipped him in the arm when he tried to get in so he whipped it back. Then the door closed on his shoulder, so he got out again and slammed it a few times, then kicked the tire until he hurt his foot, and went up front to lean against the hood. A car or two passed on the ramp, people offering expressions curious or hostile, and David returned their looks blankly, as if to say he belonged here, just where he was, and had every intention of staying as long as he felt like it. He followed them with his eyes. He hoped someone else would give him the finger. He hoped someone would try it.

Ahead of him, over the highway threading west, what might turn into a fine sunset was taking shape, clouds stacked in thin wedges across the horizon, just tingeing red. Maura loved sunsets, David remembered. She liked to sit in front of the window and watch them. He wondered if she would be watching this one. He thought of her coming out onto Oliver's porch, drawing a shawl over her shoulders—she'd probably completed an entire wardrobe for them both—Oliver following with more dirt tea. He pictured her here with him, out for a picnic, roast chicken and a bottle of wine in a hamper in the trunk, pausing on their way just a moment for the view, watching, no need to talk.

And then he saw himself as he was, hours from home, alone and ridiculous, with his car half off the road in an oleander bush, gazing at an empty sky. The pain was back in his throat and he moved angrily, as if to shake it off. He threw the car door open and climbed inside.

He thought the place was empty, maybe shut down. The big neon light was working—red letters flashing T & R—but there were no cars out front. Then to the side of the building he saw two trucks and through the window a waitress pouring coffee at the counter. He parked the car and got out.

The phone was in back, at the end of a short hallway between the bathrooms. It had a rotary dial, which confused him a moment—he hadn't seen one in years. He fumbled for change, surprised to notice his hands were still shaking, then remembered he didn't need any. A toilet flushed on the other side of the wall. He dialed the three numbers as a man opened the bathroom door, water still running behind him. David had to turn to one side to let him pass. A woman came on the line.

"Yes, hello," he said. "Is this 911?"

"Emergency services, sir. Can I help you?"

"I'm calling . . . I need to report an accident."

The man who had come out of the bathroom immediately struck up a loud conversation at the counter. David had trouble hearing. "Excuse me?" he said.

"Is anyone hurt?"

"Yes. I think so. I'm not sure."

"Were you involved in this accident, sir?" the woman asked.

"No," David said. "I just saw the car."

"And you say someone is hurt?"

"I think so. I was driving by and this car was overturned, off the side of the road. I couldn't see. I think the driver is still inside."

"Did you make certain someone was inside?"

"No, I was already past it. It was upside down, off the road. That's why I'm calling."

She asked for the location and he told her. Behind him, somebody said, "Hey, it ain't jailbait if you *marry* it," and somebody answered, "Yes it is, you dumb fuck," and they laughed. David leaned into the wall to hear better. Someone had written "Bobby" in green marker, then a number.

"Can you describe the vehicle?" the woman asked.

He told her. A black car, souped up, maybe a late-model Mustang. The kid inside had long hair and was wearing a baseball cap.

"You did see the driver then, sir," the woman said.

"Before," David said. "He passed me on the entrance ramp, before. I saw him then."

There was a pause, as if she was considering the truth of what he told her.

"Will you send someone?" David asked.

He heard a breath through the line and he waited for her to say something, but she didn't. "Thank you," he said, and the line went dead.

David turned around, unsure what to do next, and as he did, the conversation in the diner stopped, as if they had been waiting for him. One of the men at the counter made movements with a hand, as if he were entering numbers in a calculator, the second man watched. The man who had passed him was leaning against the counter, a mug of coffee propped on his large stomach. He wore a black leather vest over a cowboy shirt, a straw cowboy hat pushed back on his head. He looked at David. The other two swiveled to look at him also, while the waitress stacked empty plates on the shelf leading into the kitchen. David stood there, feeling the change still in his hand. He felt they were waiting for him to do something. He turned back to the phone and lifted the receiver, reaching in his shirt pocket for a piece of paper. He dropped the change into the slot and dialed the number.

He had had some trouble getting the car back on the road. He had to pull a branch from one of the wheel wells, and he had to rock the car several times before he could regain the asphalt. Then he had to stop to remove some twigs that had lodged against the windshield, and as he drove, a sound, new to him, rumbled dimly from under the chassis. He decided to ignore it. He had to tell himself to unclench his teeth and twice had to take his hand off the steering wheel to flex it. He realized he was shaking. There was a sour taste in his mouth, adrenaline, he supposed, but maybe, on top of it all, he really was getting sick. He felt his forehead, and the side of his neck. He decided music was what he needed and turned on the radio as he cautiously entered the highway, but all he could find was country and a religious talk show, so he upended a cassette case on the seat near him and kept one eye on the speedometer as he threw the tapes around, looking for something he liked.

Leaning over this way, he had nearly missed it. But it caught at the edge of his vision, a single tire rotating slowly in the air off the side of the highway. He eased his car left, slowed until he saw another tire, this one still, then the whole car, a black Mustang overturned in the culvert, its wheels in the air and its windshield a starburst of shattered glass. Steam leaked from the engine. He turned nearly full around but couldn't see inside it as he passed.

After three rings the phone was answered and David opened his mouth to speak. Celestial music, complete with harp and birdsong, filled his ear. Answering machine. He waited until a soothing voice—Oliver's—said, simply, "Please."

He realized he had no idea what to say. Why had he called? Behind him, conversation was picking up again, he could hear the waitress joining in. He turned to the wall.

"Hi, it's me. It's David. Maura, listen, can I talk to you a minute? Anybody there?" He waited a few seconds. From behind him came laughter, a wolf call. "Look, I'm sorry to bother you, something's happened, I'm a little upset. There's been an accident, on the road. Not me, I'm fine, some kid in a car. He flipped it. I didn't see him flip it but I saw him, that's what's weird, I saw him not five minutes before . . ." Behind him the cowboy said, "You think I didn't *try*? *Two* of 'em? Believe me, Cochise, I tried," and the men laughed. David continued. "Look, I'm sorry I took off like that. I had to go. I just . . ."

A beep sounded in his ear and a metallic voice said "Thank you." Feeling a flush come into his face, he fished for more change and quickly redialed the number. Behind him the cowboy said, "I don't know, Neptune or someplace. Wherever in the hell they come from." "They come from Uranus," another man said, to a burst of laughter. David tried pressing into the wall. He read Bobby's number three times while the phone rang.

After the music he said, "Maura, could we talk? Just me and you, just for a few minutes. I think we should, you know? Maybe we could talk some more." He twisted deeper into the corner, speaking lower. "The thing is, I really need to tell you some things, there's some things you really should hear." He checked his watch. "I'll be home in four or five hours, maybe you could call me, or we could talk in the morning . . ."

The beep sounded a second time and he hung up before he could be thanked again. He faced the diner. The three men were looking at the waitress, who was mopping the counter with a rag. She had a cigarette in her other hand and she spoke, moving the cigarette in the air for punctuation. "Well," she said, "and this is just me, mind. Okay—say it really *was* the end of the world, and you really *were* the last?" She paused for effect, pulled on the cigarette. "I guess that's when I finally learn to do without."

This was met with a roar of laughter, the loudest yet, even the cowboy, to whom David supposed the comment was addressed, laughing hard, his cup of coffee jiggling merrily on his stomach. Something was wrong with the light in this place, or maybe it was the air in here. The four of them by the counter made up a disturbing tableau, as if he had never seen one like it before. As if in walking to the phone he had crossed an invisible barrier, where the air was different, the light changed, and now he couldn't get back. He shook his head to rid it of this stray, useless notion, moved before they could again look up and see him standing there.

As he passed behind them David saw what the man at the counter was doing. He had one of those games, a triangle with wooden pegs, the object being to eliminate as many of the pegs as possible by jumping them. He worked quickly, dropping pegs on the counter, then sweeping them up and starting over. When the others laughed he joined in. David watched him leave four pegs, then two, then four again. Nobody looked up as David closed the door and went out into the evening.

It was full dusk. The eastern sky was deep blue edged with purple, and beyond the highway, to the west, he could see a still band of sunlight low over the far hills. He stood a moment, breathing the cool air, then realized he didn't see his car. It took a few seconds to figure that he'd come out the wrong door, had somehow walked right past the door he had entered through, to the side lot, where two trucks sat, one idling contentedly with its running lights on. He crossed the gravel to his car.

There were two girls, one in the passenger seat with the door open—had he forgotten to lock it?—her feet out on the ground.

She was leaning forward, examining his cassettes. At her feet lay a red plastic backpack. The other girl, maybe a year or two older, was stretched on her back on the hood of his car, looking at the sky. As he watched she made a tube of her hands and peered through it, scanning the horizon. They were twelve and fourteen, maybe younger.

He stopped again—would this insane day never end?—and looked around for another car that might be his. But there was a single car in the lot, his, obviously. He must have left the door open, these two had seen him do it and marched right in. He walked over.

"Can I help you?" he said.

The girl on the hood sat up to look at him. "Hey," she said. The younger girl smiled. In the back seat, he could see now, were two duffel bags and one of those old-fashioned cosmetics suitcases, round and powder blue.

"Can I help you?" David said again.

The girl on the hood said, "Hey, mister, you just missed a stupendous sunset. Superial. What would you give it, Ange?"

"Ten," the younger girl mumbled, her face lost in lank brown hair as she leaned over the cassettes.

"It wasn't *that* good. Nine point three, maybe nine point five, tops," the other girl said. She smiled at David and hooked a thumb at the girl in his car. "She's a romantic."

David didn't say anything.

"Cool car," the older girl said, and the younger girl looked up and repeated it, "Yeah, cool. We like it."

His eyes were adjusted to the failing light now, he could see them more clearly. The girl on the hood was older than he'd thought, still, maybe fifteen at the most. She also had long hair that, when she turned to look at him, fell in two skeins that nearly covered her face. She was dressed in jeans and running shoes, both filthy, and a man's green army jacket. She had a silver ring through a nostril and another through an eyebrow. The other girl looked even younger than twelve. She was plump and fresh-faced—even in this light he could see two red cheeks—and wore black high-top sneakers, a heavy sweater several sizes too large, and a baseball cap backwards. She smiled shyly at him.

"So," the older girl said. "How far you going?"

"Why? Why do you need to know that?" David asked, coming closer now, running his fingers on a series of wide scrapes along the body of the car.

"We thought we might ride with you awhile, you know, if that was cool."

David was at the side door now. He bent to peer in at their luggage. The younger girl had stacked the cassettes neatly in their holder; otherwise, he could see nothing changed. He stood up and looked at the girl on the hood.

"You broke into my car?"

She was off the hood in an instant, the car between them, hands up as if he were about to rush her. "We didn't," she said.

He looked at her a moment, then at the younger girl, still sitting in the car. She hadn't moved. An odd, sweet smell came off her, as if she'd been eating candy all day. "It was open, sir," this girl said, looking up. "We just sat in it to wait."

"You left the keys," the other girl said, keeping her distance. She reached in her jeans and came out with his keys. She tossed them at him. "Someone could have stolen it. We watched it for you."

He caught the keys, not believing what was happening. He ran both hands through his hair, stepped away from the door and leaned against the car. He supposed he could have left them in his rush to get inside, though he had never done anything like that before. The sensation that he was becoming ill returned, delivered on a surge of weariness. Maybe they would help him stay awake. "I'm not going far," he said, then, too tired to lie, added, "on this road." He moved to the driver's side. "I turn south a few miles ahead."

The older girl was around the car before he had finished talking. "That's cool," she said, nodding at him, motioning for the younger to climb in back. She got in and reached for the seat belt. "So do we."

He learned their names. The older was Drew, the younger was Angie, though recently she had decided to be called Sandra, Drew said. They had left Toronto that morning, heading south. They were from Cleveland, originally, but that was history. Drew spoke rapidly, using her hands, looking from him to the highway, then back, talking all the while. Here was something, Drew said. Did he realize that, statistically, more people in this country were from a certain place than actually still in it? A proven fact. He could look it up. David glanced at her as he drove. Her expression was intimate, animated, as if he could not fail to be delighted by what she told him.

"I like this car," Drew said, touching the dashboard, the door panel. "I've seen cars, you know? This one's nice."

"You've been hitchhiking all day?" David asked.

"Yup." She found the makeup mirror on the flipside of the sun visor. She turned the light on and explored her face, pressing here and there, arranging her hair with her fingers. She smelled of smoke and unwashed clothing, of leaves. From the back seat, off the other girl, came that odd, sweet smell, cotton candy or caramel. Drew opened the glove compartment and looked inside. David was about to tell her that was private when she snapped it shut and sat back in her seat. "You can tell about people from their cars," she said. "Also their accessories, jewelry and tattoos and stuff. You see that big guy in the diner?" Drew said, pulling her legs up under her on the seat. "What was his name, Ange—Newt?"

"Tex," Angela said sleepily from the back. "And call me Sandra."

"Yeah," Drew said, "Newt. All Newt could talk about was marriage, you know? He'd been married what, four times? Like who would marry him *once*." She shook her head. She pulled her hair back and examined something on her scalp in the mirror. "He had a cousin, Louise, who was married at thirteen. This was in Tennessee, he said, and he had pictures of the wedding back in the sleeper. He offered to show us. He offered to put us up at a motel and buy us dinner." She flipped the visor up, apparently satisfied, and looked at David. "He was all over Sandra, kept putting his hand on her leg, you know, like Oh, let's see, where'd I leave the gearshift this time? He said he'd take us to a Ramada Inn and buy us steak dinners, like we were cannibals or something. You mind if I smoke?"

She cracked the window and pulled a packet of cigarettes from her pocket. "Yes," David said, "I do."

She looked at him seriously, nodded twice, and put the cigarettes away. "Newt said he'd drive us all the way to San Francisco, wherever we wanted to go, right, Ange?" Drew said. There was no answer from the back seat. David pulled into the right lane and pressed the cruise control. "As if," Drew said quietly.

He drove west, looking for the turnoff to the city. He'd driven this road, but only in daylight and not for many years before today. He searched for landmarks he might recognize from this afternoon, but it was useless in the dark. Nothing looked familiar. In the back seat the younger girl slept, the smell still coming off her. Sweet, but not like candy, he decided—thicker, more chemical. Drew, beside him, ate from a big paper bag of granola, which she twice offered him. She said it was good stuff, cleaned out your system. This guy she'd met in Buffalo, Sal—you'd think that was a girl's name but not in this case—Sal ate only granola and yeast extract and legumes, totally macro. Did David know legumes? Like beans, but with fiber. Good stuff. Sal said he expected to live till ninety, more if he cut out the smokes. She put her feet up on the dashboard as she ate, and he asked her not to do that, and a few minutes later she did it again, humming to herself, and he opened his mouth to say something, but decided to let it go.

The turnoff had to be around here somewhere. This day already seemed endless and he was exhausted, with several hours of driving ahead. He couldn't have missed it. He had to concentrate. He would find the turnoff, then talk to these girls, find out where they were headed. He would find a phone and call Maura again. Maybe she and Oliver were back, or maybe they were in the house, screening calls. He did this himself, standing by the answering machine as it recorded, deciding whether to answer. He would call, and by the calm tone of his voice he would let Maura know he was okay, she could pick up the phone. He thought of what he'd said earlier, that he needed to talk. He remembered the sense of urgency that had come over him in that moment—he really did need to talk to her, though what he had to say eluded him now. It would come to him, something reasonable and heartfelt and calm that would show he'd been thinking things over, that it was okay to answer the phone.

"So I hope you don't mind words," Drew was saying.

"Pardon?" David said.

"Words. You know, talking, verbilation. I talk a lot, have you noticed? Some people do. Angie doesn't talk much, so I talk for us both. She says I'm a people person, which is why I like to talk, but I don't know, I'm not that overly fond of people as a whole, are you? I think they're overrated, as a whole. That's why we tried Canada."

"Fewer people?"

"Not in Toronto. You'd be surprised."

David looked in the mirror at the sleeping girl. She had pulled her legs onto the seat and laid her head on the duffels. He wondered if it was warm enough back there. She couldn't be comfortable, but she seemed to be sleeping soundly.

"Why does she smell like that?" he said quietly.

"Angela?" Drew turned to look at her. She patted a high-topped foot. "That's diabetes, what it smells like when you're not on your medicine. Your body manufactures too much glucenase or fructone and it exudes right through your skin membrane. That's what that smell is."

"She has diabetes?"

"Yeah. Bummer, huh?"

"Why isn't she on her medicine?"

"We ran out," Drew said, pulling a string rucksack from the floor to her lap. "That's why we came back to the States. To get more. That and that people thing we were talking about."

"Is she all right?" David asked, again checking the sleeping girl in the mirror.

Drew was drinking from a bottle of water, which she wiped off with her sleeve and offered to him. "Yeah, she's fine for a day or two. She's just tired. We'll hit a clinic tomorrow. Where are we heading?"

"New York," David said, aware he had not thought he would be driving them that far. He was confused momentarily and took the bottle from Drew. He drank some out of politeness, and was surprised at how thirsty he was.

"Le grand tamale," Drew said, taking the bottle from him. She had a way of looking at you—smiling, eyebrows slightly raised in anticipation—even when you weren't talking, that David found disconcerting. "Cool. So, what do you do?"

Ahead, the road was filled with lights, headlights pulsing at him from the opposite lane, red lights weaving in his own. The sound from the bottom of the car, a steady, dull rumble, worried him, and he knew he'd have to deal with it in the morning. The turnoff must be coming up soon, he knew, but in the meantime he was overtaken by weariness. It surged through his body and lodged between his shoulders in a blunt ache. He'd driven from New York that morning, nearly five hours each way; still, it felt as if he'd been driving much longer. Glancing in the rearview, he was met by a confused sensation, the landscape there floating unattached, streaming away from him, no relation to the ground he had just covered. He looked over at the girl next to him. She had put the bottle down and was looking at him expectantly. She gestured with her hands. "Wrong question?" she said.

"No," David answered. "No. I'm an architect. Or I've been an architect. I'll be one for a few more weeks."

She nodded sympathetically. "Lost your job, huh?"

He nodded.

"Life changes can be good," she said. "Remember Sal? He used to be a barber." From the back seat came a soft thick snoring, and Drew looked at Angela, then back at David, smiling. He smiled, too.

"How long have you been on the road?" he asked.

"Couple of years."

"And you're all right?" he said. "How do you get by? She can't be more than twelve."

"Thirteen, actually," Drew said, pushing her hair back over her ears, then immediately shaking it loose. "We do okay."

"Even if she's sick? That must be hard on her."

"I take care of her. Better than what she left."

She was slumped against the door now, looking ahead with a blank, unmoving stare. David understood she had heard this lecture before.

"So what do you like best about traveling?" he said. The weariness had crept behind his eyes now, into his head, where it weighted like sand. He was afraid he might close his eyes a moment and miss the turnoff. He needed to talk. "You must have seen some interesting things."

"Oh, yes. Absolutely," Drew said, drawing her legs up under her again, liveliness back in her face. "We met a trucker with six fingers on each hand, this was just last week. The sixth was not really what I'd call a regulation finger. It just sort of lay there, like this." She held one finger over the other hand to demonstrate. "It didn't move or anything. It was awesome, though. Superial." He nodded, encouraged her to go on. "We saw a flood in Indiana last spring. Whole town under water. We saw a rowboat go by the fire-house with three dogs in it, no people, just three dogs, two with their paws over the side, the other running from the front to the back, howling like crazy. You would've thought dogs could swim, but these dogs were scared." She stopped for a moment to see if he had anything to add, then continued. "Okay." She put both hands up near her face, as if she'd saved the best for last but couldn't hold it any longer. "We saw Waylon Jennings at a Howard Johnson's on the Garden State Parkway on August 11. We were just standing by the Coke machine and he came out of the men's room, hitching up his belt. No one saw him but us. I couldn't believe it. I said, 'Hey, Waylon,' and he waved at me and said, 'Mornin', missy.' Just like that."

She was looking at him with her raised eyebrows, as if this last piece of information couldn't fail to impress. He looked at her and had to laugh. "That's pretty good," he said.

"I know," she said, and laughed herself, a sound David hadn't heard from her before and which he enjoyed.

"And then of course there's the comet," Drew said.

"Comet?"

She looked at him, dumbfounded. "You know, Halley's comet, out *there* somewhere?" She gestured through the windshield at the skies. "Where have *you* been?"

David remembered now. The comet was supposed to be approaching Earth's orbit this week, or was it leaving, he had heard about it on the news, seen a headline on someone's desk at work. People were talking about making a trip out of the city to avoid the lights, with blankets, a bottle of wine. Someone had a telescope. But it had not come as close as predicted, or wasn't as bright, something. He had been too upset and distracted to pay much attention. "Right," he said.

Drew was still looking at him, as if his ignorance defied belief. "I remember now," he said.

"I can tell you about comets," she said, searching in her drawstring bag and coming out with a tattered paperback. On its cover was a drawing of a family on a hillside, parents, a boy and a girl, looking up in benign fascination as a burning fireball hurtled toward them from the heavens. It was called *Messenger from the Skies*. From the back seat came movement and he turned to see Angela waking, rubbing her eyes. "Oh, is she on the comet?" Angela said, as Drew riffled the pages of the book. "She's an expert."

"Have you seen it?" David asked.

The girl nodded, still sleepy.

"Comets have been visiting our atmosphere ever since the dawn of time," Drew read. "The history books are filled with accounts, and the earliest records of humankind are often concerned with the visitations of these otherworldly sojourners of the cosmic highway." She looked up at David, then back at her book. "Scientists estimate there may be as many as one hundred thousand comets journeying in mute orbit around our blue planet. Indeed, some speculate that, if not for the interference of terrestrial and solar light, we could look up at an entire sky filled with streaks of fire."

"I love that part," Angela said, leaning her arms over the seat.

"It's full of cool stuff," Drew said, closing the book. "They knew about comets in China, in Egypt even. They used to predict wars by them, famine, plagues, you name it. In 1910, Halley's comet came so close to earth we passed through its tail, which is full of radioactive gas, and thousands of people died, mostly in Europe."

"I didn't know that," David said.

"It's in the book," Drew told him.

They drove for a few moments in silence, the girls peering out the front, David willing his eyes open.

"Hey," Angela said from the back. "I bet we could see it tonight." She had her elbows draped over the seat, her head propped on her hands. Her face was flushed, from sleep or her illness David couldn't say. "We could find a field or a mountain where there'd be no lights. I bet we could."

"Hey," Drew said, looking at David, putting down the book. "What do you think?"

Somehow he had missed the turnoff. It was impossible, but he had. He was feeling absolutely groggy with weariness, couldn't remember the last time he had slept, and he had not argued when the girls had chosen an exit from the highway. They were on a hillside now, in some kind of park. They had left the car and were climbing through wet, uncut grass. There were lights from the highway and some town behind them, but if they looked ahead, to the south, the horizon was dark. The girls ran on before him, reached the crest of the hill. The younger one turned and gestured for him to hurry.

The night air was quiet, cool; it cleared his head a little. He could not remember another day like this one. Nothing in it made sense, and now, to top it off, he was lost. He should have checked a map, maybe found a hotel to catch an hour's rest, but it was too late now. He had missed the turnoff, would, at some point soon, be leaving the state entirely. He would drive the girls to Cleveland, that was all he could think of, offer them some money, drop them where they wanted to go. He supposed he would know what to do after that.

He heard the girls talking up ahead, felt his shoes soaking through in the wet grass. He could see them on the hilltop, moving from one side to the other, pointing, arguing about where to look. Drew was consulting her book; he heard her say she couldn't read the map. The night was so dark they were nearly silhouettes framed against a blank sky, a star here or there behind them.

He had a lot to do. He had not even told Maura about the letter from the partners telling him that after the Crestview collapse he should expect no promotion, suggesting, in terms so bland and restrained it took an expert to decipher them, that it might be time for him to move on to other employment. He had that to deal with. He had a damaged car. He would call the police in the morning and see what had happened to the kid in the Mustang. He would drive these girls home.

He looked around again. Below him, the lights of a small town spread out, road signs, gas stations, a string of houses on a far incline. But when he turned back to the hillside it was completely dark, nothing ahead of him but a couple of black trees and the girls moving back and forth in the grass. How he had gotten from his apartment in the city to here, wherever here was, in one day mystified him. Take a wrong turn, however slight, and you could be in an entirely new situation. Life hadn't always seemed this way to him. He had thought it was sequential, logical, you knew where you were because you knew how you got here, which is how you prepared for where you had to go next. Well, not today. All of that was out the window today.

It came to him what he wanted to tell Maura. He didn't know how to say it, and he doubted he would be able to, but he knew now what he would like to say. She had looked beautiful on the porch. It wasn't the sweater that got him, it was that. It was the look she had given Oliver, right before he had left, the way she had looked up at him and leaned into his arms. She was beautiful then. Even in the arms of another man she was beautiful. Not sexy beautiful or maternal beautiful, not beautiful like Rhonda, or like women in magazines. She was content, and from the way she looked at Oliver, David could tell she was where she wanted to be. That was it. She was beautiful in ways he could not explain, that had taken years to discover, that maybe nobody but he could even recognize. He didn't know. Whatever it was, he saw it, and he wanted to tell her he did. That was all.

Ahead, the girls were excited. He could hear them calling. "There it is!" Drew said, "Oh my God, take a look at that sucker!" Angela was excited too, and she turned down the hill to David, waving her arms. "Come on!" she said. "There it is!"

He walked toward them. He remembered something barely overheard on the news about the comet no longer being visible from the Northeast past the first of the month, which was yesterday, something else about it being due south in the sky. The girls were looking east. He approached them. He had looked up at the sky many times before, and he knew what was there, a shimmering cold, a speckled absolute nullity. They told him to close his eyes. Angela came up and took his hand. There was nothing to see and he knew it, but he walked over to where the girls led him, let them direct his face upward. He waited, and then Drew said, "Okay. Get ready." He waited with his eyes closed, feeling the night air on his face, hearing the girls move beside him. "Wait till I tell you," Drew said. She had her hands on his face, Angela her hands on his arm. "No peeking," Drew said. He didn't peek. He waited until she moved her hands and told him. "Okay," she said. "Look."

RUTH'S STORY

In a waiting room, you wait. She leaves the magazine she has read twice, three times, and goes to the window she has never seen anyone look out. Across the street the park, its gray stone wall and benches, trees beyond. She is too tired to turn her head and she stares blankly, like a camera, objects moving into and then out of her field of vision. A boy on a bicycle. A woman pushing a stroller. A man with newspapers tied around his feet. A breath too sharp brings her up short and she follows with dull attention the course of pain as it begins in her groin, travels through her hip into her back, leaving her slightly dizzy, an acrid taste, digested medicine, in her mouth.

Her doctor, a trim man thirty years younger than she, with gray feathering his brown hair like the vice president's, with silver frames on his desk, outward, so she could see his shining children near some blue water, told her kindly, "That's where the word comes from. It's an un-ease. A disequilibrium." She looked at him just tired, but there must have been more in her face because he became uncomfortable, reached for the little pad in his pocket and they discussed pills for the pain, pills for the sleeplessness, suppositories for the pills that made her sick to her stomach. When the pills no longer worked, he assured her, they would take care of her at the hospital, or at home, if she preferred. Then he asked if she needed a prescription for her blood-pressure tablets and they looked at each other a moment as if they would burst out laughing together, it would have been nice if they had; but the moment passed and the nurse helped her to the waiting room, the same magazine as last week. "Sit here, honey," she said, and Ruth said, "Thank you, darling," easing gingerly onto the couch. All these endearments between strangers—"honey," "darling," next "bubele," "sweetheart." It wasn't so bad, she thought, looking up at the nurse, a young woman in glasses, patience inscribed on her face, in her eyes, her hand lingering a moment on the shoulder.

After two years there no longer seemed to be another life before it, as she knows now there will be none after. Outside, a squirrel runs along the granite wall of the park, a green nut in its jaws. Another follows, nothing in its mouth, and two more chasing this one. She turns to see what has become of the first but they all jump into a tree and she loses sight of them. Soon the elevator doors open and Max comes out mopping sweat from his head with a handkerchief, his hat in the other hand. He is wearing the new blue plaid jacket but the old brown pants. He moves toward her twisting from the waist, confused, hopeful, smiling, scared to death as always and she turns from the window to meet him. Maybe they will buy some peanuts from the vendor, sit awhile in the sun on the stone bench before they go home.

—•—

She has never driven a car. Growing up in the city, there was no reason. Everything in the world was a subway ride away, parking was impossible. For trips to the beach or the mountains you had neighbors, later boyfriends, first Uncle Nat with his big Hudson like a room on wheels with the red seats to climb on and the windows to hang out of as he smoked cigarettes and argued with Aunt Sophie, who folded and refolded the maps.

•   •   •

Some things she always thought she would do. Go to South America. Eat shellfish. Fly in a helicopter. Make it all right with her father. Drive a car.

In Oregon her son had taken her for long drives, she up front with him, the children in their car seats happy or fussing but eventually dozing, their exhausted mother soon joining them. They would talk sometimes, mostly they would look at the countryside, which seemed to require quiet, mist hanging over the forests in midday, the long fields every color of green, behind them on sunny days the mountains' white slopes pinned against the sky. She loved the clouds in Oregon, like the clouds in Dutch paintings, the way they caught light, hovered close, assumed shapes. In the car they'd guess at the shapes, she saw castles, birds, a bull pawing the air. Daniel saw only dinosaurs, a dinosaur eating a tree, a dinosaur in a big hat, a dinosaur sleeping on another dinosaur's stomach.

They had come around a curve into a logged-out valley. David slowed down, as if he might back the car around, then accelerated, taking the turns too fast. Before them the mountainside was destroyed, harsh light on the upturned red earth, heaps of discarded wood, thick, toothy stumps. Ahead the slope was a scraggy silhouette, occasional trees, too thin or inaccessible to be logged, spindly against the gray. She saw her own skull jutting up under sparse tufts of hair, just now beginning to grow again. Wrapped in the bright gypsy scarf, her scalp began to itch but she did not touch it. David had seen it, too. He was taking the turns too fast and in the back seat Janine stirred, looked around, and said, "What's wrong?" David slowed then, still going too fast, she thought, but slower. He looked straight ahead of him over the wheel.

They were not a family for touching. A quick kiss before bed, a hug at the beginning and end of the day. She reached over now and pressed a hand to his on the steering wheel, noticing how his fingers gripped the molded plastic tighter. "I'm sorry," David said, and she kept her hand there, riding the turns of the wheel with him, and soon they left the logged-out mountain and the children woke and they drove through a small valley with black-and-white cows nuzzling grass on the side of the road and the boy said he wanted to watch and David pulled the car over and they did.

Was it called Wonderland? Could it have been? A park with a magical name, across two bridges and two rivers, with pony rides and a carnival show and a carousel from Europe. After talking about it three weeks, they were finally to go.

She wore a yellow dress, she remembers the way it flounced up in back when she leaned over, her mother saying Don't do that, she enjoying the air on her legs, doing it anyway. She remembers loading the Hudson, the boxes of food and blankets in the trunk, its huge satisfying thump when they closed it. She remembers the ride in the car, her brothers too serious to look out the window — one of them hadn't even wanted to come! — reading books and doing puzzles. She hanging out the window — her mother wanted her head in the car but Uncle Nat said She's all right, I'm watching her — in the lovely smells, the trees passing in a roar of wind, thousands of soft fists pummeling her face. She remembers singing.

Then some trouble with the maps, arguing up front, her father deeply asleep in one corner of the back seat, her brothers looking stonily ahead. On a bridge they got stuck in traffic, hours it seemed, Uncle Nat cursing in Yiddish and Aunt Sophie folding the maps. Finally, the stops and starts were too much for her and her brother quickly guided her head out the window so she could empty her stomach, miserable as she watched the vomit run down the car. Shouting then from inside, Uncle Nat about the paint job, Aunt Sophie about being lost, her father, grumpy from sleeping, about people not knowing how to read maps. She hung out the window watching the disgust on the faces of people in the next lane, some had got on her yellow dress, she didn't know how, watching the last of it disappear in strands under the back wheel.

It was recalled for years as the time her getting sick had made them turn around and miss Wonderland. But she remembers her brothers didn't even want to go. It was the traffic, and their getting lost, and the grownups shouting at each other so much Aunt Sophie got a headache until finally no one but she had the desire to go anyway.

Now she dreams about driving all the time. The car she drives is large and streamlined and elegant, and not knowing the rudiments of driving in her waking life, she is vague about them in sleep, supplying simply a steering wheel and one wide pedal which is universally responsive, speeds or slows to the touch as she wills it. There are no mirrors and no windshields, only the slightest breeze through her long hair. In this car she drives sleek roads where rivers run shining to open seas and meadows grade quickly into snow-covered mountains. Sheep graze, cougars lounge, dinosaurs relax in the grass. She punches the cigarette lighter, turns on the radio to hushed celestial music. Knowing the car will take care of itself, she lifts her feet from the pedal, her arms in the air before her, and begins to fly.

— • —

He asks if it hurts and the answer is yes. He asks if she is tired and the answer is yes. He asks if she doesn't think she should eat something and the answer is yes, yes, of course yes, she should, but she can't, where has he been, this idiot in the baggy undershirt who won't comb his hair or get dressed until she asks him, every day she has to ask him, with the fear two bubbles in his eyes, watching her from the side of the room, saying Look at me, look at me in all this, my life, and she thinks this is the hardest part, forty years I've taken care of this man, why God can't I rest even now, and she closes her eyes to relieve herself of the very sight of him and when she opens them he is there, with tea and toast and her afternoon pills, saying Won't you try, and she looks up at him and she says, Yes. All right. I think I will.

— • —

After the surgery was the greatest pain. They had told her she could go home in a week, three weeks later she was still in the hospital, trying to take short walks in the corridors, trying to sleep, trying to stay awake. A young girl was there one day when she opened her eyes, smiling patiently, wearing a new blue blazer and a nice skirt, her hair held back with combs. Who are you, Ruth said, thinking she should remember, but the girl introduced herself, she was a graduate student at NYU doing an oral-history project on women who suffered from cancer of the reproductive organs. She was here to take down Ruth's story. My what, Ruth said, looking at the girl's fresh, unmottled skin, needing to pee in the blue basin but not in front of a stranger, wanting to brush her teeth, comb her hair. My what? May I turn this on? the girl continued, putting a small recorder on the bed between them, pushing a button. Your story, she said with an encouraging smile. Begin anywhere you like.

— • —

What she could never say to anyone. She has never liked or approved of her own body. She has voted Democratic for forty years out of habit, not that the Republicans were any better. Despite everyone's good intentions, in her own experience, love hurts more than it heals. Tomatoes, which she always insisted on serving, she found mildly disgusting, with their juice and meat. If, somehow, the right man had come along at exactly the right time—who this would have been, when, she has absolutely no idea—maybe she would have gone with him. But not really. Not after all.

— • —

When they were flooding her veins with poison to kill the disease, she could not stop crying. It was the only time. The moment they came through the revolving doors, left the air of Manhattan behind them for the smell of the hospital, its hushed, efficient urgency, it started. Her stomach flinched, her head swam, the tears could not be held.

Later, Max went running for nurses, brought them back with washcloths, water pitchers, and white booties with Santa Claus on them for her feet, but she was neither hot nor cold. Honey, is there anything we can get you, they asked, one taking her hand to measure her pulse, the other checking the plastic udder by her head, dripping into her arm. The nurses wore expressions of practiced concern, they assured her by keeping their hands on her body. One had a tiny crust of egg from breakfast on the corner of her mouth. Behind them Max looked on, desperate for an answer, there must be something they could do. She shook her head No, there was nothing. The medicine went cold into her arm, soon would flush her face with blood and heat. They stood there waiting. There was nowhere to turn away from them but she tried.

· · ·

Like everyone, she had thought of age's erosive progress—the silent hardenings and narrowings, the tips of two fingers aching before rain, the hip or knee that complained every time you moved it. She knew that inside, certainly, things were breaking down or building up, wearing out. She remembers her mother had trouble with the same hip, her father the tingling in the fingers. These were the nagging reminders of time's slow siege. Next week she would begin walking, tomorrow she would prepare better foods. Time took its toll on everyone but gave you opportunity to adjust, make plans. Not like this.

They told her cancers like hers were among the most common to women, yes, her handsome doctor said, the same hormones that led to childbirth could have something to do with the disease. Nobody knew the answer. They told her her own blood system had carried the cancer from her uterus, where it had been treated, to her bowels and abdomen, where it grew now unchecked. They told her to visualize light coursing through her, blue light blasting the bad cells, freeing the good. They gave her crystals, herbal teas, tapes of waterfalls and migrating birds. They showed her the x-rays, the CAT scans, shadowy forms like berries ripening along the trellis of her insides.

She had been sixty years old, thinking of the future, regretting the past, grateful for it, making plans to bring her family together. Thinking her body, aging, collapsing as it was, was her own, going on with her life, while all along she carried this other life, growing, lifting up, a dark flower preparing to bloom inside her, not gardener any longer but garden.

— • —

In Oregon she and the baby would take long naps. She had fallen asleep with the baby on her lap when it woke her with its cries and she saw a wide bruise on its face where the child had slept heavily against her and for a wild, half-dreaming moment she thought the cancer had moved from her body into the baby's and she gasped, couldn't breathe, held the screaming infant away from her, no idea what to do.

—•—

After the diagnosis and the surgery, during the treatments, odd moments of celebration. David called from the West to plan her trip, Daniel got on the phone to sing songs for her. Max insisted they go to a Broadway musical, a movie at the Continental every week, and every Monday afternoon she spent time with her daughter. They would do silly things, wasteful things, whatever it crossed their minds to do. They would go to a nice restaurant for lunch and order only dessert. They would go to Bergdorf's and buy matching hats. They would have their hair done, their faces. Once they took a mud bath. Once they had each nail painted a different color, then went to a bar next door to have strawberry daiquiris, asking the bartender and two businessmen from Milwaukee what they thought. Then they returned to have all the nails done again, hers in Mozambique Peach, Rachel's in Aquablue.

Max worries about the boy more, she worries about the girl. She worries about the boy, too, but he seems to come out all right, always seems to find someone to take care of him. She finds herself, these Monday afternoons, wanting to leave the girl with something, some hard-won and invincible truth, something that will remain with her and make things easier. She has found nothing to say yet.

Rachel and she have developed the habit of holding hands. Walking down the street, sitting in a movie matinee, they will hold hands, lightly, the way they used to as mother and child, the way Max would hold her hand years ago. They are walking down Queens Boulevard like this, a sunny afternoon, when a man approaches from the war memorial park nearby. He is a dapper old gentleman, mustachioed, in Bermuda shorts and a cotton cap, blue canvas shoes and black socks. He stops before them with an inquiring look, each of them wondering who he is. The look becomes urgent, faraway, as if he is about to remember something important. He puts a hand up and Rachel pulls her mother back a step, then the look on the man changes, grows relaxed, near-sleepy, and they barely see the spreading stain on the front of his pants before he nods at them and continues up the avenue.

Rachel is shocked, silent, waiting for her mother to react. This is a terrible thing, especially now. Ruth feels many things quickly before, knowing it is inappropriate, looking after the man, and hoping he will not hear, she begins to laugh. From out of nowhere she is laughing so hard she has to put down her shopping bag and sit on the low wall that rings the park, doubled over, coughing with laughter, saying Yes, No, Yes, to Rachel's questions, unable to stop, wiping tears from her eyes. Rachel doesn't know what to do. She looks around, picks up her mother's shopping bag, puts it down, begins slapping her back, no help, apparently, because Ruth looks at her, laughing even harder, still coughing, and her expression, red-faced, tear-streaked, is suddenly so funny Rachel begins to laugh too, a burst through the nose and then they're done for, sitting on the low wall gripping each other, trying to stop but that only makes it worse, holding out hands, fingers, stomping their feet but nothing helps, breath coming in yelps and snorts, ridiculous, hilarious, people making room for these lunatics—on New York streets you're liable to see anything—and when they still don't stop a small crowd gathers to watch and Rachel gasps, I wet, my pants, too, and Ruth nods, points at herself, then they look up and in the crowd of six or eight people watching is the old gentleman, returned to see what the commotion is, is it a speech? a street musician? nodding and smiling to his neighbors, the stain wide and dark on his Bermuda shorts, out in the air, sunning himself on Queens Boulevard on a fine May afternoon.

— • —

On the patio out back she sleeps in the warm spring dusk. Some time ago he had brought a blanket for her and she is distantly aware of its pleasant wrapping weight and him behind her head, moving plates around in the kitchen for their dinner. She is in that halfway place she has loved since childhood, where you are awake enough to enjoy your sleeping, not awake enough to stop. The sun is nearly gone but she can feel it warm on her face. She sleeps.

In the dark she is fully awake, unsure why. She is not in more pain. She has not had a dream that scared her. She doesn't hear anything from inside. She looks into the yard and there, at the edge of the pool of light from the patio, stands a fox. She has never seen one but recognizes it immediately, its tail a sinuous curve, its alert, precise face regarding her. She has lived in New York sixty-two years and never seen a fox before. It lifts one paw and lowers its head, looking at her. She is stunned, delighted, half afraid. Max, she whispers, not wanting to frighten it. Max, come see. The back door opens with a clatter, Ah, she's awake, he announces, dinner is served, then he sees her face, looks where she is looking in the yard, but all that is left of the fox, if there really was one, is a disappearing shiver at the base of the garden's far hedge.

— • —

Things that have always scared her. Dentists. Losing her faculties, becoming dependent on others. The subway, when you realize you've miscalculated, are riding in the wrong car, or too late. Her children's unhappiness. The country at night, its sounds and shadows, something always moving. Rats. Anything that looks like a rat—big mice, possums, even squirrels in the summer when you can see their tails. Real pain, unavoidable and constant, that you can't run from or forget, that becomes your absolute center, that changes you from whatever you thought you were into simply and completely the organism that feels the pain, nothing more. Pain like this.

When her children were small and they were afraid of something on the television, the boy would cover his eyes with his fingers, spread them to look, and shut them again. The girl would sit, looking intently, Ruth would watch her sizing up the risk. Then she would slowly get up and walk to the doorway of the room, stand there, and, depending on how scared she was, move more or less of her body into the next room, leaning her head in to see.

Max every morning wraps himself in the tallis so she can see only the black box of the tefillin and the dome of his forehead. He used to pray anywhere he found himself, out on the patio, in the kitchen. Now he prays in a corner of the living room, he turns to the wall, sometimes she hears crying from under the shawl. He prays the *shemona esray*, the morning prayers, and she hears him, hears the quaver and accusation and pleading come into his voice. She prays also, at various times during the day, usually when she is tired and has to take a moment to decide what to do next. When the pain comes there is no time to pray.

. . .

It is not so different, at times it feels this way, from all the other leavings. Dropping the children off at first grade, the school bus all those mornings, the first year of college, the first apartment, the wedding, the move out of state. You say a small prayer to the teachers, the bus drivers, the friends and roommates and lovers and spouses, the landlords and neighbors and doctors and mail-men and people talking on the street. Here are my children, you pray. I am trusting you with my children.

Prayers are for ourselves, she realizes. They are for our loved ones, for the poor, the unprotected, the helpless about to be harmed, but they are for ourselves finally, always have been, for our hurt, our fear, our constant aloneness.

In the morning she lies in bed and he is praying in the next room. She turns on her side and tries not to hear. He chants, he sways, he holds the tallis in front of his face in two fists. Nowhere else to look, she looks out the window, at the dim blue radiance framed there. Help me, she prays, please help me now help us help me please help.

She wishes Rachel was here. She wishes she could go with Rachel through the door, fear just a confused babble of voices from the next room. They'd sit on the linoleum and play jacks as they used to, they'd sing and share something to eat, and there would be nothing at all to be afraid of.

— • —

Smells. The smells of her own body lifting off her. He washes her hair every day, sometimes twice, she showers in hot water, as hot as she can stand it, sitting on the white chair from the patio, scrubbing and soaping and moisturizing and powdering, and there it is anyway, her teeth moving in her gums, the skin on the back and palms of her hands growing thick and brown, her nails like an animal's, pitted and ridged and not her color, and when she tries to sleep in the fresh sheets, the laundered nightgown, it is there, under the perfumes and soaps and powders, the dim odor of rot.

—•—

They sit together one night in front of the TV. She wonders if he is watching or also dozing, if she has been asleep long. She remembers a comedy, the one with the funny fat man who has nothing to do all day but drink beer and complain about his wife. All the people on the show seem to have nothing to do all day but drink beer, make jokes together. They don't seem to have lives beyond the bar. This seems to her a pleasant arrangement. The show makes them laugh.

Now a documentary is on, about manatees. The narrator, it sounds like Jacques Cousteau—they've always enjoyed his shows—tells her that for centuries manatees were mistaken for mermaids by sailors. They float on their backs while nursing their babies, and they look like human mothers. She finds this interesting—they don't look anything like mermaids to her. Mermaids have long hair, for one thing. But the sailors thought so, for hundreds of years, so there must be something to it.

She looks over, expecting to find him asleep. There is no movement from his chair, to the side of the couch she lies on, covered in a blanket. He wears the worn gold sweater she got him for a distant birthday, the slippers with the crushed backs. A drained glass of tea with its used tea bag is on a coaster near his arm. He is not asleep. To her surprise, he sits looking into the room, not at the TV but above it somewhere to the left.

She worries she has kept him from bed, that in not wanting to disturb her he has waited for her to wake. She feels a mild flush of annoyance—she has told him a hundred times: she sleeps all day, the last thing she cares about is being awakened to be told it's time to go to bed—and then a wash of guilt for her impatience. She is looking for something to say when he speaks instead. How long had she been sleeping? How long had he known she was awake? "The children," he says.

"What?" she almost says, but she knows his exact meaning. They've not talked about the future much, about her illness, about afterwards, but when they do they've come into this short-hand that places them immediately inside each other's thoughts. She reaches toward the side table. Everywhere she is nowadays, there is a collection of pill bottles, tissues, water glasses, tubes of lotion and hand cream. Moving, she is aware of stiffness in her neck and back floating above, partly masking the other pain puls-ing quietly inside. Around them is soft yellow light except for the wall opposite the TV, which flickers blue and red. They've sat in this room hundreds of times. It must be very late. He looks tired. She waits for him.

"I don't know what to do," he says, so quiet she can't be sure he meant to speak aloud.

"I know," she says.

He looks over at her and she brushes the blanket at her side, meaning Come over, sit by me, but she only half means it, and she regrets this. His coming over would mean her moving on the couch when all day she couldn't find a position that didn't hurt. But he doesn't understand her signal, or understands her too well. He looks away, stays where he is.

"I love them," he says.

"They know that," she says quickly, not wanting to interrupt but wanting to say something.

"I love them," he says again. "I love them both. I don't under-stand the world they live in. I don't understand this world either, the world we live in. I used to think I would understand. I don't. I don't." He clears his throat, shakes his head so he will not cry.

She reaches for a water glass. It is less than half full and a scrim of dust floats on the surface. She reaches for another, fuller. "You do love them. They love you, too," she says.

"So what," he says. "It's not enough." He is beyond tears for now, angry. "Who said love was enough? What can love protect you from? Did it save my brother? Has it protected us here, in this room?" He speaks with a twisted face, as if he is tasting something bitter and wants to spit, looks around for something to spit in. She holds her water glass out to him but he looks at it, at her, and leans back in his chair.

They don't say anything for a few moments. His brother, dead over fifty years now. She has seen pictures, a smiling, handsome boy, a bit arrogant in his look, so sure of himself. On the television they are showing a resort in Florida where modern-day mermaids dance to disco music in a huge underwater tank. They breathe through hoses made to look like underwater vines. She looks away from the screen.

"What will I say to them," Max says. "How will I talk to them? After." He clears his throat again. "I'm afraid I won't know how."

She reaches for the remote, near her head on the side table. Twisting for it brings the pain fully to the surface, a deep and huge aching that her body recognizes with exhaustion. She turns the set off.

"Tell them that."

He turns to her, anger and confusion, even disgust, on his face. "Tell them what? That I don't understand?" He turns away, she can see him wrestling with his anger, he has determined not to be angry these last months. But it gets the better of him this time, pulls him halfway from his chair, his arms gripping the sides. "Tell them," he sneers. "That I never will understand them, how they live? That I don't understand what happened to you, to Rachmil—who is this God that he let it happen? That every morning I curse him for a traitor and I curse them for the unhappiness they bring." He sits back down, moves his hands apart in front of him in a gesture of futility. "You, too," he says, quietly, "for tricking me like this, for leaving. Every morning I curse you all, and then I curse myself. I should tell them that?"

He rises now, goes to the corner by the bookcase where he prays each morning, stands there, his back to her in shame.

A tremendous weariness, almost luxurious, settles over her. She examines it and for the first time without fear she contemplates the end of her life, it can't be far off, and is surprised to find it has an aspect of comfort, of cessation, of rest. At least they will be beyond this. She wants to go to him. She wants to turn him to her, she wants to take his face in her hands and bring him close so he can cry there, as he had the first night after the surgery, bending awkwardly over her hospital bed, his arms at his sides. She looks at him, the worn slippers, the stiff gray hair in all directions, the infuriating brown pants. She wants to transmit some of what she feels to him, the lassitude, the warm sleepiness—after a hard day you give in to sleep with pleasure, you close your eyes, you know tomorrow will be better. Come, she will say, Time for bed, and lead him by the hand. But she can't get off the couch, knows this without even trying. She holds her hands out but he doesn't see. She lets them rest on the blanket. This is how it is, how it has always been, throughout their lives, in the same room, the same bed, the same family—together and apart, always. She closes her eyes and speaks softly. "Yes," she says to him. "Tell them that."

She wakes in the bed. Outside, it is gray light, just as it had been earlier. From the living room she hears the television, laughter from an audience, hears Max folding the pages of the paper. She has no idea if it is nearly night or nearly day, if she has slept twelve hours or ten minutes. She doesn't dream much now, the medicine, when it works, dropping her into sleep like off the end of a cliff, sudden, bottomless black. She checks the pain. It is there, but quiet, coiled like an animal sleeping inside her. Before she reaches for the light or calls his name she wants to remember if it is night or day. It seems very important. She lies back, looking out the window, waiting to remember.

— • —

No warning. Something twisting her bones so they will crack, a fist hammering through her insides, red light behind the eyes, no air to breathe, pressing the button that releases the painkiller, again, twice more, reaching for the pills, she cannot move free, every move is to remind her she is part of something else, all joints fused to the thing inside her, she cannot escape it, take me now, you son of a bitch, take me this instant, I don't care about them, I never have, about anyone, just this, make it stop right here you evil bastard through eternity you'll hear my curses, please just stop it make it stop. Then suddenly the slightest easing, full clean breath in her lungs, the roaring in her head growing a little apart. She reaches across herself to lay a hand on his shoulder, lies there, beyond fear, nearly beyond pain, a strange quiet eagerness in her. She feels his warm leg beside hers and watches the window for daylight, hearing his breathing, hearing hers. She waits.

— • —

Her children, David four, Rachel not yet three, posing before the neighbor's new car in dirty overalls, smiles and chocolate cake on their faces. It took ten minutes to coax them to hold hands . . . her Aunt Chipka's house, where only one light is allowed to burn at a time, she herself no older than four, under the dining-room table with its massive carved legs like the legs of a lion, looking through

the fringe of the heavy tablecloth at three women on the sofa, one
of them her mother, laughing . . . on the deck of the *Queen
Mary*, twenty-one and off to Europe with a friend, new hat, new
dress, new stockings, which she bends to align while her mother
snaps pictures. Catcalls, whistles, and she looks up to see a row of
sailors at the rail above, smiling, waving down . . . in the
bathroom, her face twisted with disgust, her mother plucking
feathers from the holiday chicken, the down filling the air, landing on her mother's face and hair, the soft, insistent ripping . . .
her daughter, two, maybe three, taking a tumble down the length
of the brick stoop out front, she from the porch watching horrified, about to run, more scared still when the girl rises, blood on
her face, one tooth they would find dislodged, turning up to her
silently, refusing to cry . . . when they called the city to cut down
the dead sycamore out front and instead they came and cut the
healthy maple, the one that gave shade to the house in summer,
having to come back next week and cut the dead one, so that
stumps and soft mounds of sawdust which the kids jumped in and
threw until they were entirely dispersed were all that remained,
her mother standing out front on the sidewalk crying in full view
of the street . . . the children out back playing, the sounds coming to her through the kitchen window, bats dropped, shouts,
sneakers biting the concrete drive . . . Max, forty years rising
before her to shave and brush his teeth, his mounded back and
undershirt all she could see from the bed through the bathroom
door, humming a familiar, unrecognizable tune, she, seeing him
there, turning for ten more minutes of delicious sleep . . . walking with the children past the tobacco store on Fifty-first, she has
never been in it but this day even she is curious, walking on the
other side of the street, one of their hands in each of hers, peering
over at the dark glass, the whitewashed X's the police had put on
the windows, where last week two men, the owner and the boy
who tried to rob him, had shot each other and lay dying while
they waited for the ambulance to follow its wail up the streets to

them, too late . . . Mickey Brandwein, her cousin, a boy she was taken to visit, ill for years with some disease that made him too weak to even leave his bed and play a few minutes on the floor, in his corner room of the third-floor apartment, not ten feet from the El, with his green parrot Moishe and his timetables taped all around him, when the train passes he checking the big watch they bought him, writing a number in a box on the wall, the parrot gone crazy screeching and chattering on its perch, straining on its legs as if to fly, the boy looking from the parrot to her, smiling shyly . . . the old woman who fell in front of her mother's house one evening before dinner. She lay there on the sidewalk, holding her purse close to her chest as if that were all she intended to do. Ruth running to get her father, who came out with a folding chair, her mother with a glass of water. Thank you, the woman said in Yiddish, no, I'm fine, I'll sit here a minute if you don't mind, a well-dressed old woman in a coat with a fur collar, accepting the chair and the glass of water, allowing Ruth's mother to rearrange the hat, which had slipped across her eyes, I'll just sit here, she said, and Ruth getting up from dinner several times to look, and then after dinner when they had done eating the old lady still sitting there, her purse in one hand, the untouched glass of water in the other . . . hot summer nights in Brooklyn, all the kids in bed, up and down the street couples come out to their lit porches with glasses of iced tea, pitchers for more, a radio somewhere playing dance music to sounds of ice in glasses and chairs on the wooden boards, laughter, voices in soft conversation while fireflies recede over dark lawns in the still blue night.

LIKE NEVER BEFORE

1

Birnbaum sat on the plane facing West, trying on his new life. It suited him, he felt, like the new clothes—the thin slacks of a material the man told him "breathed," the mustard jacket with twin triangles of red peeking from the pocket, the brown fedora, snap-brimmed, the feathers of some tiny bird in its band, which he held between two fingers in his lap. Before him, a whiskey sour brought by Connie the stewardess, pink liquid in a plastic cup. He had never tasted one before, but when Connie had offered a beverage—offering herself, it had seemed—he had said, "Why not?" and ordered the most festive drink he could think of, the one Ruthie used to order at weddings. He took a sip of the sweet drink, set it on the table in front of him, lightly brushed the feathers in the hat, and hitched up the slacks, so he could feel the slide of the expensive material on his legs, so the pants could do their breathing.

He was a short man, with a wide forehead and expressive eyes. He had begun taller, but time, and his posture of shouldering a burden through the years, had compressed him an inch or two. He wore a look of unaware dreaminess, of furtive sorrow, as if his mind, behind restless brown eyes, flitted between both a past and a future he could not accommodate. A wary man, he smiled whenever he could. He believed he saw it all coming.

A retired teacher living on a pension, Birnbaum had never owned clothes like this in his life. In the airport waiting for the plane, he had felt buoyed by the energy of the high glass hall— the expectant faces and holiday clothing, the outsize murals, gaily abstract, the calm intimate announcements over the intercom. He watched pilots and stewardesses flirting through cinema smiles as they walked in procession down the wide corridors, and planes nosing toward the gates like huge sea animals dredged into the light, coaxed by young men waving orange wands. He wandered the lounges, found himself grinning at people as if they had all just heard the same joke. He paused to glance into mirrors, glassed-in restaurants and bars, again to feel the pleasant shock of recognition at the slim prosperous middle-aged man blinking back at him from under a gilded beer sign. It was as if they had all gathered here, Birnbaum thought, he and his fellow travelers, to leave the old life, journey from this place to some place new and begin again. Sipping the whiskey sour, he toasted his friend Schteiner. "Absolutely," he thought. "To good times."

In Queens, in his dark bedroom before dawn, searching the parallel mirrors he and Ruthie had bought thirty years ago, he had been held by a different sight—thin hair in all directions, domed forehead over eyes that even in the darkness could not conceal their glint of mistrust, skinny legs nearly hairless, arms weakly hanging, breasts—he watched a ridiculous tired old man, some plucked fowl. In disheveled misery he sat on the bed unable to move until Schteiner pounded the door, stuck a face running with toothpaste in the room. He wore one of Birnbaum's pajama bottoms, the green toothbrush looked familiar. "Shake a leg, Rothschild!" he had shouted. "Even for millionaires they don't hold jumbo jets."

Connie came down the aisle with a stack of magazines. Birnbaum, by the window, did not think it would be gallant to lean over the wilted-looking grandmother in the aisle seat who ignored her. Connie widened pretty eyes at Birnbaum as if to say they knew which end was up. She was young, and lovely, he thought. Her red hair was pulled off one shoulder in a loose ribbon and in her lapel she wore a white flower. She had a way of smiling, of looking at you as if really interested, which Birnbaum found alarming and tensely pleasant. He smiled back uncomfortably. "Here," she said, pulling two magazines off the top. "You kids share these," and to Birnbaum's shock and delight, she winked.

The magazines were *Cosmopolitan* and *Vogue*, with ripe, heavy-lipped models on the covers who leaned so you could see all there was to see if you looked, which Birnbaum didn't, then did. Schteiner had brought one like this back from the barbershop one day, left it lying around, and Birnbaum, then too, had looked. He saw women in skin-tight dresses with plunging necklines, with startling eyes and shiny hair flying. They seemed like exotic animals from places he had never thought to see. He turned the pages slowly, all that beauty filling his eyes until he felt, rather than saw, the lady at his side fixing him—white hair helmeted around a face bony with disapproval, tiny beads of sweat lining her upper lip. Briefly, he saw himself as he imagined she saw him, an old man in some foreigner's clothing, brazening it into the world as if he had a place there. Amid dim panic, hearing Schteiner's voice, Birnbaum dropped the magazines on the empty seat between them.

"In my line of business," he said, and paused to arrange a smile, "we'd say she's got moxie." He pointed at a model in a green dress that looked painted on. "Oh, yes." He sighed a little, as if he were tired, after all these years of models in green dresses. "This one has moxie to spare."

He crossed one leg over the other to indicate he was ready, if his companion was, for conversation. He smiled again. He wondered what he would say if she asked about his line of business, having none. He wondered what "moxie" meant, where he had heard such a word. Schteiner. He tried for an expression of amiable and worldly patience, tossed his hat carelessly on the model's face. He nodded, waiting. But the woman looked at him silently through cold blue eyes, as if coming to understand that here was the biggest fool on the airplane, and eventually Birnbaum, his smile hanging on his face like a palsy, turned to the small window at his side. The plane climbed slowly through thick oceans of cloud.

He was traveling West to see his son, whom he had not visited in years, and whose strained relations with his father had resolved, at least on the father's side, into a remote and wistful antipathy. There was a new granddaughter Birnbaum had never seen, a second wife he barely knew, though Ruthie, before her death, had made the trip and returned with pictures, home movies, and a lasting delight that had consoled her through her illness, around which Birnbaum had wandered helpless and alone. With David it was one thing, then another; it had always been this way, forever, it seemed to Birnbaum, though he carried in his mind, like a talisman, a vision of a time before the troubles began.

There had been business dealings gone bad, both their moneys lost, when David was still in architecture school and bristled with schemes, plans for a gilded future. There had been his first wife, not Jewish, and the engulfing sorrow that had brought, Birnbaum first rejecting her angrily, then grieving in his heart that his life should have turned out this way, then later, before the ugly divorce, wanting from her some kind of expiation, a key to what had happened between them all. There was his son's slovenly emotional life—behaving like an aggrieved child after the marriage fell apart, quitting the New York firm where his future lay, refusing to get his career back on track. Then his slow aimless slide across the continent—Boston, Chicago, Denver, now someplace in godforsaken Oregon—who lived in Oregon?—like a hobo, Birnbaum sourly thought, like a wandering dog. Birnbaum roundly loathed cowards, those who blamed life, God, the weather, everyone else for the trouble they called down on their own heads. Hadn't he known trouble? When he thought of David in this light, a searing taste rose in his mouth and he washed it away quickly with a swallow of the drink before him.

He put the empty glass on the tray table and came reluctantly to the last item on his list of grievances, the hurt of hurts, the one on which all the others rested the way a house rests on a foundation underground—the pain the boy had caused his poor mother, throwing his future away. God keep her, she had remained silent to the very end, though he knew, David did, could see it there plainly on her face and in her sinking spirits. And that he knew and still did not, at least for his mother's sake, become a man, Birnbaum could not forgive him.

But now she was dead, and Birnbaum was old. He felt the circle of his life drawing to a close, and his son, whatever his life was, was living it. So if they had not been in the same room for years, still, what did they have, after all, but each other, and Birnbaum, this last time, was determined to try. And now, because of his uncle Levine, he had the means.

The check had dropped out of the blue, a lightning bolt, a total surprise. Starchy pink paper with a cross-hatching of gray lines, numbers embossed in black. Birnbaum sat on the sofa with the check in his lap, running his thumb over the raised characters. "Pay to the order of Max Birnbaum, Twenty-five Thousand Dollars."

Schteiner, who had come home with him from the pool, sat dripping chlorinated sweat on Ruthie's living-room rug, searching among the newspapers and fruit rinds on the table for an ashtray.

"My God," Birnbaum said again. "Is it real?"

Schteiner lit a cigarette, dropped the match in an upturned tangerine peel. He took the check from Birnbaum and held it to the light. He flicked it with a fingernail, put it to his nose. "Real," he said. "One hundred percent."

"What do I do with it?"

"Do with it?" Schteiner spoke through smoke. "You eat it. You let me take it in the kitchen and mix it in an omelet for you, with tomato." He looked at Birnbaum crosswise. He was a gray-skinned man with a large head and teeth that always showed. "Do with it, he says. Wake up, Birnbaum! Your ship has come in, for God's sake! The bell is ringing!" He held the check up by his ear and shook it. "Twenty-five thousand!" he said. "Dollars!" With two fingers he pointed the cigarette at Birnbaum. "What do you do? You go to Las Vegas, that's what, you don't wait, you just go, boom, goodbye! Miami, Birnbaum! Paris, France! Istanbul! You meet a girl, a young foreign girl, extremely young. She loves you and you marry her. Better yet, you don't. There's moonlight all over, headwaiters, schnapps. There's carriage rides, there's opera—what you don't know you'll learn—there's walks to put your spotty hand on glaciers." He paused to smile, raised his hands near his ears as if he would snap his fingers. "You live a little, that's what. You do whatever you want after sixty years of wanting, that's what you do." He nodded definitively, left for the kitchen to find an ashtray, shaking his head so that ashes flicked from the cigarette in his mouth first one way then the other. "Birnbaum, this is your lucky day, you son of a bitch. Wake up and smell the danish."

Birnbaum, who had seen his habits deteriorate—grow closer to Schteiner's—in the months since Ruthie's death, reached for a near-empty tea glass with two cigarette stubs floating in it. Schteiner wasn't looking. It impressed Birnbaum that after nearly a year of friendship—if that's what it was—Schteiner still looked for the ashtrays, as if Birnbaum, who had finally quit when Ruthie got sick, still smoked secretly, as if he had stocked up on them since yesterday.

Birnbaum sat in thongs, the plaid trunks and short terry-cloth jacket he'd worn from the pool. The pool was in an apartment building where Schteiner knew some people—was there any-one he didn't know?—and they had taken to going there every morning, sometimes again in the afternoons. Lately, Birnbaum had adopted Schteiner's habit of not changing in the tiny, dank locker room, just walking the six blocks on Metropolitan Avenue with his towel over his shoulder. In late summer the sidewalks no longer steamed but the air was heavy, exhausted, and they walked not speaking between small storefronts and graystone apartments that seemed to sag in their weariness over the street. Schteiner was a man at the synagogue, something to do with contracting, another old Pole always talking by the door in his heavy accent, pumping hands, the last to leave. When he had showed up at Birnbaum's door one morning with a box of twenty-four doughnuts, the rookie widower, not acknowledging his lone-liness to himself, saw it in the other man's face, and let him in. Schteiner turned the radio on loud in the unnaturally quiet house, made dinner, a big cooked chicken from the freezer and four baked potatoes. Soon he was staying, stretching out under the afghan Ruthie had knitted, on her striped couch, a cigarette like a tiny ship's mast sticking out of his face, saying, "Get some sleep, Birnbaum. You look like what the cat dragged back out." He would stay two days, three, then go for a while to his apart-ment on Lefferts. Birnbaum would come down in the morning to the sound of the radio, Schteiner behind the *Daily News* and a glass of tea, half a dozen eggs sizzling in a puddle of butter on the stove. "Look," Schteiner would tell the paper, "he's alive." Today, when Birnbaum had wondered at the propriety of marching down Metropolitan Avenue in their swim shorts, Schteiner had said, "What, you're Cary Grant all of a sudden? Excuse me, Mr. Tyrone Power. Who's looking at your skinny legs?"

From the kitchen, drawers slamming, cabinets being opened. "First thing you do," he heard Schteiner say, "is buy one goddamn ashtray. *Then* go to the Riviera and good luck to you."

Schteiner wore dark glasses and iridescent blue bathing trunks with fish circling back to front. On his head sat a powder-blue beret. He walked in from the kitchen, smiling with strong, snaggled teeth. "Okay," he said. "How about a nice glass'le tea?"

While Schteiner banged pots in the kitchen, Birnbaum sat on the sofa and reread the letter that had come with the check. A lawyer in Toronto telling him his uncle Levine was dead, leaving the enclosed sum to him. Birnbaum had barely known the man, his mother's cousin, rumored to be a millionaire in Canadian real estate. They had sat together a few years back at a wedding, he and Ruthie and a few other people, old man Levine and his college-age girlfriend. Sharon. No, Sharee. Levine kept sending her across the room for fresh drinks, food from the buffet table. A few times it seemed to Birnbaum he asked for something just so he, so they, could watch her walk across the room, and once he turned to Birnbaum with a knowing nod, as if here were two gentlemen who could appreciate a young pair of hips in a black skirt.

"Twenty-two," Levine told him. "I found her at the university library, licking stamps."

"A nice girl," Ruthie said, smiling politely.

"Nice!" Levine shouted. "Not *too* nice! Don't you worry about that! "

A pretty young woman who seemed happy to meet some of Levine's family, Sharee did most of the talking, hoping for a response, which Ruthie most often obliged her in supplying. They talked about travel, shopping, Sharee's major at the university. She was a sweet girl and Birnbaum tried not to wonder how she had ended up with such an old mongrel. Levine himself did little talking. He drank steadily from the glass Sharee tended for him and watched her with a cold, unappeased hunger. He was old, Birnbaum could not say how old, and all energy seemed to have pooled in his bright eyes, which moved like distant lights in his mottled, collapsing face as he watched the young girl across the table.

Now he, too, was dead. Birnbaum felt no real emotion, certainly not grief—shock, if anything, at this present from a man he didn't know. He wondered vaguely what would happen to Sharee, then brought his hands together slowly in front of his face as an idea took shape in his mind.

"Lucky bastard," Schteiner said from the kitchen, where he was searching for cookies to go with the tea. He appeared in the doorway with a box of graham crackers. "First, you get some better cookies, you know? A little strudel wouldn't kill you, some assorted pastries." He shook a cracker at Birnbaum, sending a shower of crumbs to the carpet, then turned back into the kitchen. "You can buy you a baker, Birnbaum, a live-in, from France, a little girl baker in short skirts to bake cakes for you all day long." He appeared again with two glasses of tea, thick slices of lemon and broken graham crackers on one of Ruthie's trays. Another cigarette was in his mouth. He grinned at Birnbaum over the food. "Lucky bastard."

As the plane leveled off, they still had not cleared the cloud cover. Droplets of water trailed in jittery lines across the plastic window and Birnbaum thought of the heart monitor in Ruthie's hospital room and turned away.

It was a new plane, in clean blue-and-orange brocade. The uniforms Connie and her comrades wore were crisp and freshly laundered, and the seat controls, which Birnbaum touched but did not try on his armrest, were tight plastic blisters, pleasing to the fingers. The walls were a seashell pattern, barely visible, meant to soothe, and the wing, the tip of which he could see, gleamed dully in the light from the cabin, slicing without apparent effort through sudden scuds of cloud. Still, he was uneasy. He looked up the cabin at the singular geometry of a plane in flight, angling on a vector some computer had decreed, the heads in ordered rows before him, the luggage racks minutely vibrating, voices in conversation, and under it all the throbbing drone of the engine, plowing them through limitless sky. He looked until fear bloomed in his gut, spreading upwards, taking with it his holiday mood. He determined to recall it.

The woman beside him stared at the seat back before her so intently that Birnbaum for a moment looked at the blue material to see what she might be seeing. She had a book in her hand — Birnbaum couldn't make out the cover — and reading glasses on a string around her neck, but she hadn't turned a page yet. As he watched, Birnbaum saw tiny flickers in her cheek as her jaw muscles worked underneath. A tremor seemed to start up in one of her hands. He realized she was intentionally not looking his way. *Cosmopolitan* and *Vogue* were on the seat between them and Birnbaum wondered if she was offended by what he'd said. "Who is this lady?" he heard himself think. "Who made her judge over me?" He noticed the beginnings of a sour dislike in his chest. He flicked out one sleeve of his Italian jacket, located a piece of lint on the arm to remove. His bladder was full and the captain had just announced they were free to move about the cabin. He wanted another drink — the first had been nice, sweet and tingly at the same time. He wanted to compliment Connie — another drink and, yes, some time to read one of the magazines before he tried to sleep. But before rudely pushing past her to the aisle, Birnbaum decided, for politeness's sake, to try conversation one more time. He turned in his seat, maneuvered his hat directly over the blonde on the cover of *Cosmopolitan*. He waited a moment to give her a chance to notice.

"Vacation?" he said.

The woman did not respond at first. Then she turned her white head slowly with a smile so thinly stretched across her face that Birnbaum felt rage jump in his belly.

"No," she said.

"I'm visiting my son," Birnbaum offered, thinking she can hear me out no matter what. "He's in garden supplies. Landscaping. Near Portland."

The thin smile did not waver. He'd seen this woman before, dozens just like her. A religious nut, grandmother to thirty boys in military school. Some dried-up old nag who thought her troubles, whatever they were, entitled her to look down on everyone she met. Ruthie had a way of talking to such snobs. She could talk to anyone, but not Birnbaum. He plowed grimly on.

"I called last night, midnight. I'm coming, I said, just like that. Meet me at the airport. Gave them a nice shock, I'm sure."

The woman now remembered the book in her lap. She carefully adjusted the reading glasses across her ears and began flipping pages.

"Just like that," Birnbaum repeated. "Meet me at the Portland International Airport, 12:45 p.m. tomorrow. Don't worry about work, I said. Take the day off."

Birnbaum leaned a bit forward to see the woman's book cover. A long-haired man in a torn white pirate's shirt embraced a reclining woman in a tiara. Metallic blue letters curved around their heads. She's got a nerve, Birnbaum thought, looking at his hat. He had the sudden vivid urge to reach out and grab one of the flaccid arms that hung in her pink sweater and give it a good shake.

"That's what I said. No, no, no. No questions, just be at the airport, 12:45. The rest you leave to me." He lowered his tone confidentially. "I've got a surprise. They have no idea. A trip. Wherever they want. Hawaii. Mexico. Disneyland. I've got the tickets right here in my pocket." The woman didn't look but she seemed to pause in her reading. Birnbaum pulled his jacket open. "Five vouchers, they call them. Look, I asked them special to make them up like tickets." He pointed at the destination line. "See? Anywhere you want to go. Anyplace. It'll knock their heads off, you wait," and with a laugh he reached across to give the woman a soft friendly jab in the shoulder. She did turn now, the look on her face so flat, so full of determined anger and disapproval, Birnbaum was shocked. He felt a chill in his upper arms and chest. He sat back.

"I've never been west of Chicago," he heard himself say without any idea why.

The woman returned to her reading and Birnbaum immediately tried to stand, forgetting first to undo his seat belt. Then in his haste to get out he stumbled and placed his hand flat on his new fedora, crushing it. "Excuse me," he said, "bathroom," and not looking at the woman, pushed past her legs into the aisle.

At first, the doctors did not know what caused Ruthie's symptoms. And what were they, really—aches, cramping, fatigue—in a woman her age. Birnbaum did not like to recall this time, though it was the last he would really have her, before the medicines then the doctors and finally the illness itself took her away. But it made him unbearably sad to remember how, with the diagnosis undetermined and his wife in pain, he had prodded her simply to put it out of her mind, where he insisted it originated, and pay a little more attention to him, with his back pain real, God knew, and his bursitis and the rest. And she had tried, making them dinners to eat in front of the TV, reminding him to eat his salad. But when she would invariably fall asleep, her head sagging over her full plate, she looked old to him, beyond weary, and Birnbaum, frightened, would see the sickness the doctors couldn't in her face. He would wash their dishes, then nudge her softly and tell her it was time to go upstairs.

Then one night he awoke, Ruthie was not in bed with him. He understood, dimly, that she had been gone a long time. Half asleep, he called to her, realized she was in the bathroom, had been calling his name. He reached for his glasses, felt with blind feet for his slippers under the bed. In the bathroom his wife sat on the toilet, her nightgown hiked up, a pink towel from the rack held between her legs. What he remembered most was the towel, a fluffy towel which she liked to wrap around her head in a turban after bathing, stuffed between her legs on the toilet. And her smile. "You'd better call Melman," she'd said quietly, and then looking at him, no doubt reading the fear on his face, had smiled. "Go on, Max," she'd said. "I'm all right here." In the bedroom, sitting on her side of the bed near the phone, he'd seen blood pooling on the mattress, glistening dully in the light from the streetlamp. He didn't need to touch it to know what it was. That was the moment his life changed. He picked up the phone and sat on their bed, alone, and waited for the doctor at the other end of the wire to be roused from sleep.

In the hospital, at the end, they moved in a small bed for him to stay with her. Right until the last day, the last hour, no one talked about dying, not actual death. She was ill, certainly. The disease had spread, encamped all over her body. They had operated, done all they could, but the disease had been merely held at bay for a time. It would win, yes, but not yet, surely not so soon. He had nearly lost her before and she had rallied. Some days she looked so much better. So he brought in her crosswords and they watched TV. They shared a running joke about the hospital food. She spoke to David on the phone and they made plans for another visit once she got out of the hospital. This time, Birnbaum would come along. She laughed about the baby and listened sympathetically, gave advice and talked to their little grandson, Daniel, about his dog, Barney, and when she handed the phone to Birnbaum he could barely speak, so full of anger was he that here was this woman, this saint, severely ill, in constant pain, and across the entire continent their failed son complained to her about diaper rash and food bills.

The last night, Birnbaum lay unsleeping. He remembered the night of their wedding, forty years earlier. The prayers had been chanted, the rings exchanged, the glass shattered, and the cake cut. Now the couple were to be alone. Ruthie went first, parting a thick gray curtain that revealed a wooden door. Birnbaum was delayed, talking to some teary aunt, and when he finally got away, pushed the heavy door open with a shoulder, there she sat, on a chair by a table holding two small wineglasses. In the old days, this was the moment for the couple to consummate their marriage. But Birnbaum had no thought of that. It had been a long, tiring day, the effort of being happy in public for so many hours as trying to him as the small bickerings among family about food, seating, who knew what else. He closed the door behind him. All he really wanted was to sit near her, now his wife, for a quiet moment, maybe empty a glass of wine in hopes of a kind future. He turned to Ruthie. Wax from the candles they had held in the procession shone bluely from one of her shoes. Birnbaum's pack of cigarettes lay on the table, by the wineglasses, by the yellow flowers Ruthie had just put down. She faced him in her white dress, the veil he had lifted moments ago flowing back over her dark hair. Wife. She held her arms out to him and smiled and Birnbaum walked slowly toward this vision in white, toward everything he had ever dreamed of having.

He was slapped from memory by the sound of voices, machinery. Two doctors were pulling the covers off Ruthie, a nurse was pushing a red cart up to the bed. A silver box was on the bed, a nurse hurriedly rubbing two paddles together. Alarms beeped from the wall, more doctors came in and a nurse tried to close the curtain around Ruthie's bed, but Birnbaum's cot was in the way. He stood, working his way toward her until the same nurse held him back. He watched the monitor over her head, through the bodies and arms, through the noise of machines and the doctors' orders growing more severe, trying, though the nurse held him back, to catch a glimpse of his wife's face.

Before last night, Birnbaum had not spoken with his son in nearly half a year. The last time had ended so badly, the two of them screaming into the phone, that it had taken this long for the healing. On both sides there were grievances, Birnbaum was ready to acknowledge this—no relationship was perfect. Yet, even at Ruthie's funeral, David had arrived late, after the services, to stand behind the last row of mourners at the grave site, not up front with Birnbaum where he belonged. Esther, Ruth's aunt, who wouldn't know her own business if it had a sign around its neck, walked over to Birnbaum after they had thrown the handfuls of dirt, nearly coming apart with tears, one of those women who appear in public only as an occasion to cry, as if it weren't *his* Ruthie in the cold ground. "Talk to him," she'd said. "Max, look at him. Today's not a day for fighting."

Birnbaum had been willing. He took a last breath, looked at the white pine coffin nearly obscured now by shovelfuls of dirt, and let his daughter walk him over to where his son, long hair and leather jacket—who still dressed this way at thirty-nine?—wet from the rain, stood wanly by a tree, smoking. As they approached, Birnbaum was ready to do anything, cry, laugh, throw his arms around the boy, anything. His Ruthie lay there in a box, she was not coming back. All they had left now was each other. Wasn't it her final wish that David and he be reconciled? Isn't this what Birnbaum prayed for each night, through mouthfuls of bitterness and regret? He would embrace the boy, take him home, forgive everything. They would start again. But as he and Rachel came close he saw David's face. Not on it the need for comfort, the contrition Birnbaum expected, but that look so particularly David's own—quiet outrage, detachment, the aloof expectation of pain.

In that pale tearless face, closed down on its own sorrow, Birnbaum saw all his defeats, all that he had every right to expect from
life and would never, he saw it again now, would never receive
from it. A few feet from David they crossed a path and Birnbaum
turned down it, rage tinting his vision red, Rachel calling after
him, "Wait, Abba. Would you wait a minute?"

Now, on the plane, Birnbaum reflected that any hardship in
this world is easier to bear than a disappointing child. He asked
God about this in his prayers, requested guidance, solace. After
prolonged self-examination he had determined that, like all fathers,
he might have done better, could certainly have done worse. He
prayed in private to his God of sad retribution, asked, politely, for
miracles. In early mornings after sleepless nights in the big bed he
cursed God from the bottom of his aching heart, and God, in his
heedless, unending silence, seemed to curse him back.

His appetite ruined by heartburn, he watched the lady next to
him pick four tiny shrimp one by one off a bed of green pasta and
tear at them with her small front teeth. Her meticulous movements dipped him in melancholy. He tried to read an article in
Cosmopolitan about the sixth marriage of a beauty queen from
the forties and, still reading, fell asleep. He dreamed of flying in
an airplane, of blue fish swimming through the aisle between the
seats. He dreamed Connie was in the seat next to him, laughing
at something he'd said, leaning toward him in a green dress to
take hold of his arm. He saw himself and Ruthie running before
yellow waves on a black beach. Up on the sand Schteiner and
David played a game, tossing a beret back and forth. He dreamed
of being in a box, lying on satin, turning into a warm embrace,
then the box was being lowered and he couldn't get his breath.
No air. No light.

When he awoke, the pilot was announcing their descent into
Portland. He brushed stiff fingers through his hair, was surprised
to be in daylight. The woman beside him was trussed in her seat
belt, immobile eyes trained forward. He picked up his crumpled

hat from the seat and waited. Outside, rain fell in fringes on a landscape startlingly green and lush, and white birds flew on long wings toward the treeline beyond the river.

2

They were there, the four of them, as Birnbaum, still groggy from sleep, emerged into the waiting area. Janine held the boy in her arms and made him wave—or maybe he waved himself, Birnbaum couldn't tell—while David, with the baby to the side, found an ashtray for his cigarette. Janine came up to him through the crowd. They embraced, the shoulders of Janine's and Daniel's jackets wet with rain, and Birnbaum felt punchy, elated, frightened, confused by emotions that came at him from all directions, like noise. He tried to shake the remnants of dreaming from his head. The little boy put his face up dutifully to be kissed and called him Grandpop. Automatically he put his small warm hand in Birnbaum's. David walked over, eyes scrunched as if still bothered by smoke. "Well, you made it," he said, and held the baby, asleep, up for Birnbaum to see. "This is Erin. Say hello to your granddaughter."

Birnbaum wasn't sure if David meant for him to take the child. He was willing, just let him put down his bag. "She's beautiful," he said.

David smiled curtly, as if this was what he had come over to hear. He turned and began walking with the crowd toward the baggage area. Watching him, Birnbaum felt a familiar mourning bloom, loss fingering his throat from the inside. He swallowed it down with the smile he'd been practicing all day. "So," he said to Daniel, "how's my biggest grandson?"

The boy looked first at his mother. "Wait," he said. "I'm your only."

"Absolutely," Birnbaum said. "And the smartest, too." The boy

glanced at Birnbaum a moment, puffed his cheeks in exasperation. He began dragging Birnbaum by the hand, as if to pull him
after his father.

"Daniel," Janine said quietly. She felt the lapel of Birnbaum's
jacket, stepped back to look him over. "Who is this world trav-
eler?" she said, smiling.

"I bought some clothes for myself."

"I'm impressed," she said. "No offense, Max, but I never
thought I'd be outdressed by my father-in-law."

The airport was smaller, quieter than New York's, the carpeting
a cheerful blue-green with staccato dashes of red and orange. Illuminated photographs on the walls showed vast green pastures,
placid lakes, serene mountains. Outside the windows was rain
and fog and on the way to the baggage claim Daniel tugged on
Birnbaum's hand and they stopped. A jet was taking off, careen-
ing through its own roar until it lifted off the runway. "Look,
Grandpop," the boy said. They watched until the plane banked
and turned out of sight in low cloud. Daniel was a light-skinned,
round-faced boy, with brown hair just now losing the curls he'd
had as a baby. Looking at him, Birnbaum saw Ruthie and the
boy's mother, perhaps something of himself around the eyes. The
boy held on to his hand and Birnbaum felt emotion working loose
in his chest. Aiming for jauntiness, he said to Janine, "I called my
grandfather Zeide. But where would Daniel hear such a word out
here?" Janine laughed, showing pretty teeth. "He calls my father
Grandpop. I guess we should have discussed it. This is your *other*
grandpop, right, Daniel?" "Right!" the boy said, marching forward with Birnbaum in tow.

Realizing he had forgotten presents for the children, Birnbaum
spotted a gift shop and said to the boy, "Who likes chocolate?"
"Me," the boy said seriously, stopping in his tracks and pointing at
his chest. So skinny, Birnbaum thought. Do they feed him well?
"I do," he said, looking at his mother as if she could confirm this.

"I like chocolate a lot." David walked ahead and Birnbaum bought from the woman behind the counter a large, gaily wrapped chocolate bar that read "Welcome to Oregon!!!"

In the car, Birnbaum sat in back with the boy, who was small for his age, Birnbaum noted, in a car seat by his sister's, though he was nearly five. The boy sang a song about a rabbit and some mice in the forest and offered some of the chocolate to his grandfather. Birnbaum declined and soon the bar was melted and the boy's face smeared as he chewed with browned teeth and sang. When Janine handed Birnbaum a tissue, he did what he could and thought of Ruthie, how she would have been taking care of the boy, would have brought tissues of her own, would be shaking her head at him for the notion of chocolate before lunch.

They left the airport and drove south. Mist hovered low over fields on both sides of the highway, full green in the middle of winter. Trees were vague shapes in the distance and occasional stolid sheep or cows loomed unmoving in the grass. From a high stone wall rushed two flumes of water and Birnbaum turned in his seat to see more, though no one else in the car seemed to pay any mind. The whole countryside was shrouded, dampened, mute, and Birnbaum felt the unease of his dreams returning. Far ahead, sun seemed to be agitating the fog, which parted here and there, revealing layers of gray and blue cloud, brightening toward light.

"So," Janine said, turning to face him from the front. "Tell us about the flight." She had always been pretty, with Daniel's wide forehead and clear brown eyes. As she smiled, creases gathered around her mouth and eyes and Birnbaum, surprised, wondered if she could be aging already, then thought it must be sleeplessness, the new baby.

"A plane is like nothing else," he said. "A marvel. You get on, you sit, you get off in Portland, Oregon, another country entirely."

"You've never been out here, have you?" Janine said.

Birnbaum, unhappily remembering the woman on the plane, shook his head.

"Well, I hate flying," Janine said, looking over at David. "I know it's silly. It just makes me nervous."

She paused to give David a chance to join in the conversation, but he kept silent, his eyes on the road. She looked briefly at Birnbaum, who looked away and lifted Daniel's head back into the car seat. The boy had fallen asleep and his head had rolled forward onto his chest.

"This was a beautiful plane, brand-new," he said. "You would have liked this one, David. Very comfortable, actually." He went on, trying to fill the small car with his voice. "But they put me next to a monster, a real dragon lady. An old woman, what God did to her I wouldn't want to think about. Angry? My God. Unfriendly? David, you remember Landau, from the A & P, his wife? Like her exactly, only more of the same."

David, who still had not spoken, leaned forward to push the cigarette lighter. He rolled down his window a few inches, letting in the cold.

"Sorry about the rain," Janine said. "That's Oregon for you."

"What's a little rain?" Birnbaum said. "Don't be sorry."

David lit a cigarette, the smoke dancing briefly in the air before whipping out the open window. He held the cigarette close to the filter and sucked it with a sound that made Birnbaum squirm. The boy's head had fallen forward again and Birnbaum did what he could, then lay his hand on the boy's in his lap. He smiled at Janine.

"He's tired," she said. "All the excitement."

"Sure," Birnbaum said.

They drove south, tracing the curve of a gray river. Birnbaum saw more waterfalls bursting from the rockface and fields brimming with moisture, ponds the size of small lakes in a few. A large brown bird—a hawk, Birnbaum guessed, he really had no idea— lifted slowly off a fence post and something—a cat? a fox?—

chased after it lazily. He was chilled from the open window, tired, too, the unnamable emotion he had been feeling all day welling again inside. He checked the sheaf of vouchers in his jacket pocket, fingered the comforting blue envelopes.

Birnbaum looked at the back of his son's head, fragile-seeming, despite the rough army-jacket green, the skull flattened under lank brown hair. He missed Ruthie now, acutely, her presence in this silent car. David had been a sorrow to her, too—what dreams they'd had for the boy!—but she could talk to him, she could always do that, and with her as mediator they had done all right. She could see the hurt behind the hurtful things said. She could see love where he and David, it seemed, saw only anger. She might reach out now and touch their son's hair, might make a gentle joke about how long it was, a gesture Birnbaum could not consider making himself. As if sensing his father watching him, David moved, flicked his stub out the window, and punched the lighter in the dash for another cigarette. Birnbaum reached over and squeezed Janine's shoulder instead.

"Good to see you," he said.

"You, too, Max," she said. "Good to see you, too."

Their house was a green bungalow carved low into a hillside. Although it did not seem new, piles of rusty dirt sat to the sides, fresh-looking, as if the hill were slowly reclaiming its domain, and above the house, behind it, trees trailed away in the light rain. A boy's bicycle lay on the lawn, a dimpled red kickball, what appeared to be a motorcycle under a tarp, car tires, wheel hubs. To one side, in a carport, a dark sedan from the seventies sat with a sprung hood, engine suspended above it on a winch. A short man in a greasy work shirt and baseball cap scraped inside the engine with a screwdriver. He paused as they got out of the car, raised a bandanna at Birnbaum, and smiled. There was a fierce scratching at the door and Daniel ran to the house to let Barney, his golden retriever, out into the yard. The dog ran directly at Birnbaum, ears and teeth in the wind, scaring him, but after trying to put muddy paws on Birnbaum's jacket to get at his face, the dog was pushed away hard by David. Daniel, with shrieks of delight, chased the dog into the driveway, where he hugged his neck and pulled out the remaining chocolate to share.

While Janine carried the baby indoors and David unloaded the luggage, Birnbaum stood on the grass verge of the property and looked around. Up the street, more bungalows squatting on the hillside, small frame houses across the way, each with a stretch of lawn, a spindly tree or two out front. It was so moist that even in midday wisps of fog curled above the far houses. Birnbaum took a step toward the carport, cleared his throat.

"Hello," he said. "Tell me, does it ever get dry here?"

The man in the work shirt was twisting a wrench around a lug in the engine. He stopped and looked at Birnbaum. He was short, losing his hair, with a large belly and muscular arms. He had a friendly smile. "Yeah," he said. "Sometimes it does."

David came out from the house and joined the man. They turned to the engine and began talking.

Birnbaum waited by the car. In him, despite his refusal to acknowledge it, the distinct wish to get away, to run—here he wasn't familiar, maybe not even welcome. What had he been thinking? In this green house his son lived out a life Birnbaum didn't know, wasn't sure he wanted to know. His plan for them, that he'd carried in his mind across the continent, circled him, dim in outline but vivid in detail—the five of them, he and his children, in a sunlit place, full of color, walking eagerly toward sounds of some festive gathering, laughter, music, lighthearted conversation. His new shoes darkening with wet, he watched this plan fade in mist above the house. He would leave. They would understand. A mistake. At the airport, he could sit in the lounge and feed quarters to the TV until a plane came to take him home.

Schteiner would be there. They would eat, maybe go down to the boulevard and watch the old fellows play chess, take in a movie. Birnbaum had a confused image of Schteiner answering the door in Ruthie's dressing gown, ashes dribbling down the front. He shook his head to clear it. A silly man, Schteiner, probably never had a serious thought in his life. Still, a friend. Daniel and the dog came tearing into the front yard, the boy skidding in the grass with his hands on the dog's collar to keep him grounded. "No, Barney!" he said.

Through the screen door, Janine called, "Max, what are you doing out there? David, your father's standing in the rain!" David and the man by the car looked over their shoulders at Janine. The man smiled. Janine said, "Daniel, ask your grandfather indoors, for heaven's sake."

The boy ignored her. "Wanna see my swing set, Grandpop? You have to come with us. C'mon." Daniel let go of the dog, who galloped around the side of the house. The boy said, "Grownups can't ride but they can look. C'mon," and led Birnbaum to the back.

Inside, the house was as depressing as Birnbaum feared it would be. It was clean, for which he credited Janine, but cluttered without being cozy, the furniture worn, faded, the rooms smelling of the damp, of baby and dog. The carpeting was gold abraded gray where it was walked on, the close walls a cheap wood paneling even Birnbaum could tell was imitation. Nowhere were signs of David's promising career, or the framed diploma Ruthie and Birnbaum had presented him after his graduation from NYU. Nowhere a mezuzah, a single prayer book—whose child was this? Instead, a large greasy toolbox in one corner, the metal innards of a motor piled next to it on some newspaper.

On the mantel, birth pictures of the children, creased paperback novels, a wedding photo, David shyly grinning in a light blue suit, Janine in a simple dress, darker blue. The wedding had taken place shortly after David had come home to tell them he planned to marry Janine, another non-Jewish girl. He'd come to ask forgiveness, relinquishing long before hopes of their blessing. They had been invited, but Birnbaum remembered spending that day planting bulbs in the backyard, ignoring Ruthie's occasional tears by gouging more savage holes in the wet spring ground, reaching a hand over a shoulder to receive the bulbs without looking at his wife. A picture of Birnbaum and Ruthie was half concealed by a baby bottle, while above it, hanging on the wall, a couple smiled toothily from a wooden porch swing—Janine's parents, he assumed.

"Sorry for the mess," Janine said, once she had put the baby down. "Kids. But I don't have to tell you."

"What mess?" Birnbaum said.

David walked in, wiping his hands on a rag. "That damn engine's taking a lot longer than I thought." His glance grazed Birnbaum in passing, settled on Janine. "I told Pavelich I'd have it done today."

"Can't you call him?" Janine said through a bright smile.

"Yeah," David said, throwing down the rag by the tool chest. "I can call him." He went into the next room.

"He works hard," Birnbaum said.

Janine said, "He picks up extra work fixing cars. Temporarily, till I go back to my teaching."

"Does he like this new job, landscaping?"

"I think he does, Max. He really seems to like it."

"And architecture?" Birnbaum asked, again looking around the shabby room. "Does he even mention it?"

"Oh, Max," she said. "Not much." She glanced toward the kitchen, where they could hear David and Daniel discussing the boy's lunch. "We don't really talk about it much anymore."

"His professor, at graduation, said he was the best student in ten years, maybe twenty. Right out of school, they had him design his own community, houses, banks, schools, all of it himself. They wrote about it in the paper." He realized he should stop. He was telling her things she already knew, what perhaps pained her and the boy, as it did him—the failed project, the lost career, the collapsed first marriage. He shook his head over the last words, as if he hadn't meant them. Janine cleared magazines off the couch. "He wasn't happy. I can see that now."

David walked back into the room. "Pavelich won't go for it, says I've had it a week already. If I can't get it done, he'll send a truck to haul it away."

"David," Janine said. "Your father just got here."

"I know," he said. "I'm doing the best I can."

From the kitchen Daniel said, "This bread tastes funny."

"Just eat it!" David said. The sound of something dropping, then the boy's trembling voice.

"I spilled my milk."

David muttered something under his breath and went into the kitchen. "I'm sorry," Birnbaum heard him say. "I'm sorry I yelled."

"It's on my pants."

"Okay. Go get another pair. What do you want to eat? There's some macaroni."

The boy raced through the room and back, holding a pair of dry pants. They heard the microwave, then David talking to the boy as he changed his clothes. When the boy was eating again, David walked through the room, not looking at either of them, and went outside. The door slammed and Birnbaum and Janine listened to the men talk. Birnbaum's mouth ached. He looked at the musty brown couch as if he would lie down on it, shoes and all. "He can't stay in the same room," he said quietly.

She looked at him. "He has to work, Max. We'll all be together at dinner."

He sat, still in his coat, and she went into the kitchen, where the boy first complained, then grew quiet. The couch gave softly under Birnbaum, enfolded him until his back slumped forward, aching. Across the room, in a frame on the wall, hung a picture. The plastic sheeting had warped, leaving half the picture obscured by glare, but he could see the rest—leaping lines of color, swirling forms—inexplicable, aggressive nonsense, painful to the eye. Ruthie would know the artist's name, would tell him what to look for and what to enjoy. And he would listen, dutifully. But he had never had much use for these modern painters—what could they tell you about this world, the one you lived in every day? He turned away.

Janine came out of the kitchen with a tray, and Birnbaum saw she had made tea, remembered he liked it in a glass, with lemon. She sat and began cutting into a frosted coffee cake. She smiled at him wearily. She had grown older, Birnbaum decided, this woman he never got to know. One trip East to meet them, introduced only as a friend from out West, while to him, sitting shyly in their living room, the only one laughing at his desperate jokes, she had been another threat, one more signal that his life, so meagerly lit, was about to get darker still. She had thick auburn hair, brushed back over her shoulders. Her face was wide and open and Birnbaum guessed it expressed emotions directly, the way a pond reflects sky or turbulence. He admired her warily, from a distance. She had always been friendly to him and Ruthie, invariably, even when he and David could not talk. Watching her, squirming on the swampy couch, Birnbaum searched himself for what he wanted to say, what he felt, as if he had a note somewhere in a pocket he'd forgotten. He searched for friendship, kindly affection, and was surprised to find, instead, fear.

"Janine," he said, the word sounding strange in his ears—he realized he had never used it. She had always been "she" or, before, "the girlfriend." "I wanted to speak with you." Still cutting the cake, Janine looked up, indicated she was listening. "I wanted to say to you . . . I wanted to say, all that trouble, the wedding, the fights . . ." She looked at him and shook her head. He went on. "It wasn't you. I wanted to say this. It was never you. It was family, it was religion, it was many things, but not you. You're a good woman, a fine wife, I can see that. And I know Ruth would want, if she was here, to say the same thing."

"She did, Max," Janine said.

"What?"

"Last winter, when she was here. We talked all about it." She smiled. "You don't need to say any more."

Birnbaum sat back in the sofa cushions. "She didn't tell me."

"She was a wonderful woman, Max. You must miss her terribly."

"Yes."

"She knew how you really felt. She explained it all. It meant so much that we talked."

"And David?" he said quietly.

"David, too. It was a good visit."

"So much anger. All the time he's so angry, I can't even talk."

"I know."

"Me, too. Angry, for years . . ."

From the kitchen, the raucous blaring of the TV, a rasp of canned laughter. Daniel, bored with lunch, had turned on the television.

"Too loud, honey," Janine called. The volume decreased. Janine bent over the coffee table and put a piece of cake on a glass plate, which she handed to Birnbaum with a small fork and a linen napkin.

Birnbaum thanked her and took a sip of tea. This was not a day he could understand. Why had Ruthie never spoken with him? There had been months, all those days at home, in the hospital. Never a word. What had they talked about? It seemed everyone around him could speak a language he did not know. It was unfair. It was unfair of Ruthie, and Birnbaum, for the first time, was angry with his wife, who had carried this away, too, along with the secret she had always possessed of talking to their son, had gone silently to her grave, and left him, ever more alone, to find his way.

He realized he was not eating the cake. He chewed a piece and reminded himself to taste. "Excellent cake," he said. "Did you make it?"

Janine shook her head, a small color rising in her face.

"No, we stopped at the store on the way to the airport."

"It's a good cake. I have a friend at home should try it. He's got an obsession with cakes."

He chewed another piece and swallowed. He couldn't tell if it was good cake or not, the gummy mass in his jaws seeming to grow larger, refusing to go down. Then he put the plate on the table and brought a hand to his face, aware in a flush of panic that he might cry.

Janine looked up at him. Behind her a wall heater rumbled to life, air smelling of earth filled the room. In his head Schteiner said ruefully, "Ah, look. Now look at this."

Janine said, "We're glad you came, Max. I am and Daniel is, and David is, too." She had reached a hand across to him and put it on his knee. He looked at it gratefully.

"We used to talk about him," Birnbaum said. "All the time, his mother and me. What a future he had."

They drank the tea, finished the cake in silence. From the kitchen the TV droned and Daniel spoke to the cartoons, to Barney. And from outside, the men working, sounds of strain, of metal being gouged, of laughter and amiable cursing. After a few moments they heard a truck start up and David walked in.

"Keith's gone to the Napa for parts," he said, picking up the rag he'd tossed and wiping his hands again. He straightened, loosed a small smile at his wife. "Cake looks good."

"Sit," Janine said. "I'll get a plate."

David sat opposite his father on a nubbled white easy chair. "So," he said. "How's the house?"

"Good," Birnbaum said. "Big. My friend Schteiner's been staying. I'm glad for the company."

"And you? How's the shoulder?"

"Okay. A little bit so-so."

"Janine asks about the garden. She remembers Mom's garden from our visit."

"Still there," Birnbaum said. "I pull out weeds, I try to keep it trimmed."

Janine came in with a bottle of beer, a plate for David. "I loved that garden," she said. "It must have taken years to grow."

Birnbaum nodded. As they sat, he remembered all the days Ruthie would come in from the yard, flushed, smeared with dirt and loam, happily exhausted. She would tell him of the irises, the tulips, the flowering shrubs, and he would listen, half bored, enjoying her animation. He looked at his son, remembering when the yard had been his playground, many years back. David had lost weight, was wiry, roughened. He seemed actually larger, a layer of muscle around his neck and shoulders, but his face — maybe it was just today — was thin, withdrawn, with a haggard look behind all that hair. He was no longer a handsome man, Birnbaum thought. Some people simply don't age well. "And now," he said to his son, "you're the expert gardener."

"No expert," David said. "Just learning." He drank from his bottle of beer.

"Well, I can't wait any longer," Janine said, smiling first at David, then Birnbaum. "Tell us. What's the secret?"

They looked at her.

"Oh, come on." She laughed. "New clothes, fancy haircut, surprise visit. You must have something up your sleeve, Max."

Birnbaum looked at David. His son was looking at him, too, it seemed, with interest, a small smile working on his face. Birnbaum got up and went to one of his bags, which David had set near the door, and pulled out a large manila envelope. His head was burning and he couldn't seem to shake the chill in his bones. He wondered if he was coming down with something, remembered Schteiner sneezing wetly into a hand towel all week.

He sat back at the coffee table and from the envelope pulled travel brochures. Full color, with bright arcing letters and exclamation points they announced a world of pleasure and utter ease — beaches, skyscrapers, mountain vistas ending in cloud,

Old World cathedrals and picturesque natives in costume, tropical fruit and foliage, young people everywhere at play. He laid these, along with the vouchers from his pocket, on the table before them.

"What's all this?" Janine said.

"A trip," Birnbaum said.

"A trip? For who?"

"For you. For us." He tried to explain. "I came into some money. David, you remember Levine, from Canada?"

David picked up two of the brochures, looked at them in his hand, did not respond to his father.

"A relation of mine," Birnbaum said to Janine, "an old man, passed away."

"I'm sorry," she said, looking from one man to the other.

"We weren't close," Birnbaum said. "Anyway, he left a sum of cash. I'm alone now, I find I don't need as much as I thought." He fingered a brochure of some island in the sun. A bronze giant of a woman in a tiara of flowers beamed at him. "I find it difficult, some days, to fill the time." Schteiner suddenly traipsing through his mind, trailing chlorine and cigarette smoke into Ruthie's rooms. His head felt filled with sand. At the airport he would call Schteiner on the phone. A mistake. David opened one of the brochures, dropped it back on the table, opened a second. Birnbaum looked at Janine. "A vacation," he said, reaching for his tea. He took a sip, sucking breathily. "I thought maybe we could travel someplace together."

"But where?" Janine said. She had opened one of the vouchers. "These don't have a destination."

"You fill in," he said. "Anywhere," he heard himself say, but his voice sounded far off, empty of conviction. Janine was smiling, yes, but Birnbaum had expected more, something was supposed to happen. That feeling from the plane, a lightness in the chest, a heaviness in the throat and head enfolded him. "Anyplace," he said. "Where would you like to go?"

"Max," Janine said. "I don't believe it. Let me get Daniel."

She went into the kitchen. This was not how he had pictured it, the telling, and weariness contended with disappointment in his mind. He had envisioned them around a table, the three of them, a cloth-covered table in a different house, spacious, lit with light, maybe a bottle of wine or champagne, even, to mark the moment. The plates, still holding good food, are spread before them, candles, music from a nearby room, his new granddaughter asleep in his lap. Scattered among the serving dishes are brochures, dreams come to life, all the colors of imagination right there, in your hands. Birnbaum makes a simple toast, "To good times," there are murmurs of approval, kindly protestations. He soothes the sleeping child in his lap. Then, finally, afraid to, he looks at his son.

Daniel burst into the room, followed by the dog, who immediately ran to the door and put paws up on the lacerated wood, scratching. Daniel stopped in front of his grandfather, two sticky hands on the old man's Italian slacks. "Mommy said we're going to Disneyland! Are we? Are we?"

"Would you like that?"

"Of course," the boy said. "That's the best idea yet!"

"Well, let's see what your father says, okay?"

"Yes!" Daniel shouted. He ran to the door. The dog was gone through the broken screen door before the boy could get it open, and then Daniel was gone, too.

"Daniel!" his mother called after him. "What have I told you about letting Barney run off like that?"

The boy came back to the door. "Sorry," he said. "I forgot."

"Is it raining?"

He looked behind him. "I guess so."

"Don't you think you should wear your coat?"

The boy took his jacket off the hook by the door and ran into the yard. Birnbaum heard him tell the dog, "You're Pluto, Barney. I'm Mickey."

They sat and looked at David. He folded the brochures and put them on the table. He leafed through the vouchers in their blue holders, examining each separately. Birnbaum watched his tea.

"You just don't get it, do you?" David said.

"Honey," Janine said.

"What is all this?" David said to his father.

"A trip," Birnbaum said. "A vacation, away from winter for a few days."

"When?"

"Now, I thought. Whenever. It doesn't have to be right away."

"And you've thought of everything?"

"Everything? I don't know . . ."

"You've arranged babysitters, leave for me from the nursery?" Birnbaum looked at his tea, told himself to take a sip. "Did you call the school and say Janine would be gone even longer? Did you find out if they would hold her position? Is there in your magic pockets a mortgage payment on this mansion, winter clothes for my kids?"

"David, your father's trying . . ."

Birnbaum pulled his coat closer, cold. It was time to go. David stood, Janine stood beside him, took one of his arms. Birnbaum looked briefly at his face, then away, to the side. The picture, now a mass of incomprehensible lines, now soldiers on horseback before a turreted tower, shimmered before him. He gazed at it.

"Just tell me," David said quietly. "What do you want?"

Birnbaum didn't answer. There was a tower there, and a castle, with a moat. A battle going on, yellow soldiers and black soldiers on horses.

"What do you want here?" David said. "This is my house. I live here. My family lives here. Did anyone ask you to come?"

Birnbaum spoke softly. "I thought I would be welcome."

"What do you want?"

Birnbaum didn't understand. The picture shifted again, agitated yellow stripes, brown dashes, a meaningless jumble.

"Tell me what you *want*," David repeated. "What is it this time? Am I raising my children wrong? Have I married the wrong woman again? Have your grandfathers been coming in the night and whispering about me? Or is it the old indictment—I'm not the son a man like you deserves."

Birnbaum watched his tea. In the light from the window, small currents and updrafts moved in the copper liquid, fronds of steam waved from the glass and disappeared.

Janine tugged on David's arm. "David, that's enough."

He shook her off. "No, Janine. This is the conversation we've been having all my life, it's time for you to hear it. Look at him, the doting parent, the kindly grandfather bearing gifts. So," he said to Birnbaum, "what is it this time?"

Birnbaum put his hands on his knees. He would lie down here a moment, they wouldn't mind. Then a cab would take him back to the airport, maybe Schteiner could meet him at La Guardia. From his wounded shoulder, a cold hand reaching into his chest. In his mind, suddenly, an image of the High Holy Days as a child, sixty years ago in Cracow, the cantor keening in misery and exultation, Birnbaum, a small boy, wrapped close under his grandfather's prayer shawl, warm, smelling the old man's fishy breath as they rocked together in the yellow light. "I came to be with family," he said, "to see my son."

David snorted. "Well," he said. "Here we are. Take a good look. I'm an assistant landscaper at Pavelich Nursery and Shrubs and we've got a new baby. Her name is Erin. Oh, that's right, you've met. On the side, I fix old cars for rich assholes. My wife is a second-grade teacher at Garfield Elementary on leave. We have hopes, someday, of her teaching high school. This is it," he said, sweeping an arm through the air. "This is where we live. Take a good look."

The door opened and Keith stuck his head in. He blinked twice, as if the light inside were too bright.

David took a step toward his father, then stopped. Birnbaum

could see his hooded eyes, a few gray hairs in his beard. "Don't let him fool you," David said to Janine. "This isn't for us. It's not about us, it's about him. It's always about him." He stood there, looking down at Birnbaum. Keith came up to his side. David put a hand on Birnbaum's shoulder. "You're not needed here," he said and began pulling Birnbaum up by his coat.

"David," Birnbaum said. Janine walked quickly around the table.

"Hey, Dave," Keith said. He put both hands on David's chest. "I think we're ready to drop that engine in." His hands were lightly on David's shirt, just touching with his fingers. "C'mon," he said.

David looked at Keith, shook his head. He released his father's coat, raised open hands in the air. They went through the door.

"Hey, Keith," David said outside, "you want to go to Disneyland?"

"Sure, man. Anything to get out of this rain."

Birnbaum took off his shoes and pants, hung his shirt and jacket over the back of the single chair in Daniel's room. A short bed with red, blue, and yellow dinosaur linen was made up for him. Four grinning two-legged turtles in bandannas waved weapons at him from a poster. On the pillow were two plastic horses, a black with white markings and a dun with a gnawed tail. Daniel had given his grandfather these to sleep with while he used the room. Janine had pulled back the blue comforter, showed Birnbaum the towels and washcloth, different colors each, stacked neatly on the foot of the bed. He lay facing the wall, coveting sleep, but faces filled his brain instead—Schteiner, Connie, the woman on the plane, Ruthie in bed those last few weeks, disappearing before his eyes, but calm, somehow, like the cat that got the canary,

Daniel covered with chocolate, and his son, looming over him. He lay with eyes open, unable to halt the procession of faces. Then quickly, like a sudden undertow, weariness dragged these images from his mind. He pulled the fainthearted misery of this house over his shoulders with the comforter, rolled on his side, and dropped headlong into sleep.

Birnbaum sat in the chair by the window watching his grandson in the rain. Daniel had some toys, a purple dinosaur, a doll in a striped shirt Birnbaum associated vaguely with a children's television show, a G.I. Joe in full combat attire. He lined these up by a shovel in the grass and walked before them, lecturing. Birnbaum could hear snippets of his high, emphatic voice. Barney, told repeatedly to sit in his place in line, enjoyed instead grabbing one of the dolls in his mouth, especially the fat dinosaur that kept tipping soggily into its own lap, running out to the street with his head shaking, then dropping it at his feet, looking back at the boy. Daniel would shout, "No, Barney! Do you want a bad spanking?" and eventually the dog would return.

He had been awakened from sleep by noises. He thought at first some animal had got under the bed, was scratching there at the wall. Then he realized, dragged bodily from dreaming, he was hearing whispers through the thin wall, from David's bedroom on the other side. They were arguing, trying to keep their voices down, especially Janine, straining to whisper, trying to get David to do the same. Birnbaum lay without moving.

David said, "I had to *work*, remember? Or don't we need the money all of a sudden he rolls in?"

"I'm sorry, David. That car's been sitting there a week. Suddenly it needs to be done *now?* You scared him half to death."

"Good. Let him be scared."

"David, he's an old man. He's your father."

"You think I forget that? You think there's a minute I don't know that?"

"David."

"Yeah? And what about this Disneyland shit? Martinique. Fucking Honolulu. Huh? Drop in from the sky like some miracle rabbi and scoop us off to Disney fucking land?"

"David, he's asleep."

"Calls in the middle of the night, drops out of the sky, pack your bags, we're off to Disneyland. Fuck."

And almost as if he could hear it coming, Birnbaum was moving before the hand struck the wall, a palm-open slap that he felt in his body. He heard, tried not to hear, movement in their bedroom, something falling over.

"He'll hear you!"

"Yeah? Don't bet on it. He doesn't hear anything. Acts like God took my mother just to make him miserable. Who does he think killed her off?"

"All right, that's enough."

"No." David was no longer whispering, no longer shouting. His voice was changed, higher. He sounded like Daniel. "Does he see this place? What does he think is going on here?"

"Okay, okay," he heard her saying. "Shh."

"Disneyland. How about Mars? Two weeks at the beach in Atlantis?"

"Oh-kay," and she was whispering again, the first syllable drawn out, the second falling like a caress. Then someone was crying and Birnbaum didn't want to hear. Janine said, "We'll get through this. Just take it easy." Birnbaum sat in the chair at the far side of the room, looking out into the rain. Daniel, done with the lecture, moved away from the house—could he hear the shouting, too?—and tossed the sodden dinosaur for Barney to chase. White stuffing leaked from one of the purple legs. From the other side of the wall, no more words, just the unbearable noise of his son crying, then different sounds, quieter, sounds, Birnbaum realized, of pleasure. David uttered a soft "Oh." Birnbaum, trying not to hear, turned closer to the window, muttering words in his chair, a Hebrew prayer for safekeeping.

He had fallen asleep again, or it seemed so, because when he awoke, things happened out of sequence, sound splayed off from sight. David and Daniel play in the yard, the father catching the boy, tossing him in the air, the boy laughing. The crunching of fast tires, a horn blast. A man gets slowly out of a pickup. Daniel is over by the car they are working on, helping, smiling as David hands him a wrench. Screaming, somebody is crying. Daniel hooks a toss of the dinosaur over the hedge into the road. Gleefully, the boy chases the dog chasing the toy into the street. Daniel laughing. Someone shouts. Crunching of tires, a horn blast. David is in the road, Janine, Keith kneeling. A honk and a spray of wild gravel. In the street, two forms, an unmoving dog and a toy dinosaur. The boy calls, "No, Barney!" and his mother is holding him on her knees, the man from the truck is kneeling over the dog with David's friend Keith. Then the father walks to the son and takes him from Janine's lap, to embrace him, it seems at first, but he begins hitting him, hard, with an open hand, holding him out with one hand to get at him with the other, grunting. In his dream David was a boy again. He and Ruthie and Schteiner were at a school play, proudly watching the boy in a white shirt and black tights, Judah Maccabbee wielding a wooden sword. Daniel's head turns as each slap reaches face, neck, head. Birnbaum can make out "I. Told. You. Never," and the boy at first is squirming, trying to turn his white face from the hand, then he goes limp, hangs from his father's grasp impassively absorbing the blows until Janine, then Keith, then Birnbaum running into the yard in his underwear, get David away from the child.

3

In the car, Birnbaum watched David and the road ahead. Keith and Janine had taken the dog, breathing in pants and with at least one shattered leg, to the hospital. Daniel and the baby were at a neighbor's, where the still tearful boy was promised he could eat cookies all night till his parents came home. Janine had said goodbye while David sat on the hood of the car, smoking. She was cold in a sweater and kept her arms around herself as Birnbaum embraced her. From crying, from exhaustion perhaps, her face was slack, sensual, and as he kissed her Birnbaum thought of David's hands on her, his hands on the boy.

"I'm sorry," she told Birnbaum.

"I didn't want this," he said.

"I know," she said quietly. She looked over his shoulder at the truck, where Keith waited and the dog lay on a blanket on the cab seat. "We'll try again sometime, okay?" She smiled and kissed him on the cheek, then moved around him to the truck.

Birnbaum looked at the rain while his son drove and smoked. Drops ticked lightly on the glass, and over the fields rain hung in far fringes, no difference between sky and earth, clouds in tiers, striating, some so low it seemed he could reach out a hand and touch them. He had never encountered weather to look at before, not right there for you to see.

David kept the wipers off until the window was dotted with rain, lights looping in prismatic arches across the glass. Then, like a man brushing away a fly, he would flick his wrist and turn the wipers on for a single swipe.

Birnbaum tried not to think. He watched his son, this man, forty now, deep in his own life, his own troubles. He felt an intruder—more, an upsetter of some balance he had no knowledge of. He knew, simply, he had to leave. Once Daniel was inside the house, Keith had given David a cigarette and the man in the pickup, after apologizing again and shaking David's hand, got in his truck and left. Birnbaum had walked up to David, smoke in his face, and said, "What is wrong with you? How do you hit your boy like that?" David had appeared for a moment as if he might answer, then looked at Keith, back at Birnbaum, his face working. The laugh, when it came, shocked the old man, twisting out of his son's mouth as the lips clamped down on the cigarette. It was a deep laugh, of pleasure, it seemed, and something almost like affection passed through David's eyes before he raised a blackened hand to wipe them. Birnbaum had left him, gone indoors to wait. Now, in the light of a passing car, Birnbaum saw the face tight around its cigarette, the eyes glancing in the rearview mirror whitened, wide. The anger that had swarmed in his guts was gone, and if fear was there still it was overspread with weariness. He would have liked to say something to his son—he wanted nothing now; he thought, this moment, little of the future or the past. He wanted to pass on something friendly, helpful, an older man to a younger. He, too, knew David's sadness—age bringing little comfort, instead soiled prospects, dimming hope—and felt if anyone could offer a kind word it was he. But he was tired. The airport was near, he was going home, back to Schteiner and whatever waited there. He put a hand to his face and thought, with startled relief, Now we are strangers. He closed his eyes and said nothing.

At the airport, David talked with the skycap while Birnbaum gave the man behind the stand his ticket. The man, a middle-aged coffee-colored man in a white shirt and blue cap, hummed a tune Birnbaum thought he recognized but could not place.

Throughout the entire transaction, pulling the ticket, checking the baggage, stamping the boarding pass, he did not cease his soft humming or look at Birnbaum once. When he was done, Birnbaum turned to David, who was handing the skycap some money.

"I'll get that," Birnbaum said.

"Already done," David said, as the skycap moved away with the bags.

Birnbaum breathed. "Well," he said, "David."

David took a last drag on his cigarette and tossed it into a puddle by the curb. They watched the cigarette end turn in the water. "Have a safe trip," David said.

"David," he said again, aware, suddenly, of the thousands of times in his life he had said or thought that word. He became aware of his heart beating, and his breath rose in him, trembling, as if he had run here from a great distance. "We didn't get to talk. I was hoping we would talk a little."

"Yeah," David said. "Well." He looked at his father, then away, at the taxis and cars lined three deep in the street. "It's like Janine said, just not the best time. Work, you know?"

"We should try," Birnbaum said, the words riding on air that seemed forced from his lungs. "I have some things I'd like to say to you. As a friend."

"Sure," David said, reaching already for the cigarettes in his pocket. "I'll give you a call." Then, as if in afterthought, he turned back to his father. "Look," he said, "about before. I had no right . . ."

Birnbaum shook his head, stopping the boy. They embraced, awkwardly, shoulders in the way. Birnbaum moved to kiss him and saw, with surprise, David's eyes on him, reflecting back his own familiar look, the dark glittering sorrow, abiding fear, an absolute certainty that the future, no matter how far it spanned before him, would hold no change. With an inward shudder, he turned away from this sight. The two men lightly touched hands and Birnbaum headed for the glass doors. When he looked back,

David was leaning over the steering wheel intently, jiggling something in the car to get it started.

Birnbaum sat with his eyes closed by the window as the rest of the passengers boarded, found their seats. He dozed through the familiar litany of safety procedures, opened his eyes once when he thought he heard Connie, otherwise kept them closed, hoping by his posture to entice sleep, but it wouldn't come. Outside, they had not cleared the cloud cover and rain pelted the small windows.

Next to him, as if by plan, sat another old woman, white hair in a stiff confederation of curls. She was reading the same *Cosmopolitan* he had looked at earlier, and Birnbaum thought of telling her about the article on the old movie star, but he hoped for sleep instead. Though he had barely spoken all day, he felt he'd had enough conversation to last him a long time. By the woman's feet was a quilted purse the size of a footstool, and under the seat in front of them she had crammed a huge flowered shopping bag which occupied nearly all Birnbaum's leg room.

He looked up the aisle ahead, again noting the odd angles in the cabin. In here, they seemed to be level, and except for the drone of the engines and the slight strain in his back, Birnbaum could not tell they were flying. The luggage rack above him vibrated minutely and a stewardess maneuvered a cart built within half an inch of either side down the aisle. A droplet of water hit his lap, and looking up, he noticed a small trail of water inching from the light strip to the window, where it fell to the floor.

The cabin started to shake harder, first separating somehow from the background vibration of flight, then seemed to lurch to the left. The stewardess, a young woman in the same blue uniform Connie had worn, fell onto a man two rows up and apologized, laughing, and wiped the shoulder of his jacket. The seat-belt sign, two hands reaching, went back on with a ding, and the co-pilot came over the loudspeaker to explain, in tones almost laughably calm and offhand, that they were experiencing some turbulence from the electrical storms outside. "Gave us a little kick in the keester there, folks. Nothin' to worry about."

In a few minutes the plane leveled off and the ride again became smooth. Outside his window Birnbaum could see a long carpet of cloud in the moonlight and on the horizon strobing lights like conflagrations in distant cities. Far off, huge gray clouds loomed. He sat back and concentrated on the drinks cart, which had stopped just a few rows ahead of him.

Suddenly there was a change in the air—for a moment gravity vanished and they floated, poised, above the clouds. Then they were in the clouds again, water against the windows, and the plane seemed to land on something hard—though it was, must have been, only air—with a terrible jolt that brought Birnbaum's breath all into his chest. Ahead a luggage rack burst open, toppling a red coat into the aisle, while behind it a bottle of French mineral water sprang open, unhurriedly spilling onto the floor. People were screaming.

The cabin seemed to torque on itself, diving, quivering in its fall. As in a dream, everything seemed to move faster and slower at once. A sound like escaping gas filled the cabin and from a panel in the ceiling plastic tendrils with yellow oxygen masks attached dangled before the passengers. Birnbaum saw hands grab for the masks. A young woman across the aisle frantically worked a mask over her crying daughter, then reached for her own. Before Birnbaum and the lady beside him, only one mask hung down. The woman, eyes wide with fear, snatched it and pulled the elastic quickly over her head. Something came over the intercom. Birnbaum couldn't hear it. The woman breathed deeply with her eyes closed a moment, then opened them and looked at Birnbaum. She had pale blue eyes, clouded with cataracts, and with each breath she breathed, she closed, then

opened her eyes and watched Birnbaum. He looked back help-
lessly. He thought, With you?

He fought to stand and check the ceiling panel for the other
mask. There was none. He sat back down, breathing shallowly,
holding a hand to his chest to measure its rise and fall. The
woman held on to her chair with both hands. He wanted to say
something to her once he got his breath. It seemed of vital impor-
tance that he say something to her. In his mind an image, suddenly, of David, on the other side of this storm, driving behind a
lit cigarette in the rain. "My son," he said to the woman. "He'll get
caught in the storm." But she didn't hear. They looked at each
other steadily, Birnbaum swallowing air, the woman breathing
deep, and they waited to see what would happen next. He put a
hand out toward her hand.

Then the stewardess, her blond hair uncapped, falling over
one shoulder, her face distorted behind her own oxygen mask,
reached a mask to Birnbaum from a vacant seat in the row
behind. When he couldn't get it on, she helped him. She told
him it would be all right. She told him to breathe calmly and he
tried, sucking thin air with difficulty into his aching lungs. He
stared, as did everyone else, at the front of the cabin.

The plane, again, climbed steadily. The vibrating in the cabin
diminished. The co-pilot's voice, with a jocular edge to it as if this
had all been a planned joke, a prank, came back on. In the tones
of a football coach explaining a busted play he apologized for the
jolt, said those ee-lectric storms were the dillies, but they'd out-
raced the sucker. He announced that as soon as the stewardesses
made sure everyone was comfortable, there would be drinks
throughout the cabin, first round on him.

Around Birnbaum, passengers began tentatively peeling off
their masks. Somewhere a baby cried and the air filled with noises
of relief, laughter, small victory cheers. The woman beside him
took off her mask and looked again at Birnbaum. He tried to
smile but couldn't get the muscles to work. He wasn't getting

enough air. He sat behind the mask, feeling its pressure on his face, still trying, with deep swallows, to breathe. From both shoulders now, cold hands reaching into his empty chest. He had something he wanted to say. He kept his feet flat on the floor and his hands on the armrests beside him. He held his eyes fixed on the woman, who watched him steadily from behind impermeable blue eyes. He breathed. With his feet on the floor and his hands on the armrests he braced himself as hard as he could into the seat back, as if to delay, for even a moment, the plane's inexorable course home.

"TO LIVE IN TIFLIS
IN THE SPRINGTIME . . ."

In the weeks following his death David Birnbaum saw his father everywhere. Here in the battered blue cap worn by a stranger in front of the library. Here in the angle of a head, the determined forward slouch of a man pushing a cart through the produce section of the market. At the nursery where he worked, a voice in conversation would bring him up short, a pair of stubborn eyes behind thick glasses—a woman asking where they kept the perennials—make him forget what he was thinking. Twice he thought someone was standing near his bed, watching him sleep, and opened his eyes only to find the moon had risen in his window, and once he got the crazy idea someone was singing in his kitchen. He had walked downstairs, holding his breath, feeling an idiot trying not to make the wooden stairs creak, but it had been—as he knew it would be—nothing, a passing car radio, the old refrigerator's disconsolate wheeze.

They had seen each other only twice in the old man's last years, both visits ending badly. At the time of his death David had made no plans to see his father again. Still, his passing—a neighbor had spotted him on the patio one morning, lying in his pajamas— seemed the sudden truncation of a long, unfinished argument which David surprised himself sometimes by missing.

Now, a year later, these moments of imbalance, of vertiginous, panicky recognition, were fewer. He saw his dead mother in the sunken immobility of his sleeping son's face, his father in the absolute, meditative isolation of his daughter reading a book under the table, her face in both hands. Sometime after his father's death, Janine had cleared the mantel of its clutter and David looked unwillingly several times a day at the framed picture of his parents, some wedding in Canada years back, to see unyielding reproof in his father's stiff-backed, dignified glower, his mother's weary, forgiving half smile. If he had had the courage he would have turned them to the wall. But over the months they had faded into familiarity, were now hardly more noticeable than their twins, Janine's stolidly benevolent parents on their Midwestern porch.

It had occurred to him recently that his dead parents were not actually looking out at him from the photograph but at some fussy cameraman, that they were tired, probably, from the flight, the heavy food, the—who knew?—dancing. That his father always drew himself up tensely when he had his picture taken, that his mother's feet were aching (they always had when she wore dress shoes), that maybe even that evening she was feeling her illness's first alien stirrings. It occurred to him that there was something in this photograph his parents had liked, and they had wanted him to have it. He was shocked one day to notice they were holding hands.

Erin was fast asleep in the car seat, clutching her filthy brown bear. She dragged it everywhere, parts of its synthetic fur stiff with dirt, but when Janine had washed it a month ago, the child had cried for hours. As he leaned into the back seat to kiss her, David saw a pink dribble of medicine on her chin. He felt her forehead with his lips and wondered if the fever was returning.

Beyond her, Daniel was lecturing two plastic lizards. David had thought he was asleep, too, but the boy had moved into a new stage recently, preternaturally alert, and he could watch his parents silently for hours. David circled the car and opened the passenger door, saw his son in the flat airport lighting. He didn't recognize the lizards, a yellow and a green.

"Hey," he said. "You're awake."

The boy lifted one lizard above the other and David couldn't tell if they were whispering to each other or about to fight.

"Erin's asleep," Daniel said, keeping his eyes on his toys.

"I know."

"I'm not a baby," the boy said.

"No, you're not."

After a brief scuffle of plastic mouths and tails, the lizards lay quiet in Daniel's lap. "Why can't I come?" he said again, his lips pursing and letting go.

They had been through all this at home. "I'll be back tomorrow," David said. "And Mom needs your help with Erin. Should I bring you a present?"

David watched the boy struggle with conflicting impulses—whether to maintain his annoyance, which had the advantage of making him feel grown up, or give in to the childish seduction of a present, which he realized was a ploy to induce his cooperation. Did he see it that way, his father wondered, every maneuver between them a balancing act, a transaction? Daniel's dark eyes moved across his face. "Two presents," the boy said.

David laughed. "Two? I'm only leaving for a day."

"One for going," Daniel said, "one for coming back."

He leaned in to kiss the boy and smell his hair. At the curb he kissed Janine, looked around the wet night as other passengers for the red-eye got out of their cars, said goodbye to their families. He breathed deeply. He had quit smoking nearly a year ago and was unnerved by the suddenness of his craving for a cigarette.

"Maybe this is nuts," he said. "Maybe I shouldn't go. I think her fever's back."

"We're all right," Janine said. "Go." She had been sick first, then Daniel, and now Erin. Despite what she said, she looked exhausted, disheveled and cold, in rumpled sweats from his architecture-school days, her hair pushed back unevenly from her face. Last night he had risen once to give Erin her medicine, had Janine been up, too? All night? A smudge of the pink stuff was on her forehead, near the hairline. "Do this," she said. "See your sister. Come back in one piece."

Erin had been refusing her medicine, not sleeping, pawing her infected ear. Before they left for the airport they had ended up on the kitchen floor with Erin pinned between his arms and legs, her outraged red face howling, Janine, crying herself, spooning in the thick, choking goop. He could still smell it.

"Okay," he said.

She kissed him again, gave him a brief smile, and from inside the car said, "Sleep."

It felt odd going directly to the gate, no luggage to check, just an overnight bag. The terminal after dark was a strange place, cave-like, throbbing icy light. He looked around for a cigarette machine, promised himself if he happened to pass one he'd buy a pack. Then he remembered they didn't sell cigarettes in machines anymore. Or was it just in airports? At the gate, waiting to board the plane, he felt a tingling unease in the neck and arms, as if people in line were looking at him, as if there were someone among them he should recognize.

As the plane banked eastward the moon was a limpid dot outside his window, a white porthole in the graying sky. Constellations dropped one by one into place. Looking at them, David acknowledged the thin edge of panic he had been riding for days, and told himself to breathe deeply three times, then three more. A stewardess came up the aisle, offering pillows and magazines. She smiled at him. "Think you can sleep?" she said. He accepted a pillow and thanked her, closed his eyes and awkwardly laid his head against the circle of watery light at his window. He told himself he could.

He had been dreaming a vivid and confusing dream as the plane thumped the tarmac, waking him. His grandfather, dead thirty years, was not dead at all but living quietly in an apartment crosstown. All these years David had known this but had some-how—how?—forgotten. Now he was racing up the dim stairwell to the second floor, fumbling for the keys, filled with dread that, after all this time, he was this morning too late. Inside, the old man was just as David remembered him, squat, barrel-chested, in a T-shirt and gray suspenders. White hair waved thinly from his head. He had no reaction to seeing his grandson, who stood just inside the door, wondering what to say.

At the passenger gate he saw Tim first, a broad, calm face tow-ering above the others, then, beside him, Rachel. They were by the far wall, Rachel holding two steaming cups of coffee, one of which she gave David as he approached. "Wow," she said. "You look like shit." She reached up to kiss him.

"Don't try to cheer me up," David said, extending a hand to Tim. The hand which took his was huge and dry.

"Did you sleep at all?" Rachel said.

"I didn't think so, but I must have. I had the weirdest dream."

"Tell Tim." Rachel took his arm and guided him up the pas-sageway. "He has the same dream every night."

"Really?" David said, needing to look up to see the man.

"Yeah," Tim said, embarrassed. "Waterfalls, mostly. Oceans. Sometimes birds."

"He has Disney dreams," Rachel said, happily squeezing David's arm. "He sleeps with a smile on his face. We'll sit up tonight and watch."

"Not really," Tim said, and for a moment David couldn't tell if he meant the dreams or the smiling or if he believed Rachel was serious about watching him sleep. This was David's first sight of Tim Ball, Rachel's new boyfriend ("Over forty and still dating," she'd announced on the phone. "Tomorrow on Jenny Jones"). From his name, and from what Rachel had told him—he was an underwriter for some New York company—David had conceived an impression of someone small, energetic, a nervous go-getter.

She had said nothing about his height—he must be nearly six-five—or the loose, unironic smile on his face. His size only served to magnify his quiet—he leaned forward to hear when you spoke, and he walked lightly, as if careful not to make any unnecessary noise. He was nearly bald, what hair he had left fringed neatly above his ears. David had never thought Rachel would be with a bald man. He didn't know what that meant—Tim was probably younger than he was. He looked at Tim, and at his sister, some unidentifiable emotion working loose in his chest. Tim reached out and took David's shoulder bag, and David, too tired to think of how to refuse, let him.

They drove toward Flushing Meadow Park, the marina still shaded in thin autumn light. There were neon figures, stories tall, on the walls of Shea Stadium, a red batter gripping a dim neon bat. Were they there last time?—David tried to recall. He remembered hanging out with friends years ago, smoking dope under the willows by the lake, off near the muddy, weed-clogged shallows. Once, a slimy brown figure took shape out of the ooze—a muskrat, they later learned from a book—and waddled toward them as they watched in stoned amazement, until it reared up on its hind legs and they remembered to be scared and ran shrieking from the park. Behind the Unisphere were the towers of what used to be a restaurant. He had brought a date up there in high school, his first date maybe, his mother had taken him to Macy's to buy a jacket. What was her name? He remembered they stood on her front lawn and kissed for a long time before she went indoors, and that night he was so elated and full of hope he hadn't been able to sleep.

"The World's Fair," Tim said, as if David had been speaking his thoughts. "1964. I must have made my parents bring me, I don't know, ten times."

"Where did you live?"

"The Island. Mineola." He smiled in the rearview as if this confirmed something about himself. "Remember the Magic Skyway?

You sat in your own Ford convertible and rode into the fabulous future. I loved that exhibit."

David didn't remember it. He remembered the Fair—never had he seen so many people, charging across the broad concrete walkways holding maps, a landscape of bizarre and alluring shapes out of a child's storybook. He remembered his grandmother pointing out the Unisphere, saying if they somehow got separated he needed to make his way there and she would be waiting. He remembered the faceless, churning crowds, his grandmother pinning a paper with his name and phone number inside his shirt (inside, where a bad person couldn't see), and he remembered thinking if he got lost here he would never be found. But nothing about the Fair itself. He must have read all about it, planned what to see, been several times. He remembered none of it.

Under a series of highway ramps David recognized the overpass where his father and he used to stand, Friday nights. There it is, he almost said, but Tim wouldn't know what he was talking about and Rachel, he remembered, hadn't been on those walks, anyway. He twisted to the right, then the left, trying to locate the exact spot, but the car was moving too quickly.

As they drove up, the neighbor, a pugnacious-looking Irishman named Groves, stood on his stoop, holding a small white dog to his chest. He acknowledged Rachel's wave with a curt nod, looking past them up the street, as if whomever he was expecting, someone important and interesting, would any moment turn the corner. David hoped this was not the neighbor who had found his father.

The house, from the outside, looked the same. The white stucco was worn, seamed with cracks, and the wooden molding sagged here and there, but it had been that way for years. The Japanese maple his mother had planted had grown hardly at all, but there it was, living still, a skirt of delicate red leaves below it on the ground.

Tim parked in the driveway, which the neighbor seemed to register with distaste. There was no room in the garage. David could see boxes, portable files, the treadmill his mother had bought years ago and had used to hang clothes on. Deeper in the gloom he saw the handlebars of dusty bicycles, his and Rachel's, perhaps, thirty years old.

"The guy on the other side put in a pool a few years ago," Rachel said. "When they tore down his garage they found all our shit—remember that car seat? They thought vagrants must have been camping out there, Mom told me. I said, Vagrants, huh? No kidding."

They led him inside and he stood in the dusky hallway, reluctant to enter. Had the house always been this dark? He remembered, when he had come home from college, even after, his mother always assumed two things—that he had not eaten a meal in days and had not slept since she had seen him last. She hustled him first to the table and then to bed, a nap before dinner, and though he told her she was being ridiculous, and enjoyed making fun of her fussing, he came for just this treatment, his mockery concealing a deeper easing, a gratitude. Home, then.

Tim turned on some lights and David looked around the room. The old coatrack, humped in coats and hats, the overflowing Mexican umbrella pot, somebody's cane sticking out. Ahead, over the stairs, ascending portraits of him and Rachel, two grimy kids holding hands in front of a Buick, posed shots up through high school and college.

Rachel came back for him. "C'mon," she said. "I promise I won't show you around."

They had moved in two months ago, when it became clear David and Rachel would not sell the house, not right away. They were welcome to it, David thought. Now he was surprised at how little progress they had made. Books had been moved from the shelves, replaced with pottery and CDs, and the worn sofa and side chairs were gone. The terrifying batik rabbi was down and some pictures looked new, but most everything else had remained, the collection of Hanukkah menorahs on one wall, the illuminated biblical manuscripts on another. On the dining-room table, as it had always been, a white cloth was laid, the huge glass bowl half-filled with fruit.

David stood at the door, thinking of those roped-off exhibits in museums—furniture and paintings, even silverware and books, all suggesting that sometime people had lived here, though you never really believed it. But this was his own life. He had lived nearly half of it in these rooms. The past loomed at him, seeped across the walls and floor. It was no longer something to be recalled from a distance—it was there in front of him, to walk into if he dared. He stood with one foot across the white doorframe and expected to hear his mother calling from the kitchen, see his father shamble into the living room, answer her over a shoulder, and lower himself into the big chair with the evening paper.

To Rachel he said, "It's the same."

"I know," Rachel said from the coatrack, where she flung her jacket and scarf. "It's too weird, I know. The first week we stayed in my old room upstairs, the Day-Glo flowers on the mirror, that tiny bed. Tim stuck out both ends. I wouldn't let him make any noise, like they could hear us." From a side table near him she picked up a squat stone figurine, a green Mexican god from one of their parents' trips. "I didn't think it would be so hard. I'm not sentimental. I thought we'd get in here with our stuff, a week, two weeks, tops, the place would be ours."

"They lived here a long time."

"Yeah," Rachel said, putting the figurine back where she had found it.

"I couldn't do this," David said, meaning to encourage.

"Upstairs is better," Rachel said. She pulled him by a hand into the room. "We got a new bed, your room is now my studio. It always had the best light, remember? Take a look if you like."

He noticed now several of her stained-glass pieces hanging in the far window, shelves filled with art books, her collection of antique glass-working tools.

"It's a nice house," he told her, taking off his jacket and adding it to the mound over the rack. "It'll be fine."

She smiled. "There's wine, not Manischewitz, real wine. And beer. And tofu and salsa. Pot in the freezer, if you want some. *The Nation* comes now, along with *Israel Today* and the *Jewish Spectator*. I've resubscribed to Mom's crossword club."

From the kitchen came sounds of Tim opening cupboards, gathering glasses.

"Anyway," Rachel said, "welcome back. Or something. It's good to see you."

These words could have been spoken anywhere, any time in their lives. David looked at her and realized he must be making her uncomfortable. He moved quickly and sat on the new striped couch, bouncing once or twice, adjusting pillows behind his back. She followed.

"Comfy," he said.

She ran a hand slowly through her hair. "Is it?" She smiled. "I let Tim pick it out."

He examined her closely for the first time, saw she had put on weight, it looked good on her. Her thick black hair was shorter, she wore dangly silver earrings, a sweater that looked expensive and handmade. His sister appeared prosperous and happy, a successful artist nearing middle age. He realized he had not hugged her when he got off the plane, that she had several times held his hands or touched him and he had not responded. Familiar disappointment coursed warmly through him. She pulled back her hair again and David understood, suddenly, that she probably hadn't slept any more than he had these last few days. He turned and put his arms around her, leaning awkwardly from the waist. She lifted her arms about his neck.

"This doesn't have to suck, does it?" she said.

"No," he answered. "Not the seeing you part. And Tim. He seems great."

Just then Tim came out of the kitchen. He carried one of their mother's scrolled-aluminum trays, and on it three glasses of tea, a plate of lemons, and a plate of cookies. He was so big and solemn, watching the amber liquid in the glasses, approaching quietly so as not to interrupt. He put the tray down on the wide coffee table and started to hand out napkins. He looked at them. Rachel brought a hand to her face, David tapped meditatively at his jaw with two fingers. No help. She snorted first and then they were both laughing, David trying to without noise, Rachel's laugh ringing through the room. She moved over to Tim, who stood there, smiling himself.

"We're sorry, honey," she said, reaching up to kiss his cheek. "It's just, Mom's fancy tray, and the nice glasses." She bent over the tray to appreciate it, but began sputtering again. "Linen napkins," she gasped. Then, "David. Would you like a cookie?"

Tim looked at David. "I thought you might want some tea."

"I would," David said. "Thanks. Ignore us. It's just, you coming through the door, holding that tray, you looked . . ."

"Like Mom in drag," Rachel said, laughing again and shaking her head to stop. "Adorable," she said. "Sweet and adorable. Really." She fell back onto the sofa and covered her eyes. "Jesus, I'm tired."

They leaned over the coffee table and passed around the lemon, honey for Rachel, sugar for Tim.

"Do you want real breakfast?" Rachel said. "Eggs and bacon? Chorizo?"

He looked at her.

"Just kidding. Strictly vegetarian. Mom's kitchen is still kosher, I guess. But there's eggs, cereal."

"This is fine," David said.

"Tim's the first man I've dated who likes tea," Rachel said.

"You'll have to marry him, then," David said.

Tim broke into a wide, open-faced grin. They drank the tea. David ate three cookies.

So," Tim said, "is it safe to ask? What exactly is an unveiling? Rachel tried to tell me, but I still don't get it."

"He's not Jewish," Rachel said, and David wondered at how casually this sentence could now pass through these rooms. "Christians put the stone up right away."

"Well," David said. "Jewish tradition, or maybe it's law, is that you wait a year until you erect the headstone."

"It's so the earth has a chance to settle, I heard," Rachel said.

"Maybe," David said. "Abba told me once it was because sometimes the spirit lingers by the body, wandering around. This gives the spirit a chance to, I don't know, to leave, I guess."

Tim looked interested. "Why do they linger? The spirits."

David looked at him. "I don't know," he said.

Tim nodded, Rachel reached across him for a cookie. David looked into the dining room and thought he saw a figure sitting in one of the chairs. Tim's jacket draped over the back. He felt a flare of heat in his chest, the dizziness from the plane returning. He heard an unrecognizable sound and closed his eyes, and when he opened them it was as if, without warning him, someone had altered the room, turned it a few degrees on its axis, done something to the light. He heard a soft chattering from the kitchen and it took him a few seconds to realize it was the kettle, boiling for more tea.

Rachel went to turn off the flame. Maybe she was right, he should try to eat something. He leaned back on the sofa and rubbed his eyes.

"I know it's stupid to say," Tim said, "it being your home and everything. But we're very glad to have you here."

David opened his eyes to see Tim looking at him, extending a hand across the table. Did he want David to take it? He awkwardly put out his hand, and Tim took it, covered it briefly with his other, then went to the kitchen to join Rachel.

David remembered last night. Driving to the airport, working through the streets of their small town to the highway, Janine and

Daniel were singing a song to Erin, the one about animals coming in twos to the ark, trying to get the baby to sleep. Daniel
changed some of the words to make them funny, he and his mom
did different voices. Erin was alternately enthralled, looking with
wet eyes at them in turn, then screwing up her face and howling,
squeezing hot tears onto her cheeks. David tried to concentrate
on the road, driving through a fine misting rain that made colored
streaks of all the lights, peering in the mirror for signs the baby
was quieting.

Ahead of him, to the side, a bicyclist. As he neared, the rider for
some reason swerved directly in front of him, into the middle of
the street. David cursed, thumped the horn hard, swung the
car sharply left, jolting the baby into a new series of breathy
howls, bringing Janine's panicked face forward. As he passed, he
pumped his fist in the rider's direction, saw, in the drifting illumination of his headlamps, a boy, a college kid maybe, dark lanks of
hair plastered above a face pitted with red marks and angry clus-
ters of scarring—some idiot kid out, God knew why, near midnight on his bike in the rain.

"Dumb fuck!" David shouted. He remembered raising his fist,
Janine bringing her hands up quickly, a reflex action to brace herself as she felt the car swerve, then looking at him, keeping them
up as she saw him, not the boy on the bike, but him with his fist in
the air, ready to strike.

Then, like a colder current drifting upward from the sea bottom, another memory—the dream he had been dreaming midflight, when he had woken to see the moon had set outside his
window, leaving a barren sky flecked with ice. He didn't remember the beginning of the dream, how he had reached this part, or
where this part led to. In a room somewhere he is pushing his
father, who faces him, hands hanging, no expression, if not
encouraging, then allowing. He shoves his fists into his father's
chest again and again, he can feel the thin clothing, the flesh and
bones underneath, hear the old man's escaping breath. Behind

him, unrecognizable sounds, somebody saying something, not his father, who stumbles to keep from falling and waits for the next blow.

David stood. "I have to," he said. "I never." He took a step toward the kitchen and stopped. "I need to call Janine," he said. "Is there a place I can wash up?"

Rachel and Tim were at the kitchen door, looking at him. "Upstairs," she said. "The blue towels are for you."

In the bathroom, with its oddly repellent lime-and-maroon tiles—when had this style been popular, to whom?—he washed his face, put his head low in the sink so he could splash his neck with cold water. Then he took off his shirt, his shoes and pants and underwear, and let them drop in a pile on the floor. He reached into the tub and turned on the shower. The spigot coughed several times, then shot out water, ringing off the tile walls. He stepped in. It was too hot. He let it hit his back and neck, turned so it could hit him in the face.

That day, a year ago, he had been working with a crew down by the river, planting cherry trees in a newly cleared park for the city. The autumn sun worked through early clouds, lighting the tree-tops on the river's far bank in red and yellow. Some bird, a hawk or an osprey, circled high above. The two men with him were talking about a fishing trip and David stopped work repeatedly to watch the river as it curved northward around a woody bluff. When, for some reason, he felt it to be the right moment, he left the crew and walked to the edge of the riverbank where mounds of freshly turned earth steamed in the late-morning sun. He climbed one and looked at the water. He waited for whatever would fill his head to arrive.

Rachel and Tim were dressed, ready to go. They sat a little apart on the sofa, waiting quietly. The tea tray had been cleared and a vase filled with purple mums now lay on the coffee table, near it a candle burning in a short glass. David came downstairs wrestling with a tie he had taken from his bag. He used to put one on every morning without even having to think. Now his fingers fumbled the cloth and he had tried three times but couldn't get the ends right.

Rachel met him at the foot of the stairs. "Here," she said. "Let me."

He felt he should apologize, but couldn't put his finger on exactly what for—for taking too long? Had he? For his strange behavior earlier? He tried to shake off his confusion and said, "What time are we supposed to be there?"

"Two. The rabbi said it would take about twenty minutes. They unveil the stone, say some prayers, then leave time if anybody wants to say anything."

She finished the tie and smoothed it on his chest with a couple of pats. He walked to the mirror over the mantel to check his face and hair.

"It's a nice spot," Rachel said. "I like the little hill, and the tree nearby. I go there sometimes to talk to them."

"You do?" David kept his eyes in the mirror. "What do you say?"

"It's silly, actually. Silly stuff. I tell them secrets. I tell them how I feel. I say things to them in the ground I could never say when they were alive."

David turned and saw them together on the couch, Tim in a gray suit and white shirt, looking like a benevolent school principal, Rachel in a short pastel dress and sweater, one hand in his lap.

"Sometimes I tell them stories," Rachel continued. "I just stand there and make things up, or I tell them stories they told me when I was a girl. Remember the one about the girl who keeps asking her parents to take her to the amusement park so she can see the Ferris wheel, and when she gets there she's too scared to get on? Remember? I tell them that one. I don't know why, it makes me feel better."

David and Daniel had been making up stories together, about the Green and Pleasant Land where King Daniel ruled over a happy people with Queen Amanda—a girl Daniel liked in his class—and fought with the Blue No-necks across the river. In each story King Daniel and his advisors saved the day by relying on their ingenuity and endless knack for improvisation. The boy loved the stories and would demand one whenever they took a walk or went for a drive, fiercely guarding their integrity, correcting his father when he got a name wrong, or missed a chronology. "No," he'd say, looking at his father with puzzled annoyance. "That's not right." Stories had unity, the boy believed, things added up.

On the phone Janine had said the baby was better, that Daniel had hit his head but was fine.

"What happened?" David asked.

"He's having a backwards day," Janine said. "Walking backwards, wanting dessert first, all his clothes are inside out. He bumped his head on a door."

"Is he okay?"

"Yeah. He stood there and thought about it and said, 'Head my oww.'"

"Tell him I'm having a day like that, too."

"He misses you."

"Me, too. Tell him. And you," he added.

"See you tonight," Janine said. "We'll be at the gate."

Rachel picked up a small cardboard box from her feet and held it in her lap. He went over and sat by her in a side chair.

"I've been saving this," she said. "It's from Abba's night table, what we found there. Some of his things. I thought maybe you'd want them."

He took the box from her and held it unopened.

"I just thought you might want them," Rachel said again.

Tim rose from the couch and said sometimes his Civic was balky in the changing weather. He'd be outside warming it up, whenever they were ready. They both watched him get his coat and leave, as if this were part of a sequence that would reveal what needed to be done next. After he had gone, Rachel came over and sat on the arm of David's chair. She ran a hand briefly over his head and took one of his hands.

"It's okay," she said. "I tell them about that, too."

"What?" He had to turn his body to look at her. Her being so close was overwhelming, her hair, some scent she wore, the proximity of her arms and legs.

"About you. That Janine and the kids are great. That you're becoming a terrific landscaper. That you'd come when you were ready."

He let out a short breath, meant to be laughter. "Am I?" he said.

"I don't know," she said.

He gave her hand a small shake. "I wish I could have told them some things, too."

"Like what? What would you say?"

"That I'm okay, I think. I think we're happy, Janine and the kids and me. That they don't have to worry."

She took her hand from his and put her arm around his shoulders. "Well," she said, "maybe they know that already."

"I'd apologize, maybe. I don't know. Say I was sorry."

She touched the back of his head with her fingers, moved them through his hair.

"For what, David? Everyone's sorry, everyone knows. We all meant to do better." She tugged gently on his hair. "I'll be outside," she said.

He watched her stand and get her jacket from the rack and go out through the open door. He heard the car revving and, intermittently, the sound of their voices.

He reached into the box on his lap. Inside he found two pens, a worn Parker and a Bic, a bottle of stomach tablets. A notebook with memos the old man had left himself: "Monday, dentist," and "Vitamins, milk," and "Call about shoes." There was a battered hardcover book with a collage of gray numbers—years, he realized—on the jacket. Isaac Babel, white letters read. A plastic ruler marked a page. He opened to the marker and read a sentence: "To live in Tiflis in the springtime, to be twenty years old and not to be loved is a terrible thing."

He started to read the story, something about a printer's apprentice in a strange town, lonely, looking for love. The letters were small and the browned pages gave off the sweet, musty air he recalled from his father's library. It made his head swim. He closed the book and put it down. He would read it later. He took the last items out of the box, his father's broad-faced Bulova watch, a faded handkerchief, clean and neatly folded. Sixty-two cents in change. A creased photograph of the four of them at a lake one summer years ago.

He knew the story behind Daniel's backwards days. Last year the boy had gone through a difficult period. Ill twice in one month with strep throat, he had missed school, and returned to find he had a lot of catching up to do and that his two buddies, Eric and Ben, had, at least temporarily, consolidated their friendship without him. They had code words they wouldn't tell him and a special handshake. There had been some crying, he had slept badly a couple of weeks, didn't eat well. One Sunday he came out of his bedroom backwards, tried to speak that way, asked for dinner instead of breakfast. After watching him struggle to dress backwards, come and go from the yard only through the back door, they had questioned him. "Well," he had said, looking at them solemnly as if to indicate he would break his discipline momentarily for their sake, "I'm not so happy about the way things are right now. I liked them better before." Doing every-

thing backwards, he hoped, would help return things to their earlier, happier order.

It was a story his parents would like to hear, David thought, pic-
turing them together in this room, listening to him tell it. They
were a family who liked stories, liked to read together and have
guests over for conversation and debate. His father would enjoy
telling stories from the old writers, Berkowitz, Peretz, Babel.
David remembered the story about the girl and the Ferris wheel,
his father used to tell it, and one his mother had about an old aunt
who used up all her words. There were stories about Moses and
Abraham, about Elijah, who would appear disguised as a poor
man whenever a Jew somewhere needed a miracle. Once his
father had told him about being a boy, falling into a dry stream
bed in Poland and breaking his leg, lying there, unable to climb
back to the road. Cold and scared he had started to sing and a Polish farmer he had never seen before heard the singing and carried
him home. His mother had wanted to be a doctor, had planned
privately to be one all her childhood, but it hadn't turned out that
way. He remembered Rachel and that guy from Rumania, what
was his name, Alex, all the trouble she had had. He thought of
Janine before he knew her; of his first wife, Maura, a potter now,
somewhere off in the woods. Of Daniel's fierce tales of combat
with his lizards and warriors and imaginary kings; of Erin, staring
out at the world, patiently waiting for her stories to begin. This new
guy, Tim, he had stories, his meeting Rachel was one, the World's
Fair was another. If he wanted to tell them, David would listen.

They're everywhere, David thought, forgotten, saved up, never
told, stories told over and over until finally someone believed
them, until they worked. Maybe that's as close as you could come
to knowing anyone, he thought, hearing their stories. His own
confused him, seemed so fragmented and without pattern, cru-
cial pieces missing, some of the mistakes he had made so irre-
deemable, at times he felt frozen with loss. From the midpoint,

maybe beyond, he struggled to make sense of it. If he had a story it was one he didn't understand. Maybe his parents, at the end of theirs, understood more.

He looked at the snapshot in the pile by his feet. It was taken one summer, maybe the last they had all spent together. They had gone to a lake upstate for a week. David was in college, if he remembered right, Rachel finishing high school. There was a photographer staying at the hotel, some amateur trying, in his inept, smiling way, to make some moves on Rachel. He had suggested a family shot, a commemorative portrait, and though Rachel was embarrassed by his clumsy attention, and David and his father had ignored the man, his mother, to everyone's surprise, had thought it a good idea.

On the last day, before they were to return to the city, they had ended up by the lake, this oafish man, smiling over his tripod, leering at Rachel's thin peasant blouse, hustling them around, endlessly looking through his lens, holding up a light meter he wore on a ribbon around his neck. Somehow he had gotten the idea of them all sitting together in one of the rowboats tethered to the dock. Why not? They had clambered in, helping their mother, who was scared of the water, and when they finally sat down the boat wouldn't stop rocking. The photographer was taking readings, scuttling up and down the wooden dock. "The light's perfect," he called. "When I tell you, look at me and smile." But they weren't paying attention. The boat would not stop rocking, however they tried to balance themselves, and then they had all seen their mother's face, sternly worried and taking on a green cast. "Is it safe?" she asked them. They were laughing, even she, at her own fears, and the boat would not stop moving. They had just reached out to put their arms around each other, thinking that might help, when from the deck the man with camera said something and they all looked up together.

For Marnie Pavelich

EIGHT RABBIS ON THE ROOF

Feeling his way through darkened rooms, he is downstairs for the third time this night, stumbling over aching feet to the bathroom. Before him black shapes of furniture sit immobile, consoling reference points. But in the kitchen, to his right as he passes, his father is scraping plates at the sink. The lighting is unnatural, stage-set, which should be a tip-off, but Birnbaum is in a hurry, can't right now be bothered. He makes it to the little room, closes the door behind him, urgently grapples for the light.

Then nothing. Not five inches away, his bladder shoots emergency messages to the brain: What are you waiting for? Hey! Anybody up there? But all he can manage is a few lank drops, strangled, they plat despairingly in the toilet. Used to be he would fill the bowl with foamy gurgling noise, golden water. No longer.

So he concentrates, plants his feet. Pulls, shakes, closes his eyes. Thinks: Niagara Falls. Suggests opened floodgates, bursting tropical cascades. Nothing. He gives up, washes his hands with one of her leftover soaps for guests, a pink seashell rubbed featureless. No towel, he uses the sides of his pajamas. Then heads back upstairs to where sleep, a blue bastard, sniggers just out of reach near the ceiling.

In the kitchen, still, is his father, sleeves rolled on his pressed white shirt, drowning plates, grabbing glasses by the neck and slamming them in soapy water. Thick hair-covered arms, suspenders, belly propped against the sink's dripping ledge. Expression so familiar Birnbaum can read it like a billboard—who lives like this? a *chazer*, that's who, needs a dead man to do his cleaning. He makes faces, holds a nice pot out by the handle, drops it, soup and ladle and all, in the trash.

From the doorway Birnbaum watches impassively a moment, massaging his chest, registering his incapacity these days for surprise. Good. He wants to clean, let him clean in the dark. He chops the light switch, pauses on the seventh step to enjoy a painless, trumpeting fart, and climbs the stairs to bed.

Downstairs, not even sure what woke him. Something remembered, something overheard—sleep spread out before him like paradise, endless, with open arms, then something rattles his head and he is downstairs stubbing toes in the dark, a clumsy thief in his own house. Anybody sleeping here? he wants to shout. For a nap he would slice off three fingers smiling.

So what is it, the bladder? Probably. Dead weight, a soft unstopping punch in the belly. It sags on him, begging for attention. Let it.

Sometimes walking helps him decide—ready or not. He wanders, turning on lights, turning them off, looking into corners. He never realized they had nine chairs, twelve if you count the three in the kitchen. The coatrack looms suspiciously a moment, then subsides—coats, a couple of hats, somebody's red scarf. From the bookshelves faces goggle at him, stunned, as if they, too, despaired of sleeping. Only over the mantel a batik rabbi exults, souvenir of their last trip together, lifts a Torah and his shining face toward heaven. Show-off, Birnbaum thinks, moving unhappily away. He picks Ruthie's afghan off the sofa, familiar bristle on his fingers, stale wool smell in his nose. Maybe he could lie here a minute, a quick doze, forty winks, thirty, even—who could argue? But no, he came down to do something. What was it? He

folds the afghan once, again feeling in his chest a curious lightness, a suspension, like something about to drop. He counts
glasses and saucers on the coffee table: six, seven. Must be a glass
somewhere. Two coffee cups. In a saucer, four orange seeds. He
begins counting oranges in the glass bowl, stops himself.

In the center of the room he catalogues body parts: head a little
achy, eyes also. Shoulder like he's been hung by it for a week—
nothing new there. Feet frozen solid. Stomach? Not so bad, could
be worse. So wait. And inside? At the hospital, when he woke up,
lying there hooked up like Frankenstein's monster, they asked
would he like to listen. He listened—a window shade flapping in
the next room. Traitor, banging his ribs, no longer pleased with
the accommodations. Who's pleased? he asks. Do I look pleased?
At least it doesn't nag, like the bladder, which he now remembers—ready or not? Maybe ready. Move yourself.

In the bathroom a gay trill, a little brook burbling, then turns
off suddenly like someone's in there with a wrench. He curses,
squeezes, shakes, waits. Turns on both faucets and closes his eyes.
He looks at the short rumpled hose in his hand with dispas-
sionate unfriendliness. You. It looks back, unmoved. You, too. He
reaches for the faceless soap and searches the room for a towel.

But, on his way upstairs, lights blazing in the kitchen like a
party, like a pogrom. When was he in there? Not this night. By
reflex he wants to raise his voice—listen, you want to burn money
let's build a fire, do it right—but no one is here to hear it. Pity. He
leans in, fingers the switch, and sees, at the head of the table, by
the napkin holder and the box of Sweet 'n Low, his father reading
the Yiddish paper under the lamp. He is in his underwear, the
striped boxers and yellowed undershirt, as if it is summer, Brooklyn, 1967. His glasses are propped on his domed forehead and he
licks two fingers to turn a page. He sighs at some piece of news
and makes noises just like a man reading the paper.

Enough, Birnbaum decides. It must be two in the morning.
Enough is enough.

He approaches, pulls a chair out, deliberately scraping. He sits noisily, feeling with satisfaction his dense, fleshly bulk settling around him, as if this is the first card he plays. He looks at the typeset letters as if to bore a hole in them. He reads a few. So that's how you spell Giuliani in Yiddish. With renewed respect for the vigors of the imagination he suggests to himself some improvements in conjuration next time — Cyd Charisse, for instance, on a beach in Havana.

He pokes the newspaper, just to see his hand glide through, bumps instead the bony gristle of his father's thumb. "Ooof!" says the ghost, lowering the paper in dismay. At Birnbaum he directs outrage, shocked vanity, positioning his glasses over his eyes to heighten the effect. "Sorry," Birnbaum mutters, pulling his hand away, thinking, Congratulations, now you're apologizing to dead men. His father continues to look at him. Birnbaum gestures with both hands, palms up, Sorry, again, thinking Who invited you, anyway?, thinking Thirty years and not so much as a hello. Even up there they couldn't teach him manners.

He recalls some dreams in movies, maybe he could reach out and twist a little pink skin on the old man's arm, chase him back to dreamland. Light a match. Show him a mirror. Looks real, anyway — sparse white hairs on his head adrift, a vein over the left eye throbbing. Excellent detail, Birnbaum concedes, always ready to admire good craftsmanship.

He clears his throat and waits. He can sit also. Eventually the old man will tell him what he wants. His father reaches for the paper, pushes up the glasses, brings two fingers to his lips, making it clear he has no such intention.

That's it for Birnbaum. He stands, ready to go. He says sourly, "They don't even have a Yiddish paper now. Only English. Only once a week."

The old man looks at him now, around the paper as around a shower curtain, immortal exasperation covering his face. Birnbaum understands this look. In his head he hears the words as if somebody is whispering in his ear. Seventy-two years, it says, and some people still can't see what's in front of their noses.

Birnbaum dreams. Inept, infuriating dreams, they chase him from sleep and are useless, ridiculous to him awake. Jacob wrestled with angels, saw ladders to heaven. He:

Two folding chairs, someplace. Next to him a man in a green suit unwraps gum, pulling a stick from the package, teasing the paper without ripping, an expert, taking his time. He chews thoughtfully a minute, then pulls out the pack and begins again.

Some hotel, he can't find his room. His key opens every door, but in one room he finds a young couple looking at a TV, in another two men cooking eggs. Another room is empty, even of furniture — a blue candle lies on the carpet — and in the last room all the windows are open, wind knocking curtains back against the wall. It is a big hotel and already his feet hurt — rooms stretch as far as he can see on either side of the corridor.

In an airport lounge, he watches planes. One taxis slowly, a stewardess waving from the window. He feels a bump against his shoe. A young boy pushing a truck across the carpet. Something wrong with this boy. The seats around him are full of people, something wrong with them, too. The boy looks up and Birnbaum realizes what it is. He looks at the people. They have the same noses, every one of them — there must be a hundred — the exact same nose, slightly wide, a little bumped maybe, not too bad, actually, as noses go, the boy looking up at him is a handsome fellow, but, still — everyone?

He dreams he is dreaming, from the ceiling he watches himself, blissfully, utterly reposed, sleep like he has not known in forty years, the sleep of the clear-conscienced, the empty-bladdered, on clean sheets in a more comfortable bed. Dreams flicker across his sleeping face like pictures on a distant screen. He drifts around the bed, watching himself.

Then awake like the bed is on fire, fear thrilling the blood, heart walloping, downstairs before he knows it, feet aching stones on the cold floor, swimming through black water for the kitchen's yellow light.

Surely it is near morning. Where had he left his watch? At the kitchen table, his father, thirty years dead, sits reading the paper. With him are two old gentlemen, unpleasantly familiar to Birnbaum. They, too, have papers, Russian, if he had to guess, and some Oriental lingo, designs Birnbaum has never seen before. The light from the lamp is not good, and they lean toward it, as if for warmth. No one notices him come in.

He should have found his slippers first, his feet are ice. He puts a hand to his chest, rubs there. Slow down, he tells its airy, fluttering tenant. Something got him going, something he ate, maybe, or a dream. He moves to the sink. If he waits long enough someone will say something, at least look up. No one does. He fills a glass with water, he drinks. He shuffles his feet, clears his throat—Listen, who's the ghost here, anyway? Wearily, he gives in, and walks over.

"Abba," he says. "Look. It's me."

The old man lowers the paper, pulling his glasses over his face. He nods, confirming something to himself. "I didn't make tea," he says and raises the paper again.

"I'll get it," Birnbaum offers.

"Sugar," he hears from behind the paper. "Lots sugar." The other men look, too.

"No lemon?"

"No. No more lemon."

Birnbaum boils water, pours it in four steaming glasses, cuts lemon for himself, and brings spoons, the yellow box of sugar to the table. He remembers a bag of cookies, finds it on a shelf. There are six left, not counting two broken and one with a bite missing. He arranges a plate, wondering, Do ghosts like cookies? Maybe cake? But cookies is all he has.

The old men fold their papers neatly, Birnbaum's father puts them on a chair. As Birnbaum watches, his father pours a stream of sugar for several seconds into his glass. It collects in a thick sediment at the bottom. The other two men watch with interest; when it is their turn they do the same. Birnbaum busies himself squeezing a lemon over his tea, dropping it in. One of the old men offers him the sugar, smiling with one brown tooth exactly in the center of his lower jaw, blue eyes filmy with cataracts. Birnbaum puts up a hand, No, thank you. His guests lift their glasses in unison. They smile.

"Beautiful," his father says to the men. Then to Birnbaum, "This they haven't got."

"What?" Birnbaum says. "Tea?"

His father takes a sip, a long sucking sound, as he had taught Birnbaum to do, mixing air with water so as not to scald. The others try theirs. They move tea in their mouths, savoring, raise their chins to swallow. For a moment they sit with eyes closed. Then his father says, "Anything?"

They shake their heads sadly, first one old man then the other.

"Nothing," Birnbaum's father agrees, shaking his head, too. He puts his glass down.

"It's not good?" Birnbaum asks.

"No taste," his father says. "Smells, yes, even better than before. But taste—nothing."

He leans back in his chair and Birnbaum examines him closer. You would have to say, for a man in the ground thirty years he looks terrific. His round bald head, with its full lips and vigorous, bushy eyebrows, sits firmly on shoulders which sprout tufts of thick white hair. His arms are solid, if not muscular, and his skin, if it's possible, looks even better than Birnbaum remembers, ruddy pink, healthily glowing. He looks more alive than I do, Birnbaum thinks, resentfully. The others, too, appear remarkably healthy. Birnbaum reaches out a hand to touch, but his father raises both hands to stop him.

"Please," he says. "No contact physical."

"No?"

"They got rules."

"Even there? There's rules even there?"

"Rules they got everywhere," his father says.

They drink the tea in silence, the old men clearly not enjoying it. One stops several times to stir in even more sugar, until his glass is sandy water, shaking his head after each morose sip like a master chef who has suddenly forgotten how to cook. They are wearing shapeless, colorless robes, the kind handed out by institutions, caps the color of old linen.

"Who are they?" Birnbaum asks, gesturing with his head, whispering to be polite. His father is holding two cookies, smelling one, then the other.

"You don't recognize?"

Birnbaum looks at the men. Both have high-domed foreheads, wide serious faces, expressions not quite friendly or un-. "No," he says.

His father nods, again the familiar bloom of long-suffering disappointment.

"Why? Should I?" Birnbaum asks.

His father opens a hand, closes it: Who's to say? He takes a small nip at a cookie.

Birnbaum sits back in his chair, gives the two men a smile to show they are welcome, even though, strictly speaking, they aren't. "So tell me," he says. "What's it like?"

His father shrugs. "Not so bad."

"No?"

"No. At first a little strange. Not painful so much—more

uncomfortable." He looks at his son. "You been to the doctor, you have to wait with the magazines?"

"Yes," Birnbaum says.

The other two men nod. "Then you know," his father says.

"That's it?" He feels foolish, as if he is being lied to. "But what do you do all day?"

His father nibbles the other cookie, puts them both down on the plate. "Day is not a permanent useful concept."

"No?" Birnbaum looks around the table. "No day? No night?" They shake their heads. The man with one tooth opens a hand, lifts both eyebrows—he doesn't understand it either.

"Still," Birnbaum persists, "you must do something to pass the time."

"You wait," his father says. "You discuss, you argue, you remember. What you did here, you do there. You liked to talk, you talk. Not, not. Mostly, you wait."

"Wait? For what?"

"For the next thing."

Birnbaum opens his mouth to say something else, decides against it. The men look into the air before them, one scratches something under his dingy cap. Birnbaum sighs. If his vision of the afterlife is a ward for senile old men, who can he blame but himself? The tea is giving him heartburn. He should be in bed. He looks around for the clock but can't find it. He looks beyond the silent men to the windows but there's not much he can tell—indeterminate gray, sometime past midnight, not yet morning.

He must have turned the heat down by accident, first his feet, now his legs are so cold they throb. And it must be the tea, or the cold, now reaching into his chest, tightening around his ribs. The middle of the middle of the night, he suddenly thinks, then remembers that's what his father would say to him, sixty-five years ago, when he couldn't sleep. "What time is it?" he would call, propped in his bed in the corner room, the sound of rain, moon-light or its absence having woken him. "Abba, what time is it?" "The middle of the middle of the night," his father would say, just his top half leaning in the room, illuminated from the hall behind him. "Go back to sleep. Plenty time to dream." Birnbaum looks at his guests, patiently, amiably bored under the lamp.

"And my mother?" he asks. "Rachmil?"

His father doesn't look at him. "They send regards."

"How's the hip? Is she well?" The old man starts to make a face and Birnbaum interrupts him. "Not a useful concept?" The old man nods.

Birnbaum slides a hand across the white tablecloth, pushing aside cookies and a discarded wedge of lemon. All three men look at him and he leaves his hand where it is. He doesn't want to ask but he does. The words seem to force themselves from his throat. "Please," he says. "My Ruth. At the end, so much pain . . ."

His father distributes the newspapers, still won't look at his son, who can barely breathe now, emotion pressing from all sides. His father opens his paper to the middle. "Waiting," he says.

He counts. The number of candles on his mother's table, Cracow, 1935: nine. The number of shoes in Ruthie's closet: forty-seven (how, forty-seven?). The number of times he has voted for President, ten, no, nine, 1992 he was out of the country. The number of pills in a bottle of Anacin, magazines by the TV, shelves in the refrigerator: sixty-eight, twelve, three—who needs to know such things? The number of knobs on his dresser, tooth-brushes in the bathroom, spoons in the kitchen drawer. He counts desperately, greedily, moves in and out of sleep like a man stuck in a revolving door. Ejected finally, he sprawls downstairs, counting the steps as he goes.

. . .

Awake, entirely, as if he has not slept, the blankets massed around
him, the sheets he lies in wet. Through the open bedroom door
he sees the open door of the bedroom opposite, framed through
that the window in the room's far wall. Absurd, he tells himself,
in his own house, don't be crazy, roll over and close your eyes.
But he doesn't. The three rectangles loom, recede, then, as he
watches, move again toward him slowly, unable to turn away,
three square-shouldered men approaching silently in the dark
house.

He wakes suddenly, his arm numb where his head must have lain,
his jaw aching, mouth sticky from slobber. He hears noises from
downstairs. Robbers? Did he leave the TV on? He sits at the edge
of the bed and feels for his slippers underneath. The two mirrors
opposite him are wells reflecting darkness. He looks away. He
moves carefully to the door, the top of the stairs. He works to get
his breath. Below him, where the stairs turn to the kitchen, an
edge of light dimly pulses, carrying sound. He cocks his head,
pushes an ear forward. He hears prayer, singing, laughter. He
hears drawers rummaged, chairs moved, the shimmer of bottles
in the refrigerator as it is opened, closed, opened again. The
whiny scratch of violins. He takes two steps down, hesitates. He
keeps a hand on the banister, cranes his neck forward to see.
There, on the third step, he waits, afraid to move.

His kitchen is full of old men. Every light is blazing, by the sink,
in the oven hood, the two concentric ceiling rings, the lamp

above the table. All the cabinets are open, ransacked, puddles of rice, dry beans, conical mounds of flour and spice litter the floor. Upended boxes of cereal, baking powder, bread crumbs. A tub of yogurt sits on its lid, oozing fatly; a stick of margarine stands at an angle on the tile, a yellow salute. The radio has been moved from the living room, and it plays klezmer music from behind a sweating whitefish by the sink. Birnbaum takes a cautious step into the room and stubs his toe on a potato, which sends the Quaker on his tube spinning, then skitters across the tile to thud against the back door.

At the stove three old men tend a cooking pot. They hover, hold ladles, wooden spoons, a spatula. Birnbaum steps closer and sees, in the pot, tea bags, all he had, maybe three dozen, flailing in the brown swirl like drowning men coming up for air. The old men sniff, carry spoonfuls to their noses, poke each other's bony ribs, and smile. They are in holiday clothing, unbelievably tattered, fur hats that look gnawed on, long coats with peeling colored patches, fringes the color of cat's teeth trailing to the floor.

Two more are at the refrigerator, one passing food, the next examining it, dropping it. Peppers, lettuce, detonated tomatoes form a heap of compost by his feet. The man on his knees passes two eggs, which he barely looks at, adds to the pile. They locate a lemon, take turns holding it, bringing it to their noses. The man in charge of disposal licks it, then tries to fit it, whole, in his mouth.

At the table Birnbaum's father sits in a dignified blue suit, like the ones he wore to shul on High Holy Days. Another man, even older than the rest, is in the chair beside him. His father leafs through a stack of index cards, reading, making notations with a pencil stub.

"You people have trouble with your landlord?" Birnbaum says, pulling out a chair.

His father is not amused. "Show respect."

"For what? For who? I should call the police on you." At the refrigerator they have found onions. The man on his knees peels one while his companion looks at another closely, then takes a big bite, right through the crinkly brown skin. He straightens and looks before him with startled eyes. "Who *are* these people?"

"Family," his father says, making notations on a card.

"Family? Whose family?"

"Yours."

"Mine? I've never seen one of them before, not one."

His father turns over a card, gives him a bland look. "So now you see."

Birnbaum leans closer to observe the man near his father. He is wearing a belted robe, but so faded and worn Birnbaum couldn't begin to guess the style or color. His face, too, is so aged it seems partially effaced, rubbed away as if by time or weather. This might explain the odd shimmer around him, of movement, of displaced light, slightly green, as if his clothing had hairs, nearly invisible, waving. On his shoulders a fine sifting of dust, like salt, but another color. Birnbaum, with an effort, looks away.

"And him?" Birnbaum gestures. "More family?"

"No. Not him."

"Who then?"

"A guest."

"Whose guest? You're inviting guests now?"

His father shakes his head, that annoyed confirmation of some private misgiving about his son rising in his face like bile. He goes back to shuffling the cards. At the refrigerator the old men have reached the freezer. They take out a frozen turkey and drop it to the floor, where it bounces.

"Hey, you!" Birnbaum calls. "Cut that out! Leave that stuff alone."

The men at the stove look up a moment, nodding, as if this is good advice. One begins singing to a tune from the radio, the others join in. Together they upend a five-pound sack of sugar into the pot. Birnbaum's father takes the stack of cards and organizes them neatly before him. He turns his eyes on his son.

"Adler, the dentist. Did you pay?"

"Who?" Birnbaum says, looking over his shoulder. "Sure. Of course."

"Here it says funds are on account. One hundred seventy-four dollars thirty-eight cents."

"Where? Let me see that." Birnbaum reaches out but his father draws back. He holds the card closer to read.

"Two fillings, one x-ray, left bite wing. Plus scaling and cleaning the teeth."

Birnbaum sits back in his chair.

"Also Greenberg Martinizing, twenty-four dollars; Kew Gardens Red Apple, seventy-two-fifty; also electric bills over two months' standing." He shakes his head at Birnbaum.

Birnbaum slouches, suddenly drained of energy. The older man, the gray ghost, looks at him with a mild forbearance which Birnbaum finds no less infuriating than his father's displeasure. "I've been a little behind with my bills," he admits.

"Also, with your son David you had words," his father says. "You never called to apologize."

"Me?" Birnbaum sits forward again. "Why me? He said worse."

"And," his father continues, reading, "one Arno Schteiner, certain promises made."

"What, he's complaining? He's dead, for Godsakes!" Birnbaum smiles wanly at the older man—he meant no impoliteness. "I haven't forgotten," he says, quieter, "I haven't had time." A friend, a promise, he'd ship the bones back to Poland if he could. He could, and he would, as soon as he found the time. He opens his mouth to explain.

His father raises both hands, palms forward, indicating he is finished, or not looking for excuses, or it's too late now to go into it. Birnbaum sags, his head inclined, as if the air has become a medium he has to press through. He is tired, remembers his room upstairs, the dark warm bed.

"Look," he says. "I don't mean to be disagreeable. Is it five in the morning? Later?" He looks at his wrist, above his head, but cannot locate a clock. "I need to lie down. Just a little while. You wait here. When I come back, maybe you'll tell me what you want."

He looks from his father to the older man, who has closed his eyes and is silently moving his lips. Behind him, too, the music has stopped, the giggling and cooking and food being thrown. All he can hear is his own breathing, and even that, barely. He looks around and all of them, his father included, are watching the gray ghost who sways gently, muttering to himself. Birnbaum takes deeper breaths, louder, so he can hear them, and turns to his father, still waiting for an answer. When nobody says anything, he supplies it himself. "Now?" he says. "Tonight?"

They are on the roof. Even in his dreams he heard them. It had been a wonderful sleep, sleep like he has never known. He was on a staircase of some kind, endless, warm, thousands of arms drawing him upward gently, caressing him as he moved. Each arm had a hand and each hand fingers, many, and each finger had a face and each face had eyes, and each face had a mouth that was singing in a voice so low Birnbaum could hear nothing beyond the soothing imminence of sound, not the song, but the silence right before the singing.

Then, even before he is awake, he can hear them up there, over his head, stamping their feet, keening into the night. They will wake the whole neighborhood. He grabs his robe and runs downstairs, feeling eerily alert, light on his feet. In the kitchen he kicks aside a potato some idiot has left and opens the back door, steps into the wide warm night.

There they are, at the roof's steepest angle, seven old men in bright-colored robes, holding each other, swaying back and forth, bearded faces lifting a tuneless song into the air. He looks around the yard. Someone will hear, someone will look out a window and see, the police will come. He looks for faces in the windows, lights. Nothing. Still, one of them could fall, all of them could, and then what would he do?

He steps to the fence at the edge of the deck, waves his arms. "Hey!" he whispers gruffly. "Get down from there! What are you doing?"

They ignore him. He sees them link arms until they are one lilting mass, chanting words he can't hear. Looking around him again, feeling a fool, he puts one foot on the fence's bottom rail, raises himself so he can be seen.

"Get down!" he calls, trying to whisper, determined to be heard. "I don't care if every one of you breaks your goddamn chicken necks, but not on my roof, you hear me?"

He lifts himself to see better, looks around for something to throw. Maybe he'll turn the hose on them. Behind them he imagines, for a moment, a boy wearing a gray scarf on a donkey, two women sitting under a tree. He shakes his head to clear it.

He makes one last effort to get their attention, rattles the drainpipe to the side of the roof. Still they ignore him, lift their faces higher, if anything, seem to sing louder. The sons of bitches, he mutters, realizing there is only one way to get them down. He sizes up the terrain, looks at the fence's top rail, the window's painted ledge, the rusted bolt where a light used to be. And along these the ridged tin drainpipe, trembling in his hands.

Nothing else to do. He says a small prayer for safekeeping, looks up one last time with a curse at the rabbis on his roof, hitches up his blue pajama leg. Then thinking, I'm really too old for such nonsense, he takes the pipe firmly in his hands and begins to climb.